RESISTANCE

JENNIFER A. NIELSEN

RESISTANCE

SCHOLASTIC INC.

Copyright © 2018 by Jennifer A. Nielsen

Photos © United States Holocaust Memorial Museum: 394 (courtesy of Guenther Schwarberg), 395 (courtesy of Rafael Scharf), 396 top (courtesy of Leopold Page Photographic Collection), 396 bottom (courtesy of Instytut Pamieci Narodowej), 397 top and bottom (courtesy of National Archives and Records Administration, College Park), 398 top (courtesy of Louis Gonda), 398 bottom (courtesy of Instytut Pamieci Narodowej), 399 top and bottom (courtesy of National Archives and Records Administration, College Park), 400 (courtesy of Leah Hammerstein Silverstein).

This book was originally published in hardcover by Scholastic Press in 2018.

ISBN 978-1-338-14850-3

10 9 8 7   23 24 25 26

Printed in the U.S.A.   40

This edition first printing 2022

Book design by Christopher Stengel

A note to readers: While some of the dialogue spoken by real historical figures in this text, including Aharon "Dolek" Liebeskind, Gusta Draenger, Shimshon Draenger, and Mordecai Anielewicz, was actually spoken by these men and women, and recorded in various volumes, the author has also created portions of it. Among other sources, the author employed extensive research in the archives of Yad Vashem (yadvashem.org) and a book written by Gusta Davidson Draenger, titled *Justyna's Narrative*, published by University of Massachusetts Press, Amherst, 1996.

Additionally, German, Polish, and Yiddish words will be italicized upon their first appearance in the text.

To *those who resisted,*
in every way they resisted, this book is for you.

For the young Jewish couriers,
I hold you in the highest respect.

Defense in the ghetto has become a fact. Armed Jewish resistance and revenge are actually happening. I have witnessed the glorious and heroic combat of the Jewish fighters.

—Excerpt from the last letter of

Mordecai Anielewicz,

April 23, 1943

· PART ONE ·

ONE

October 5, 1942
Tarnow Ghetto, Southern Poland

Two minutes. That's how long I had to get past this Nazi.

He needed time to check my papers, inquire about my business inside the ghetto. Maybe he wanted a few seconds to flirt with a pretty Polish girl. Or for her to flirt back.

But no more than two minutes. Any longer and he might realize my papers are forged. That it's Jewish blood in my veins, no matter how Aryan I look.

"Guten Morgen." This one greeted me with a smile and a hand on my arm. I learned early not to smuggle anything inside the sleeves of my coat. You only had to be stupid once, and the game was over.

This officer was younger than most, which I once believed would give me an advantage. I'd thought the younger ones would be more naïve, and maybe they were. But they were also ambitious, eager to prove themselves, and fully aware that capturing someone like me could earn them an early promotion.

"Guten Morgen," I replied in German, but with a perfect Polish accent. I smiled again, like we were old friends. Like I wasn't as willing to kill him as he was my people. *"Wie geht's?"* I didn't care how he was doing, on this morning or any other, but I asked because it kept his attention on my face rather than my bag.

Like other ghettos throughout Poland, Tarnow Ghetto had been sealed since nearly the beginning of the war, cut off from the outside world. Cut off from Jews in other ghettos. This isolation gave total power to the German invaders. Power to control, to lie, and to kill.

For the past three months, I'd worked as a courier for a resistance movement known as Akiva. My job was to break through that isolation, to warn the people, and to help them survive, if I could. But we were increasingly aware that time was running out. We'd seen people being lured onto the trains with promises of bread and jam, pacified into thinking they were being relocated to labor camps. Then they were crammed into cattle cars without water or space to move. And their destination was never to a labor camp.

They were headed for death camps, designed to kill hundreds or even thousands of people a day. I'd seen them. Been sickened by them. Had my heart shattered by them.

The Nazis called these camps their solution to the so-called "Jewish problem."

Yes, I very much intended to be their problem.

Which required me to stay calm now. Just inside the ghetto, I saw an open square that used to be a park. Now it was a place for trading, for begging, for a population with little more to do than wander about and wonder when their end would come. Maybe some even wished for it.

As was generally the case at the gates, there was one other Nazi on duty, this time a man in an SS uniform, the more specialized military force. There were also two Polish police officers and two members of the Jewish police, whom we called the OD. They often were as brutal as the Gestapo, and no more trustworthy.

I offered the soldier my *Kennkarte* before he could ask, because he'd need to see the identification anyway and my two minutes were halfway up. The passport-sized bifold contained my picture and fingerprints. Everything else inside—the dates, the stamps, the personal information—was forged.

One of our leaders, Shimshon Draenger, did all the forgeries for Akiva. He was so talented I believed he could forge Hitler's signature and fool Hitler himself with it. We sold Shimshon's forged papers inside the ghettos as our way of funding the resistance.

"You are Helena Nowak?" the soldier asked.

I nodded, a lie that I'd told many times over the last three months, and one that I would certainly tell again. A thousand other Polish girls might have the same name, which was the plan. If all went well, he'd believe me, then in the same instant, forget me.

"Why are you coming to the Tarnow Ghetto today?" he asked in German.

I scrunched my face into a pout, a careful balance between hinting that I wished I could go on a picnic with him instead, but not enough to actually encourage him to invite me. I replied, "Shawls for the women. Winter is coming. I can make money in there."

He frowned. "Where do you get these shawls?"

"My grandmother knits them."

My grandmother, whom I recently smuggled into hiding with a Christian family in Krakow. She sews, cooks, and cleans for them. In exchange, they don't have her killed. They saw it as a fair bargain, and maybe it was. If they were caught, they'd be killed too.

"Let's see your bag," the officer asked.

It was worn on my back, and was narrow and deep. Deliberately sewn that way. I had packed the top half of the bag tightly, making it difficult for him to dig around, if he felt the need to do so. But I hoped he wouldn't because today, the thick shawls hid the potatoes I was smuggling in, along with some forged identification papers. For sneaking in a single potato, this Nazi could shoot me here on my feet. For the papers, my punishment would be far worse.

I turned and hummed a little tune while he looked the bag over. This was by far the most dangerous part of my mission.

If I'd raised his suspicions. If he wanted to impress his commander. If he looked at me and saw the Jewish girl inside, the one who has trained herself to look these evil men in the eye and to smile and make them think I sympathize with their slaughter of my people. If he saw *that*, it was all over.

But I'd get in today. And tomorrow I would lie my way into another ghetto, and do the same every tomorrow after that until my last breath, or theirs. After three years of war in which I'd felt helpless against the overwhelming force of the German army, I was finally doing *something*. I was bringing my people a chance to survive.

Ghettos themselves were nothing new to the Jews. Many times throughout our history, we'd been forcibly segregated, often behind walls. Which made it harder to get people to listen now. They believed the German lie that if we cooperated, we would get through this, as we had in the past. They wanted the ghettos to be what they'd always been: a separation, and nothing more.

But it was different this time. The German plan was not to divide us from the population. It was to eliminate us from the population. To exterminate us.

The ghettos played a key role in their plans, suspending the Jews in a halfway point to everything. Half-starved, treated as much like animals as humans. Existing halfway between hope and despair.

Halfway between life and death. The one became the other in the ghettos.

And I was doing everything I could to stop it.

It began with smuggling. I'd become creative about how I brought things in: weapons baked into loaves of bread; fake identification papers sewn into the linings of my coat; or, occasionally, the smuggled object might make my bust appear larger than it really was. Whatever I was secretly carrying, I always brought information to the residents of these sealed ghettos about what was happening elsewhere, and then learned everything I could to warn the next ghetto.

But that was only the beginning. My mission today was bolder than usual, and I was nervous.

"You must leave before the ghetto curfew at seventeen hundred hours," the Nazi told me, then with a smile added, "Come out through this gate, pretty girl, no?"

I offered him a smile of my own, one that shot bile into my throat. I couldn't come out this gate now. Not if he was specifically watching for me.

He let me pass, and then I was in.

I wondered if he'd sensed how hard my heart was beating back there, if he'd known my palms were dampened with sweat. I'd talked my way past the soldier by making him think I was Polish. Now came the harder part: convincing my own people that I was one of them. For if they did not trust me, coming here was a waste of time.

I turned down the nearest street, hoping to get out of sight if any guards looked back. It was time to be Jewish again. I put the necklace with the Catholic crucifix in my pocket and repeated my true name under my breath: Chaya Lindner.

I was named for my grandmother, as she was named for hers. Every time I passed myself off as a Christian girl named Helena, I wondered: Was I dishonoring my name, or preserving it?

Maybe it didn't matter. I was committed to my fate. I'd be a courier for as long as a courier was needed. I'd be a fighter if that was needed.

If a martyr was needed, I'd be that too.

But for now, this ghetto needed to see a Jewish girl. If it was difficult to pass myself off as a Pole back at the ghetto gates, it was no easier now to make the people here trust me as a Jew. I was a stranger with a Polish look, and that made me suspicious.

I was supposed to make contact with a resistance member here, but until he found me, I began distributing the potatoes. Like everything else, I passed them out as quietly as possible. I didn't want to be recognized, or remembered. Even among my own people, there were some who might point me out to a Nazi if they thought it'd buy their family another day to live.

So whenever possible, I distributed food to children, slipping a potato into their bag or coat pocket, then quickly moving on. I sometimes looked back to see their eyes light up when they felt it with their hands, but they were always smart enough not to bring the potato out in the open, and too excited to look around for me. Usually, I didn't look back. It wasn't worth the risk. I moved fast, eyes down, trying not to think about who got the potato and who I'd passed over. They didn't deserve hunger more than the child whose bag happened to be open, but such was the randomness of life. I would never be able to bring in enough food for everyone.

At my best, I could not save them all.

That thought always destroyed me. Always.

Far too soon, the supply of potatoes was gone. So what if twenty families had a potato to eat today? Couldn't I have snuck in even one more? I lowered my eyes and clutched my bag in my hands. I couldn't give out the shawls—no matter how cold it was about to become, I needed them for the second part of my mission. But I had to find my contact soon.

The German invaders had taken everything from me: my home, my family, even much of my faith, which had once been the center of my life.

So I had no problem taking something back from them: my dignity, my fight. My will to live.

But if I'd learned anything from this war, it's that we can never go back.

TWO

September 1, 1939–April 22, 1941
Krakow, Poland

Over my sixteen years, I'd lived three different lives. The first was my childhood, full of peace and beauty and memories that lingered in my mind like a faint perfume, sweet but always just out of reach. My father owned a shoe repair shop, and Mama used to sing as she cooked us masterpieces of fish baked in cream sauce, or lamb dumplings, her specialty. My brother, Yitzchak, was two years younger than me, mischievous and playful. My sister, Sara, a few years younger than that, had hugs that were made of magic and she gave them freely. Our lives used to be perfect.

Used to be.

The Germans invaded Poland on my thirteenth birthday, a *Blitzkrieg* that came with tanks and bombers and thousands of deaths before our country surrendered that same month. Poland became occupied territory under Germany's control and Krakow replaced Warsaw as its new capital city. With our country's waving of the white flag, thus began my second life: enduring the occupation.

New laws and regulations were immediately instituted, most of them targeting my people. German tanks rolled through the streets, particularly the Jewish quarters, issuing orders through bullhorns that all Jews must register with the new government.

"Don't do it," I warned my parents. "Don't give them our names."

"You heard them." Papa always preferred to be cautious. "The penalty for refusing to register is death."

Maybe it was. But I had a terrible feeling that the penalty for registration was also death.

Within weeks, the invaders barged through our front door with orders to search all Jewish homes. They combed meticulously through our drawers and cupboards and wardrobes, even cut open the mattress on Sara's bed to search inside it. Officially, they took our jewelry and foreign currencies, which we were forbidden to keep. Unofficially, they took anything they wanted. My mother's fur coat that had been an anniversary gift from Papa. A violin that Yitzchak had saved up for months to buy. They tossed our prayer books into the square and burned them, simply because they could. At the time, I'd been relieved, thinking that they had taken nothing from me.

But they would. Very soon, they would take everything.

Like a hungry fire, their destruction continued throughout the city. Our national monuments were looted, synagogues were burned, and the bronze statue of our national poet, Adam Mickiewicz, was taken for scrap metal.

One month later, forced labor began. Jews were made to dig ditches, pave roads, and drain swamps. If they were paid at all, it was with a mouthful of bread and little more.

Papa and I were on the streets one day when I happened to look down at a man cleaning out sewage from a broken pipe.

"That's our rabbi!" I whispered.

Papa took my hand and quickly pulled me along. "Don't look," he whispered. "Learn not to see anything, or to be seen."

I did learn, better than he could have imagined. There were ways to move about the streets so as not to draw attention to oneself. Those who did it well got home safely each night. I perfected it.

Which was important, because I'd also learned that the Nazis held us in particular contempt. They wanted the Poles to see that if we were given the work of animals, we would do the work of animals. They wanted the world to think that we were less than human.

At first, I thought it would be impossible for any civilized person to believe such absurdities, such ugliness. But that was only the beginning . . .

By November, all Jews were required to wear the yellow Star of David on an armband, which created an entirely new set of problems for us. Now that we were easily identified, we became easy marks for Poles or Germans who considered harassment a cheap form of entertainment.

One day, Mama took us into town. We were supposed to meet Papa at the corner outside his shoe repair shop, but then we heard a commotion nearby. Mama let out a small cry and tried to pull us away, but I recognized my father's black fedora.

"No," I growled as I broke free. "What are they doing?"

He had been stopped by a Polish police officer who was making him stand at attention while he ripped out pieces of my father's beard, one fistful at a time. With every tear, my father grunted with pain, but he said nothing and offered no form of resistance. The crowd that had gathered pointed at him and laughed, as if humiliation and pain were some kind of joke. The closer I got, the angrier I became. How could they do such a thing? These were people who had been peaceful toward us in the past. Some had even been our friends.

I started forward, determined to defend my father, but Yitzchak grabbed me from behind and dragged me away from the crowd. "We have to help him!" I said, still fighting.

Mama was by my side then and spoke firmly. "Don't make it worse, Chaya. Let it be."

By then, the officer had finished with my father, and he was waving the crowd away. At one time, this would have been shocking behavior, but gradually such abuse became common. Now it was accepted. The officer saw me glaring at him and only smiled, receiving pats on his back from members of the crowd. If he knew what I'd been thinking, he'd have arrested me.

Late that night, I heard my father crying with my mother at his side. I'd never heard him cry before, and it crushed my heart. Afterward, he avoided going out on the streets, and if he had to, then he walked with his eyes down, hands stuffed in his pockets. They had not just taken pieces of his beard. They had robbed my father of his dignity, which was far worse.

The new year, 1940, brought the tightening of the noose. My father lost his business and most of his savings. We sold my mother's china, my father's typewriter and books. We traded extra clothes and household items for food, and my brother and I worked endlessly for Polish families, cleaning or doing odd jobs, to earn less than a tenth of what we could have charged before the war. Then we were told our neighborhood was to become part of a German-only district and we would have to leave.

A member of the Jewish governing council of Krakow, known as the *Judenrat*, suggested that my father ought to seek housing for our family in the Podgorze District, set aside for the Jews. Thousands of others would soon be trying to get in, they warned us. Every apartment would be shared by four families, but the crowding was better than homelessness. Once winter came, that would be a certain death sentence.

"*Four* families per apartment?" my mother asked, her voice thick with concern. "That's uncivilized."

"War is uncivilized," came the reply. "Take what we've assigned you, or the next family will."

My family had never been wealthy, but our home was always clean and comfortable. The Judenrat directed us to a rickety apartment building that should have been torn down years ago. It had no heat or running water, and the room we were to share with another family was little more than a large closet.

"Five of us won't fit in that space," Papa protested.

"But four of you will." The Judenrat official in front of him shifted his eyes to me, and I will forever remember the tone of his voice as he spoke: without emotion, or concern. Perhaps already, with his soul pieced away to his Nazi overseers. "A new order has come from the Germans. Most of the Jews still in Krakow must leave the city. Your daughter's name will be on tomorrow's list."

That's when my world caved in. I was being sent away from my family, my city, the only life I'd ever known. My name was only one on a long list, but it was the only name I saw through my teary eyes. The next morning, others left mostly by wagon or on foot, hoping to stay with family members elsewhere, or to find other ghettos that might admit them.

"Your grandmother will take you in, if you can get to her home," Papa suggested.

If I could. She lived a very long way from us.

"I can get there," I said, fully aware that I probably couldn't get that far on my own. But from the looks in my parents' eyes, they needed to believe I would end up somewhere safe. I hugged each member of my family good-bye, lingering longest with my mother, who couldn't seem to let me go any more than I could release her. Then I picked up my handbag, the remnants of what few possessions I had left, and took my first step into the countryside, entirely alone, with little chance for survival and no idea of where I should go next. Those steps marked the end of my second life.

A few days later, my third life began, though in a most unexpected way.

THREE

April 25, 1941–October 5, 1942
Kopaliny Farm, Poland

I didn't make it as far as my grandmother's. For the first three days after leaving Krakow, I wondered if I'd make it anywhere at all. Papa had warned me to be careful about who I trusted, so I trusted no one. I stole eggs from untended chicken coops, hid whenever a car or wagon passed by, and slept in cold ditches at night, covered with reeds or grasses, wondering how long I could last this way.

Not long. I'd known that since the moment I left Krakow.

Then on the third day, I wandered past a sign for the village of Kopaliny, and a memory sparked within me. A farm there was run by a couple named Shimshon and Gusta Draenger, both in their early twenties. Before the war, they had been the leaders of my Jewish scout group, Akiva, which taught us about our culture and history, and who we might become one day. I'd lost track of them after the invasion, though I had heard Shimshon was arrested for a while for some of his anti-Nazi writings.

Late that night, I showed up on the Draengers' doorstep, tears already rolling down my cheeks. I hadn't seen them for two years. What if they didn't remember me? What if they did . . . and couldn't take me?

By the time Gusta answered the door, I was almost shaking with worry. She was a pretty woman with a serious nature and a warmth that immediately began to calm me. "Chaya Lindner?" she said, clearly surprised.

I took a deep breath, hoping that what I had to ask wasn't too much. I knew it was. The last thing anyone needed these days was another mouth to feed. "Will you let me stay the night? I can leave by morning if—"

"Nonsense!" Gusta wrapped an arm around my shoulders and led me inside. "Of course you'll stay here, for as long as you want." If there was a way to love her more in that moment, I didn't know it.

I did stay, and it wasn't only me. One by one that first summer, other Akiva scouts came to the farm, all of us suddenly on our own, but slowly becoming family. We worked the farm during the day and gathered each evening to socialize and study. It was a good life.

Until we thought of those we had left behind. Of our true families, most of whom were now trapped inside the ghetto during what turned out to be a very cold winter, locked behind walls with too little food and too much disease. The problems worsened with every new wave of Jews brought in from other areas of Poland. Then selections were made, and hundreds disappeared by train or were simply shot down in the street. So far, my family was not among them, but I saw other Akiva members crying, and prayed that I would never have to fully understand how they felt.

Most of the news about the ghettos came to us from another Akiva leader, a man a little older than the Draengers whom everyone called Dolek. I'd heard it was a fake name, but I never asked him about it. If he was hiding his true identity, there had to be a reason.

Where both the Draengers looked distinctly Jewish, Dolek had more Polish features. Thanks to Shimshon's forgeries, he was able to travel nearly anywhere in the country and returned as often as possible, telling us of a war that seemed to be spreading all over the world, of Jewish resistance groups forming up in Warsaw, or worst of all, what happened to those who were taken away by train.

Which meant I was already anxious on the day he arrived from Krakow and motioned me over beside him on a bench at the back of the house. It was early in the summer of 1942, and I'd hoped the warmer weather would bring better days ahead. How wrong I was.

Dolek had just come from the Podgorze Ghetto, where my family lived.

No.

No, it couldn't be that.

Surely there was another reason why his mouth looked grim, his eyes so heavy, why the tone of his voice was flat when he said, "I have some terrible news for you."

My heart constricted, enough that I could barely mumble, "Please don't say it."

He paused. Too long. And if he was struggling to force the words out, then it was even harder to make myself sit here, when what I really wanted was to run, somewhere, anywhere, and to keep running until the war couldn't touch me anymore. Where it couldn't hurt me, or those I loved.

But that was impossible.

Finally, he said, "It's about your brother and sister. I'm so sorry."

I stopped breathing, and the corners of my vision blurred. This wasn't happening. Not this.

He continued, "Sara was taken away on a train . . . to Belzec." Dolek's tone was gentle, but his words struck me like a blow to the chest. "I thought you should know."

"What is Belzec? A labor camp?"

At first, he didn't answer. He only furrowed his brow, his somber expression full of compassion. "I've told you what I've seen there, Chaya. You already know what it is."

A death camp.

Sara was barely eight years old. She knew nothing of war or violence. She'd fallen victim to a level of hatred she couldn't begin to comprehend.

Enormous tears spilled onto my cheeks, which I was certain would never dry. But he wasn't finished. I squeaked out, "My brother?"

"The same night as your sister was taken, your brother failed to return home."

Yitzchak was twelve at the time. He loved to build things with his hands, but my father had hoped Yitz would join him in his shoe repair business instead. Like my mother, he used to sing.

Used to.

Maybe he was still alive.

Maybe not.

We might never know for sure.

On the day my little sister was sent to her death, I had been planting seeds in the ground, congratulating myself on having escaped the worst effects of the war. That evening, when Yitz disappeared, I'd been laughing with my friends here, planning the feast we might have when the harvest came in.

I was utterly ashamed of myself, and vowed in that very moment to find a way to remember them, to honor them. A way to bring some meaning to their loss, if I could. I just didn't know how to do it.

My answer came later that same night as we gathered around the supper table. Dolek reported on what he'd seen and heard around Poland. About the mass graves of Jews shot dead in the forests. Our people packed so tightly onto the trains that many never survived the trip to the so-called labor camps. And if they did survive, they were likely killed upon arrival anyway.

"We know the truth," he said. "But most of the Jews do not. They refuse to believe it, or can't comprehend such horrors." His eyes flicked to me. "Even when it touches their own lives."

Then Dolek told the others about my family. There were tears and expressions of sympathy, but I was hardly the first to receive such news. Only the latest in a long line of Akiva members who were mourning friends and families still trapped in the ghettos.

Or . . . not in the ghettos. Not any longer.

Shimshon stood. "Our situation is becoming clear. It is time for Akiva to make a choice. Do we remain a scout group, pretending the war isn't happening to us and never will? Or do we become something more? Let us decide our fate before it's decided for us."

Standing beside him, Gusta said, "Let's be clear. Any decision we make will end with our deaths. If we do nothing, if we wait here, it's only a matter of time before the Germans come for us and put us on the same trains."

Dolek leaned forward to add, "Or there is a second option. What if we die on our feet, fighting back?" He grinned. "What if we prove to the Nazis, prove to the world, that not all Jews will go like lambs to the slaughter?"

Shimshon clapped a hand on his friend's shoulder. "We

21

will join other resistance groups. We will disrupt the Germans when we can. Above all, in every way possible we will try to save the lives of our people. *If* you all agree."

As I lifted my eyes to him, I was flooded with competing emotions: fear and doubt swirling with my sadness and guilt, blending strangely into something I could only describe as excitement. I didn't understand why I should feel such eager anticipation. None of us had military experience, or for that matter, life experience. We had no money, no connections, and no training. Our Akiva leaders weren't pretending we had any chance to succeed.

But if we did nothing, if we continued living behind this sheer veil of safety, then we would certainly fail.

More important, I owed something to Yitzchak and Sara, and to my parents, who might eventually be forced into the death camps too. I wanted revenge for every single Jew who had already fallen, and a chance to save the life of every Jew still standing.

I was one of the first to raise my hand and say, "I'm in." Other hands followed, both boys and girls, the youngest of us teens, and our leaders not much older. I didn't know how someone like me could possibly make a difference, but if this was my way to honor Yitzchak and Sara, then I would do whatever my leaders asked of me.

Their request came that same night. After everyone else had left for bed, Gusta pulled me aside. "Have you heard of the couriers, Chaya?" When I shrugged, she added, "The courier's primary job is to get in and out of the ghettos. To get in, you'll have to forget everything that makes you Jewish." She pursed her lips. "I've noticed your accent is less Jewish than the rest of ours."

"We lived in a Polish district . . . before," I said. "My parents sent me to the public schools with Poles."

She smiled, obviously pleased. "Were you often mistaken for being Polish?"

"More than I was thought to be Jewish." In contrast to many Jews, my hair was blonde, my complexion a little lighter. I spoke Polish as fluently as I did Yiddish, the language of most Jews in Poland, and I even spoke a little German.

Gusta's face became grim when she said, "I won't lie to you, Chaya. This is a very dangerous job. As a courier, you will smuggle in food or money, maybe forged identification papers or items of greater risk. At all times, you will have information about the resistance. If you are caught, you might be shot on sight. More likely, you will be tortured first."

My eyes widened. "Tortured?"

She didn't hesitate. "The invaders will do whatever they can to extract the information they want. If they don't succeed with you, they will threaten your loved ones or fellow prisoners. They might kill them right in front of you. But under no circumstances can you ever tell them what you know. Not one word, Chaya, or everything we are doing here is lost."

I couldn't pretend that her words didn't frighten me, and she saw my hesitation, quickly adding, "Focus on the goals of the resistance. Remember why we are doing this. If you can focus, you will lose the fear. Lose the fear, and you will save lives."

"What about my friends?" I asked. "Jakub, Rubin . . ."

"Boys cannot be couriers—with the circumcision, it's too easy to identify them as Jewish. And only a few specific girls can do the job. Girls with your look. Girls with your courage."

Girls like me with little to lose. Which meant my decision was made.

"I'll do it."

My training began immediately. Within a month, I had completed my first successful mission inside the Lublin Ghetto. The second month, I smuggled in my first weapon. By the third month, I was arranging safe houses for Jews in hiding. And now it was October 1942, a month after my sixteenth birthday, and I had just made it inside the Tarnow Ghetto to undertake my most dangerous smuggling operation yet.

FOUR

October 5, 1942
Tarnow Ghetto

I didn't have to wait for long inside the Tarnow Ghetto before a tall, gangly boy approached me. He might've been my age, sixteen, but his bony face made him look older than he probably was. He looked at me as if he knew who I was, and I gave him a distinct nod of confirmation.

"Did Dolek send you?" he asked cautiously.

"He did." If this boy knew Dolek's name, it was enough proof that we could trust each other.

The boy sighed, obviously relieved. "My name is Fishel. I arranged this meeting."

Fishel probably wasn't his real name either, but I wouldn't ask for anything more, nor would I tell him my name. Information was a dangerous currency. We were better off knowing as little about each other as possible.

He added, "We expected you here earlier. We're running out of time."

Maybe he wasn't aware that among other challenges of living in an occupied country, the Nazi soldiers were hardly going to make it convenient for a Jewish courier to smuggle stolen items in and out of a sealed ghetto.

But I pressed my lips together, reminding myself that he couldn't know that. Fishel was trapped in here, as isolated from the outside world as any other resident. I only said, "Then let's not waste time standing here."

Fishel immediately led me deeper into the ghetto, obviously in a hurry. "Is there any news from outside?"

"No good news. Is the . . . package ready?" The question set my heart pounding. Smuggling out of a ghetto was far more dangerous than smuggling in.

"It was. I hope nothing has changed."

We passed a boy lying on the street, half-clothed, without shoes, and so still that I'd thought he was dead. But his eyes tracked us as we passed. Why were we just passing him by?

I touched Fishel's arm. "Should we—"

"He'll be gone by morning. Our efforts must be for those who can be saved." Fishel's tone wasn't cold, just realistic, which was almost worse.

We left the boy behind, but his eyes would follow me forever. He wasn't the first person I'd seen who was starving. First, they begged on their feet, then they sat, then all they could do was lie on the ground, as this boy was doing. In ordinary times, I would never have walked away from someone in such desperate need.

But these were not ordinary times. How often must I be reminded of that?

"Someone will collect his body tomorrow." Fishel had chosen his words carefully, and I understood them. The boy wouldn't be buried tomorrow. A burial required the Judenrat to make a record of his death. But if a family kept his body in hiding, they could use his ration card to get an extra share of food. Use his death to give themselves a better chance for life.

We entered an apartment with crumbling plaster walls and a door with a spray of bullet holes through its center. "There was an *Aktion* last month," he explained, still in that matter-of-fact tone. I tried not to look, tried not to think about who had hidden here and why, and how futile it had been. Anywhere outside the ghetto, this building would have been condemned long ago, but here, the Judenrat was forced to consider these adequate living conditions. They wouldn't be adequate for one's worst enemy.

Trying to survive the ghettos was like treading water. You might keep your head up for a while, but if you didn't get out, eventually you would go under.

"Is that her?" A woman stepped from the shadows, squinting against the light and looking as ghostly as if she had been an actual apparition. She had a rash on one arm that spread up and across her neck. When she began coughing, my suspicions were confirmed.

This woman had typhus, the plague of the ghettos. Whenever possible, we tried to smuggle in vaccinations, but even if I'd had one, they were almost always kept for the children.

Which meant that she was already as dead as that boy on the ground outside. Only neither of their bodies knew it yet.

When Fishel confirmed that I was the courier, she closed her eyes and whispered a prayer under her breath, then widened her coat to reveal the package, my purpose for coming.

It was a baby girl, probably no more than five months old. She was bundled up in a knitted blanket that likely contained the same lice that gave her mother this disease.

"I made this blanket for her." The mother fingered it tenderly. "I hope it will always be her special gift."

I'd have to dispose of this blanket as soon as possible, as well as the clothes, and anything else that connected the baby to this ghetto.

"My daughter's name is Cypora."

A Jewish name that had already been changed on the forged birth certificate I was carrying. From the moment I left the ghetto, this baby would be known as Irena, a good Polish name.

"We have to go," Fishel said nervously. "The sleeping pills will wear off soon."

Which explained his worries about me arriving late. They gave the baby the pills too early.

"Will my daughter grow up knowing who she is? Knowing who I am?" The mother's eyes became bright with tears, wondering if she was doing the right thing, if it wouldn't be better to let her daughter die here as a Jewish child.

It was a question that always filled me with guilt. If this war ended—no . . . *when* this war ended—the parents of these infants would never know where to begin looking for their child.

I touched her arm, speaking softly. "Your daughter will grow up. That is most important."

My words seemed to satisfy her, so I emptied my bag of the shawls. We'd already sewn a mesh patch into the bottom of the bag that would allow in enough air for the infant until I was safely out of the ghetto.

The mother kissed her daughter and whispered, "My dearest Cypora," likely the last time her true name would ever be spoken to her. But when I held out my arms, she couldn't force herself to give the baby up. Fishel leaned in, taking the baby. "It must be this way," he said. "Give her a chance to live."

The woman agreed, and immediately sank to the floor, quietly sobbing.

I choked back my own tears. If I was going to assure this woman that she had made the right choice, then I had to stay strong. But inside, every sob that emptied from the woman cut my heart a little more.

This was the right thing to do. I knew it, and also knew I'd have to remind myself of that again at least a thousand times before this mission was over.

I hoped this was the right thing to do.

Fishel lowered the infant into the bottom of my bag;

then we put down a thin piece of wood to be sure Cypora wasn't suffocated from above. The shawls went in last of all. Hopefully, that would be enough.

He helped to raise the bag onto my back, but before I left, I offered the weeping mother the best hope I could. "The family who is taking your daughter are good people. They always wanted a child of their own and never could have one. They will love her as you do, and protect her as courageously as you have until now."

The mother looked up at me, her eyes empty of light. "May God go with you."

Fishel promised to check in on her again, then led me from the apartment.

"I have to go out through a different gate," I said. "They're watching for me at the one I entered."

He clicked his tongue. "That's farther away. We have to hurry."

But with a sleeping infant tucked into the bag on my back, we couldn't go too fast, nor could we draw any attention to ourselves, especially since we were passing the Judenrat offices now, which were usually shared by the OD. We picked up our steps and took whatever shortcuts we could, but it was all done with our heads down, the same as most other people trapped in here.

When the west gate came into view, Fishel shook my hand, grateful but eager to see me go. "I hope to see you again."

I hoped so too. That would mean both of us had

survived today's smuggling job. That would mean I'd safely escaped another ghetto.

I chose the guard who looked most likely to give me a pass, this time a German about my father's age. I didn't like to interact with the Poles or the OD. They were usually more adept at recognizing one of their own.

I had my papers ready for him and he made the same inquiries as the officer did when I tried to get in. I showed him the shawls and complained that the women inside the ghetto must not have any money left to purchase them because these were very good shawls.

"What do the dead need with money?" His cynical laugh was like a drill on my chest. He thought we were sharing a joke. I thought about sharing my knife with his gut.

I bit back the response I wanted to give, but before he gave me permission to leave, I heard a soft coo coming from my bag. Quickly I asked, "May I go, sir?"

He frowned. "Why the hurry?"

The bag shifted behind me. The baby was rolling over. Waking up.

"I have a long way to go home, and curfew is coming. My mother will worry."

The coo became a sleepy cry, and I coughed loudly enough to cover it, then added, "Also, I might be getting sick. I should get home, sir."

The Germans feared typhus. If he thought I might have it, maybe it would help me get out of here faster.

"Go," he finally said, shoving my papers back at me.

That was all I needed to hurry away from the gate. I ducked into a nearby Catholic church and sat in a pew to unpack the bag. The baby was already awake but still lethargic from the sleeping pills. She was too thin but seemed strong. Her tiny body wanted to live.

"May we help you?" a priest said, appearing in the aisle beside me.

I looked up, startled and empty of words. My pulse was still racing from leaving the ghetto and I wasn't thinking as clearly as I needed to.

Before I could answer, he noticed the baby and seemed to understand. "Ah, it's you."

He held out his arms for the baby, assuring me she'd be safe with her new family.

"One day." I hesitated a moment, making sure the priest heard me. "One day her adoptive parents must tell this child who she really is. The sacrifices her mother made."

When he promised they would, I gave him the baby and left, hoping this child, who would be raised saying Catholic prayers and attending Mass, would retain a kernel of her Jewish origin within her heart.

I hoped.

But whatever happened, at least I could end this day knowing one life had been saved.

For now, that was enough.

FIVE

October 12, 1942
Podgorze Ghetto, Krakow

While I was at Tarnow Ghetto, the decision was made for Akiva to leave Kopaliny Farm. The neighbors had noticed the number of people who came and went, and were asking too many questions. Dangerous questions with answers that could send every single one of us to the losing end of a firing squad.

We'd relocate inside Krakow's ghetto, a place that had been sealed from the outside world for a year and a half. It was home to my parents now, and would've been my home too had I not been sent away. One of our members offered us his empty apartment on Jozefinska Street. The scouts snuck in through holes in the wall, talked ourselves in with fake papers, or joined the shift of workers returning to the ghetto at the end of a workday—those who left were counted far more carefully than those who returned. I was one of the last to enter, because although I understood the need to be closer to our people, to work where we were needed most, I didn't want to go. I'd seen enough ghettos by now to know how difficult it was to live in them.

No one laughed here, and smiles were fleeting. They spoke often of the past and rarely of the future. Bread wagons, a source of life, came through occasionally, but trucks to collect the dead were part of the daily routine. Oftentimes the body could not be buried, so it was simply covered with newspapers, and soon the shock of seeing bodies left this way became commonplace.

Death had become normal here, inevitable. And since there was nothing to fear from the normal, attempting to delay one's death seemed almost illogical, like resisting the urge to breathe.

I'd visited my parents a few times since becoming a courier, but today was going to be different. My father sat cross-legged on their worn wooden floor and gestured that the small chair against the wall was for me. When I sat in it, he asked, "What is the news from the outside world? You always seem to know."

Everything I knew was awful. So instead I said, "Grandmother Lindner is well. She asked me to say hello."

The first part was true, the second was not. Tensions were already high in the home where my grandmother was staying. I wouldn't make it worse by paying her a visit. She was kind without exception and baked a babka cake that made my mouth water just to think of it. But she was also fixed in her ways: her Yiddish language, her Jewish proverbs that seemed relevant to every possible conversation. If the family who was hiding her was ever raided, my grandmother would be easily identified as Jewish. I checked in on her as often as possible, but neither she nor the family ever knew I'd passed by.

"And are you well?" Papa asked, hopefulness in his voice. "You look good."

"You need to worry about yourselves, Papa, not me."

"We're still your parents." His eyes creased. "My little bird, of course we worry about you."

I hadn't heard his nickname for me since I was small, and it was hard to hear it now. I only shook my head, stuffing my emotions down. "I'm good, Papa. You can see that."

"Not always."

He looked around for any signs that someone was listening to our conversation, but my mother was the only other one in the room and she was staring out the window, barely aware that I'd come. Something had collapsed inside her when she lost her two younger children, like part of her died with Sara and vanished with Yitzchak.

Although we appeared to be alone, Papa lowered his voice. "Sometimes you're here in the ghetto . . . sometimes you're not. So we worry."

Mama mumbled my name but remained looking out the window. From her view, she could see the entrance gate to the ghetto, one I sometimes used while smuggling. I wondered if she'd ever seen me come through.

I leaned in close to my father and withdrew two bifolds from a pocket in my coat, which I passed to him. He unfolded one and then the other, then looked up at me, clearly confused. "What are these? They look like—"

I shushed him and whispered, "They're identification papers. Polish papers for you and Mama."

"These aren't our names. How did you—"

"I can get you and Mama out of the ghetto. I know of a safe house near Krakow."

He closed the bifolds. "These aren't our names, Chaya. That isn't our life."

"Just until the war is over, Papa. I can help you."

"Yitzchak's coming back here, to the ghetto," Mama said. "We'll wait here for him."

I turned to her. "No, Mama, Yitz isn't—"

Papa placed his hand on my arm. "This is where Yitzchak will look for us *when* he comes back."

If he was put on the trains like Sara, then Yitzchak wasn't coming back, because the kids who were taken away on those trains never came back. Those trains carried passengers in only one direction, ever. Away from the ghettos, to an almost certain death.

But now my father was whispering to my mother, telling her everything was all right, and I knew our conversation had to end here, for her sake. Robbing her of hope would've been almost as cruel as the Nazis had been to rob her of her children.

Papa stuffed the fake identification papers into his pocket. "Your mother and I will talk about it later."

"Will you promise to look at what I gave you? To really think about it?"

He nodded, and I hoped he meant it, that they would look at what surrounded them and realize that taking a risk out there was far better than the certainty of remaining here. I wanted to shake him and beg him to say yes; then I would take care of the rest. I would take care of them.

I stood to leave, but Papa gestured to their small half-room. "You could stay here, with us," he said.

"I have a place nearby, with friends." I tried not to see the hurt in my father's eyes when I spoke. I loved my parents more than anything, which was probably why visiting them had become so difficult. Where was the father of my child-hood, who always knew how to make everything all right? Where was my mother, who sang me to sleep every night and was the sunshine in our home each morning? There was no Yitzchak, no Sara.

Even I was nothing like I'd once been. I'd grown stronger, bolder, more proud of my identity than I'd ever been before, and I needed to be with others who felt the same way. Maybe Papa understood that. He never asked me to stay again.

The easiest excuse was to tell myself that they couldn't

know about the work I was doing, that my staying there would have endangered them. But mostly, I stayed away because I knew the papers I'd just given my father would probably never come out of his pocket again, and I didn't know how to save people who no longer cared to save themselves.

Beyond that, I was drawn to the energy in the Jozefinska apartment: our secrets, our goals. We had started as a handful of teenagers led by an amateur newspaper editor, his young wife, and a job counselor. Our leaders had become unlikely generals in our acts of resistance, and I was as willing a soldier as anyone on the front lines. We'd become an organization formidable enough to gain the respect of larger resistance movements in Warsaw, and we had begun discussing ways to get the Nazis' attention here in Krakow.

"How far are you willing to go?" a fellow scout named Rubin asked me one night. He was a couple of years older than me, with slightly wavy hair and a dimple in one cheek when he smiled. Like me, he'd been sent away from Krakow by the Judenrat last year, though he'd lost all of his family soon after in an Aktion on the streets. Also like me, he was eager to do anything he could for the resistance. Rubin had become one of my closest friends within Akiva, the person I always went to first for ideas or advice.

"How far?" I grinned. "I'll do whatever it takes to make them regret coming to Poland."

He was echoing the same thoughts our leaders were already debating. It was no longer enough to do courier work, or to respond defensively to Nazi aggression. The time had come to take a few bites of our own. Perhaps we were only fleas nipping at the heels of a giant, but if our actions stopped the giant from crushing everything within his path for even a moment, then it was worth it.

Despite our leaders' lack of experience in the world, they were learning fast and passing on to us everything they could. Rubin compared it to being thrown in an ocean and being told to learn to swim.

So we did. And we still are.

Rubin showed me how to fire a gun. I taught him to lie. All of us learned about grenades, studied the routes of Nazi patrols through Krakow, and began to scavenge, buy, or steal anything that helped in our cause.

Within weeks of our move to Jozefinska Street, Dolek returned from a meeting with other resistance groups up north, announcing that from now on, Akiva would be divided into cells of five. We were not to ask for the names of people in any other cell, and especially not for any details of their missions. If we were ever captured, the less we knew, the better.

My cell was assigned to begin raids on German storehouses. Acquiring weapons and ammunition were the top priority, but medical supplies, money, and food would also be valuable.

Rubin acted as the leader of our cell, simply because he was oldest and took direct orders from Akiva's leadership. A younger boy named Jakub worked with us too. He was brilliant and willing to do anything asked of him, but since he'd attended only Jewish schools while growing up, he spoke very little Polish and no German, which limited his usefulness. Hanusia was brave and clever, though she lacked the specific look for a courier. Finally, Meriam was an experienced courier who'd taught me a lot over the past few months. It was good to have her along.

"Where are we going first?" I asked Rubin.

He smiled over at me. "How would you feel about taking a ride on a train? It should be loaded with supplies meant for the Germans."

I grinned back at him. Perhaps with our help, it would arrive at its destination a little lighter than when it began.

SIX

October 20, 1942
Bochnia Countryside

Waiting at the apartment until it was time for the raid seemed to take forever. In keeping with the requirement for secrecy, we didn't discuss any details there, so I was anxious to know what my specific role would be, but Rubin said only, "Wear dark clothes."

Finally, the time came. Each of us was to smuggle ourselves out of the ghetto by five o'clock and meet in Old Town. From there, we borrowed a wagon from a sympathetic Pole whom Hanusia used to work for—under the agreement that if we were caught, he would claim it had been stolen—and drove east to the outskirts of Bochnia. A supply train would pass our way at precisely 10:14 p.m.

As we rode, Rubin assigned our tasks for the evening. Hanusia would guard the wagon at the final stop, our end point for completing the mission. Three of us would station ourselves along the tracks to gather up any boxes thrown from the train. They might be heavy, had to be snatched up as soon as they were dropped, and would have to be carried all the way to the wagon, up to three kilometers ahead. Jakub and Rubin were obvious choices for that job.

"I'll be at the third drop point," Meriam offered. "I'm older and stronger than Chaya."

Both of those were true, but I decided she was also wiser than me, choosing the job that didn't require her to climb into a moving train. That task fell to me.

Meriam dropped me off first by the tracks outside Bochnia, right before the train would pick up speed on its way to Krakow. A small station was here, but there'd be no passengers boarding. It'd be a safe place to hide while I waited for the train to pass by. When it did, I'd have five minutes to get inside a boxcar, then would make a supply drop every five minutes after that. Jakub had carefully calculated the places each of them should hide along the tracks to find the boxes as soon as I dropped them. After the third drop, I was to get myself off the train when I found a soft place to jump.

No problem.

I hoped.

Once Hanusia left, I waited for the train from behind a wide oak tree, on a night that had suddenly become far too lonely. I had no fear of the dark, but no love for it either. The moon would've made it easier to see had it not been dimmed by thick clouds, but I supposed not being seen was the whole point of our raid.

Right on schedule at 10:14 p.m., the train rounded a bend, its engine a steady hum, its bright headlight blinding me. At the last minute, Rubin had cautioned that Nazis could be on watch from platforms outside the trains.

"Whatever you do, don't open a car next to one of those guards," he had warned.

"How will I know which one has guards before I'm up on the train?" I asked.

"You won't." He gave my cheek a quick kiss, then added, "Just don't get caught."

With such encouragement in mind, I took a runner's position, ready for the train to pass. I was aiming for one of the boxcars in the middle of the line, hoping not to see any guards there.

Hoping not to see guards anywhere at all. Or that, at least, they never saw me.

The engine passed first, then a passenger car. A single Nazi was indeed standing watch on a platform at the rear of it, but he was leaning on a railing, looking away from me. I let four more cars pass, then began running alongside the train, near a line of boxcars. My heart had already been pounding with anticipation, but that was nothing compared to now, running as fast as I ever had, trying to get close enough to a bar on the train doors. Cool wind smacked me across the face and the engine noises were all I could hear. If a soldier was shouting orders at me, I wouldn't know.

My first attempt at grabbing anything attached to the

door failed, but I did better with the car after that, taking hold of the bar and swinging my feet onto the thick metal rod that braced the car from underneath. So far, so good.

It was a trick to unlatch the door with only one hand, but I opened it enough to slide my body inside, then widened it a little more. Against the passing city lights, I checked my watch. 10:20. Only four minutes before the first drop.

It was too dark inside the car to read the writing on the boxes, so I opted for the heavier ones, figuring they were more likely to hold weapons or food.

Four minutes later, I pushed a box out of the car and watched it tumble down a hillside. I didn't dare look out to see if Rubin was ready for it, or if anyone had seen what had happened, but I didn't hear any whistles or shouted orders, and that gave me courage.

Exactly five minutes later, I did the same, but with two boxes, since they were lighter, and hoping Jakub was nearby. This was his plan. If I'd missed the mark, it was because he'd done his calculations wrong.

At the third drop, I rolled out the heaviest box yet, smiling as I did. Meriam had mentioned how strong she was. I figured she'd want to be tested.

Then I looked out for a safe place to jump. This was the part of the mission I'd dreaded most. Surely, I wasn't the first person ever to jump from a moving train. Surely, they'd all survived it.

Or someone must have survived a train jump. Somewhere.

Hadn't they?

As soon as the ground looked relatively soft, I closed my eyes, crossed my arms over my chest, and jumped. I hit the ground hard, scraping my elbows on the gravel beneath the surface and hoping the stinging was the worst of it. I rolled with the momentum and kept going until I was behind some bushes alongside the tracks.

That's where Rubin and Meriam found me twenty minutes later. My arms were still across my chest, but at least my pulse was normal again.

"Are you all right?" Rubin asked, helping me to sit up.

"You said it'd be easy if I rolled," I told him. "You said the ground would be soft from the fall rains."

"Are you all right?" Meriam echoed.

"That depends." My smile at them was hopeful. "What did we get from that train?"

"What did we get?" Meriam laughed. "My friend, we have one crate of canned stew, two crates of potatoes, and some military field supplies that should fetch a good price on the black market."

I leaned back against the slope and tried to do the math. It was enough food for the residents of a single building in the ghetto for a single night. The field supplies might provide bribe money to obtain twenty blank identification papers, or to smuggle two or three children out of the ghettos.

"It isn't enough." I stood, determined to ignore the first aches of oncoming bruises. "When is the next raid?"

SEVEN

October 26, 1942
Krakow

Almost daily, Akiva continued to evolve, both in mission and in tactics. Gusta often spoke about how we should fear death—not for ourselves, but because death would shorten our mission.

When rumors began swirling in the ghetto about a coming deportation, Dolek found us a safe house outside the ghetto walls.

"It's to protect us," he explained, "and those inside the ghetto. If we're caught, we can't risk them being blamed for our actions."

I had a reliable safe house ready in Krakow, used as a temporary stopping place for anyone we smuggled out, but Dolek chose an apartment nearer to the ghetto. That would serve as our new bunker, and just in time. Two days after we left, six thousand people were removed from the Podgorze Ghetto by train. Thankfully, my parents were spared.

This time.

There was another change too, one that affected my cell. Dolek took Meriam and a few other couriers with him on a trip north and returned with a new, fifth member for us, a girl named Esther Karolinski, who intently studied the floorboards as she mumbled, "I've never done resistance work before, but I can't wait to learn."

I arched a brow, deeply concerned. How could a girl who wouldn't even look us in the eye be of use for what we had planned?

"Do you have any particular skills?" I asked her. When her only response was to stare blankly back at me, I added, "Can you pick locks? Aim a gun? Speak German?"

"I have a good memory," she said, keeping her eyes on the floor. "And I can knit, though I'm sure that's not what you meant."

No, it wasn't.

Esther was petite, with a shy voice, an uncertain smile, and every possible look and mannerism to radiate her Jewishness. None of us were perfect, but we all brought something of value to our jobs. I saw nothing in Esther that would help our cause, and plenty that endangered both her and us.

I immediately pulled Rubin aside into the small kitchen of our safe house. Esther was at the other end of the room, but although we whispered, she probably could hear me, and I didn't care if she did. Akiva was not a nursery school for helpless young girls.

"If we get in trouble, will she knit us weapons to escape?" I said.

"You were a beginner once. We all were." Rubin was far more patient than I ever was.

"I never lacked confidence like she does. And I was trained before I did my first mission."

"We don't have time to train that way anymore, Chaya. She'll learn on the job."

"If she can. Look at her."

When I peeked back, there Esther was, sitting alone in the corner, jumping at every passing shadow and pretending not to hear our conversation—probably because then she'd have to defend herself. If she wanted to learn, then she should train in a cell with less dangerous work than ours.

"Dolek wants her to come with us," Rubin said.

"I can do it," Esther mumbled, still not looking at us. "Trust me."

Rubin shrugged back at me, and the decision was made. No matter what I said or thought, Esther was coming.

Tonight, we left even later than the 10 p.m. curfew for Poles. The streets were watched at all times by Nazi soldiers, though Akiva knew their routes and routines. We took the quietest roads, the darkest alleys, and understood where to hide if we heard a whistle and an order to stop.

Rubin had a gun tonight, a Nazi Luger with only three bullets in it, but we weren't to use it unless we had no other choice. That was fine by me. Our cell's mission was to steal supplies. Gunfire hardly helped keep us secret.

This time, we planned to raid a train station on the outskirts of Krakow. Several trains had come in during the day, but because of heavy rain, the Nazis were waiting until the following morning to unload them.

Rubin took the lead to get us into the station, then motioned us beside him. We hid behind a tree with gnarled roots that threatened to trip us every time we moved and with tendrils of branches that soaked us with dripping rainwater. But it'd take more than that to stop us.

I leaned out just far enough to count a small group of five Nazis clustered together beneath a metal overhang, the dim lamplight overhead converting their green uniforms to gray. The soldiers looked cold, but at least there they might stay dry. They should not have left their posts, but even if they had intended to monitor their assigned positions, the lure of casual conversation had apparently distracted them.

I briefly wondered what they were discussing. How much they missed home? How cold and wet they'd be when their shift ended? How many Jews were murdered that day?

Did they ever discuss that? Did they even think of us as people?

"This is a bad idea," Esther whispered to Rubin. "We shouldn't be here."

"But we are," Jakub replied, brushing her aside to take

the first step into the train yard. The rainy night offered us little help to light our way and had created small pothole ponds that we tried to avoid so there'd be no sounds of splashing. Hanusia went next, then I made sure to keep Esther ahead of me as we ran. Rubin followed last of all.

We passed several train cars nearer to the Nazis. Some of their doors were partially opened, full of wood boxes and metal crates, promises of supplies we urgently needed. But entering any of those would put us in full view of the soldiers. The train car we chose would have to be better positioned.

On the set of tracks farthest from the soldiers, Jakub slid open the doors to a car, quietly, and no wider than was necessary. I climbed inside and immediately smiled. Most of the boxes were stamped as food items, which Hanusia began gathering into a load she could carry.

I handed Esther a box of first aid supplies, then said, "Stand watch near the door."

While she did, I joined Rubin to study a crate at the back, marked as hand grenades. Since that was probably the most valuable thing we could take, and the heaviest, Rubin handed me the gun so that he could carry the crate.

"Is it safe to take those?" Esther's eyes were wide with worry.

Jakub picked up a box of dried meat, and while I looked around for something else of value, he jumped from the train car.

Without warning, a gunshot rang through the night and

Jakub yelped with pain. There was no time to think or to consider what I was doing. I darted from the car and found my target, a Nazi running toward us with his pistol out, shouting for his comrades. I raised the gun Rubin had given me and fired.

It created an echo through the air that put a hard lump inside my gut. What had I just done? Had I really shot someone? The soldier fell and went quiet, though I didn't know if I'd killed him or if he was just unconscious. Either way, we had to run. Other soldiers were already shouting from the distance, and coming closer.

We dropped everything and jumped from the car, then spread out in whatever direction we could think to go. I followed Esther because she was slower than the rest of us and finally took her hand to pull her along with me. We headed up the tracks, ending up at the back of the station on an overpass covered with vines. Silently, I pushed her to climb over the railings and then motioned for her to get behind the vines. Worried that I'd been spotted, I dropped to the ground and squeezed beneath the bottom railing, then grabbed the same vines before rolling over the ledge. I had hoped we'd have time to climb down to a thick patch of weeds below, but German voices were close behind us and growing louder. I didn't want them to see the leaves rustling, so I folded myself behind them and hoped Esther had already done the same. Once we were inside, I couldn't see her, but I heard her breathing and knew she was crying.

"Stop that!" I hissed. I was already angry enough. If those tears caught anyone's attention, even God wouldn't expect me to forgive her.

She stopped, and just in time. At least two Nazis stood on the overpass directly above us. My grip on the wet ivy was not as good as I wanted, but my foot was tangled and that helped to prop me up. Esther couldn't have weighed much more than the ivy itself. She should be safe, though I was sure I could hear the tremble of her lower lip, as if at any second a sob would burst out in all its devastating glory.

"Two of them ran this way," one of the Nazis said. "One with blonde hair, the other was darker."

"Poles?" the other replied. "The Jews wouldn't have done this."

Whatever they believed made no difference to me. I was a Jew. I was a Pole. Depending on the day. Depending on the need.

"The blonde is the one that shot Schmidt. But we'll find them all, eventually."

"Do not report that there were five," the second man answered. "If we report five, we'll have to answer for how five people snuck in here. We'll report that there were two Poles, both girls. If they are Jews, we'll have to explain that too, and neither of us wants that. Go tell the others."

He sent his companion on his way, but I heard him kick the overpass in anger. If he was the one in charge, then he'd take the punishment for our raid and his fallen man, with no prisoners to show for it.

Unless the others from my cell were caught. Unless Esther and I were caught. Then we'd take the punishment instead. I closed my eyes, vowing the same things I always did when I knew I was in trouble.

No matter what they'd say, no matter what they'd do, I would never tell them about my cell. I would never tell them about Akiva. No matter what.

Above Esther and me, the Nazi wasn't budging. I wished he would leave too, but instead, he lowered his rifle by the stock and brushed it through the ivy. The thick leaves swished against my face, flicking rainwater on me. It was close enough that I could smell the metal.

I pressed deeper against the wall and prayed he couldn't get at any better angle with that rifle. If he did, I'd grab the stock and pull him over the railing. I'd likely lose my own balance in the vines to do it, though, so for both our sakes, I hoped that wouldn't be necessary.

He gave up on the vines, then fired a spray of automatic bullets into the grasses below. If Esther and I had had five seconds longer to hide, that's where we would've been.

We'd have been there if Esther had been a faster runner.

That thought sent a shudder straight through me.

We remained there for what seemed like hours, all the while the echo of my gunshot ringing in my ears with the enormity of what I might've done to that soldier. I tried telling myself that Jakub would be dead, that all of us would be dead if I hadn't fired. Besides, it was nothing compared to what the Germans were doing to my people. When none of that worked, I silently repeated the goals of the resistance, to do whatever was necessary to disrupt the German occupation of Poland. So I had.

The rain finally let up, and still we waited, until my knuckles were swollen from gripping the vine, until I was chilled to trembling. Until I was certain it was safe to shinny down the vines to the road below and get back to the safe house.

Esther followed me the whole way, her head down, silent as the night. Our mission had failed and it was her fault. She was supposed to have been keeping watch.

It was a great relief to find the others were safe, including Jakub, though we'd have to figure out a way to dig the bullet from his leg with the few supplies we had here. Nothing we had could numb the pain from the wound, and from the haunted look in his eyes, I knew he was thinking the same thing.

Beyond that, we'd returned with no supplies, and that train yard would be too heavily guarded from now on for us to return. And every soldier in Krakow would be warned to watch for a girl fitting my description.

The last words I spoke to Esther were "Don't ever ask me to trust you again."

EIGHT

November 20, 1942
Akiva Bunker, Krakow

Our numbers were growing, and resistance members from other groups frequently came and went from our bunker. Maybe from the outside it appeared to be a normal Polish apartment, but inside, the bunker was packed with bedrolls, Shimshon's typewriter and forgery equipment, and the spoils of our raids. If a stranger ever came to the door, a quick glance inside would be enough to justify a call to the Gestapo.

Akiva carried on with our traditions, though, including Shabbat—the Sabbath—tonight. Looking at the faces around me in our crowded front room, surely I wasn't the only one who felt the tension in the air. It was thick, pressing against me from every side, weighing on me, making it hard to draw a complete breath. We all understood the same unspoken thought: Another change was coming.

Akiva members usually tried to celebrate Shabbat together. No one pretended that our humble gathering could replace the rituals we'd once shared with our families, but for most of us, this was the only family we had left.

At sundown, Gusta lit the candles, made of squares of margarine with a string wick. They would burn out fast, long before we were ready to lose their light. Somehow tonight, that felt particularly meaningful.

With each candle, Gusta pronounced her hope for light to return to Poland, and to the world at war. We said the blessing together, but I covered my eyes with my hands, giving myself a private moment with God to ask for health, happiness, and prosperity. I didn't exactly mean what I said that night. I knew our leaders were going to tell us what they were planning, something bigger than we'd ever done before. Despite the words of my prayer, in the deepest reaches of my heart, all I really wanted was to live long enough to complete my part of that mission.

We stood for the singing of the prayers, though with thin walls and neighbors who'd gladly fatten themselves by blackmailing us, it was little more than rhythmic whispering.

Shimshon passed around the wine while reciting the blessing, the kiddush; then we lined up for the washing of hands and breaking of bread.

My mind was supposed to be focused on the holiness of the moment, the sacred nature of each part of the meal. But I kept thinking of my parents, who probably had no bread at all tonight. If they did, it wasn't challah bread, and their share would be little more than a mouthful.

The rest of the meal was simple and there wasn't nearly enough meat to go around, but it was delicious considering the trouble it must have taken to acquire everything, and I was more than grateful to be part of it.

Grateful . . . and nervous. The closer we came to the end of the meal, the sooner I would hear Akiva's plan.

Following a teaching from the Torah, Dolek gathered us in a circle and stood in the center, looking us each in the face before beginning.

"There is no turning back," he said. "If you want life, don't look for it here."

We knew that. We'd always known that this was never about winning, only about dying on our feet, as fighters, not on our knees.

From behind the circle, Shimshon took over. "Look at what we have already accomplished. We have provided forged papers for hundreds of people to escape the ghettos. We have warned as many as would listen to get themselves into hiding and not to board the trains. We have fed our people, clothed them, armed them when possible. We have smuggled out children who now have a chance to live, thanks to you. Never let it be said that the young are powerless or incapable. Never let it be said that youth is a liability. No, we feel life within us more intensely than most, and whatever happens after tonight, never doubt that you have done God's work."

Dolek pointed to a girl in the corner. I knew her only as Anka, and that she was a courier, same as me. Her cheek was badly bruised, and she'd had difficulty sitting up straight all evening. She'd been released only a few days ago after having been arrested by the Nazis.

"Anka fights for us," Dolek said. "She withstood their questions, their brutality. She told them nothing."

We honored her courage, but the possibility that what had happened to Anka could also happen to me was constantly on my mind. Even now, she looked strong, resolute, so much of what I wanted to be whenever I stepped into dangerous territory. I wished I could be more like her.

No, I intended to *make* myself more like her, armored with courage and determination, and a renewed vow that if I was ever caught, I would live—or die—having remained fully loyal to the resistance.

Dolek brushed back a lock of dark hair, damp with sweat, that had fallen over his forehead. Then he laid out his plans for our next attack, one very different from anything we'd done before. It would happen shortly before Christmas, one month from now. He promised that specific assignments would come soon, and that no matter what our jobs were that night, we were to carry them out to the best of our ability.

My eye shifted to Esther when he said that. Ever since our failed raid last month, she had remained as far from me as possible, and rarely spoke to anyone. Whatever her assignment for the upcoming attack, it had better not involve me.

The night ended with words I would never forget. Dolek's eyes were bright and he spoke with a clear voice as he said, "We will not win, we will not get glory, not in this life, anyway. We are fighting for our three lines of history just so that it will not be said that our youth went like sheep to the slaughter."

Seated in a room filled with people I considered heroes, I doubted that my name would be included in those three lines. Nor should I be remembered, not when my job as a courier was to be forgotten whenever possible. But I understood my purpose, and was glad to have any role to play.

I would do my best. For Akiva's fighters. For Poland. For the Jewish people, as long as God preserved us. And for myself. I had no intention of going down without a fight.

I was ready to claim our place in history.

NINE

December 22, 1942
Cyganeria Café, Krakow

The week before we attacked the Cyganeria Café, I barely slept. How could I, when every whisper around me was filled with questions about what might happen that night. What if we failed? What if in the end, all our efforts amounted to nothing? Or, somehow more frightening, what if we succeeded?

Over the last month, Akiva's membership had grown to forty people, the swelling of our ranks coming as a response to the rapidly worsening conditions in Krakow.

Half of all residents still in the Podgorze Ghetto had already been transferred to the Belzec extermination camp, and rumors were growing of other camps expanding their machineries of death, in Auschwitz-Birkenau, Chelmno, Treblinka, and other places throughout Poland.

The Nazis were preparing for the complete annihilation of the Jews.

Occasionally, I heard whispers from other Akiva members that we were fools to think our efforts would make any difference. My response to them was always the same. "Let us be foolish, then, because if we save even one life, we are the best of fools."

The timing for this attack had been carefully chosen. The German invaders wanted to celebrate Christmas, to buy last-minute presents for their loved ones at home, and to take a break from the war. We'd heard reports of some Allied troops calling for holiday truces at the front. That was fine for them—their war was very different from ours, and their temporary declarations of peace mattered little to us.

Our Akiva leaders had been planning tonight's attack for a month, ever since the Sabbath evening we now called our Last Supper. It would be far more dangerous than anything we'd done before. Over the past two months, most of our missions had happened after curfew, in secrecy and silence. But tonight's mission was meant to draw attention to our cause. We wanted the Poles to see it, the Nazis to feel it, and the world to hear it.

First to leave the bunker were the less experienced girls, assigned to post anti-Nazi flyers around Krakow, calling on Poles to resist, to fight back. Even if only a handful of citizens were encouraged to join resistance efforts, at least it ensured that our movement continued, regardless of what happened to us.

Next to leave were the boys assigned to post Polish flags at key locations around the city, places where our flags had always stood. We wanted the people to remember Poland as it had been, and that we were not a conquered people as long as we refused to accept it. There was another strategy at work, one I credited to Dolek's genius. He hoped the Polish flags would make the Nazis suspect that this was the work of the Polish underground, not the Jews.

The third part of the operation was important symbolically. Two of our members were assigned to lay a wreath at the broken statue of Adam Mickiewicz, our beloved national poet. Many Poles were nearly as angry about the destruction of the statue as they had been about our country being invaded. We hoped the wreath would remind them of that anger. If they would not fight for millions of living Jews, perhaps they would fight for the memory of a single dead poet.

Those Akiva members who lacked enough experience to go far from the bunker were to call the fire department at coordinated times, reporting fires at various places around the city. There wouldn't be any fires, but we wanted the confusion.

I expected that would be Esther's assignment. She could do the least amount of harm there. But that was not the plan. Shortly before we left, Rubin pulled me aside. "You should know, Esther has been assigned with us to the Cyganeria Café."

My jaw fell open in utter disbelief. "What?" By far, the most dangerous part of tonight's attack was the Cyganeria Café.

I'd watched Esther earlier today, and already knew she'd spent most of the afternoon knitting. Knitting, while the rest of us prepared for the biggest attack we'd yet attempted!

"She's part of our cell, Chaya."

"So is Jakub! He still walks with a limp, thanks to her."

Rubin tightened his lips, then said, "The plans are set. I just thought you'd want to know."

I would've argued further, but it wouldn't have made any difference, and besides, it was time to leave. My backpack was loaded with my identification papers and layers of clothing in case I was searched. Buried beneath the clothes were three grenades. If I could have, I would've brought more.

In total, Akiva would be attacking three cafés known to be frequented by German officers. This late into December, the nights were brutally cold, so the cafés would be full. Busiest of all would be the Cyganeria Café, a simple and pleasant restaurant where my family used to eat.

My fellow cell members and I left separately, each of us taking different routes to the café, and each of us aware that regardless of who did or didn't make it there, the attack must go forward. Other Akiva cells would be there too, though I didn't know how many or which ones.

The route I was given took me through a German district, since I was less likely to be stopped. Not only because of my looks, but because I knew the expectations for my behavior around the Germans. I walked in the street like all Poles did—the sidewalk was for conquerors, they said. I kept my head up and eyes focused on the road, but never looked directly at anyone. Confident, but not arrogant. Purposeful, but not driven. Formidable, but not dangerous.

I smiled at that thought. Whether I made it to the café, or if some unfortunate soldier stopped me along the way, these grenades I was carrying were going to be thrown.

One way or another, I intended to be exceptionally dangerous.

Because of my longer route, I was one of the last to arrive, but I took my place across the street, biding my time by pretending to window-shop. The Cyganeria Café was on a busy street, surrounded by other shops and businesses, all decorated for the Christmas season. The building itself was made of large bricks and stone divided by tall arched windows. Through them, I could see the café was full of German soldiers. Civilians bustled along the streets, hurrying home with their holiday packages. We had no wish to harm them. The timing would have to be exact.

Outside the café, other Akiva members had quietly gathered. I recognized a boy who'd recently joined us, leaning against the bricks, reading a newspaper. Rubin stood beside a street sign, eating a pastry, and others still were milling about, engaged in any activity that wouldn't draw attention their way. Dolek was near the café's entrance, off to my left. He would give the signal for us to begin.

I checked my watch—fifteen minutes before seven o'clock, our start time. I lowered my wrist but immediately felt desperate to check it again, eager to see the minutes tick away. But I couldn't do that. I couldn't look as anxious as I felt.

Staring in the window across the street, I returned to watching the reflection of the Cyganeria Café behind me. Inside, soldiers were clinking together mugs of Pilsner, perhaps laughing about how easily we had become a conquered people. I thought again of the grenades I carried, itching to throw them.

I'd also been mentally counting down the time. Five minutes must have passed by now, then ten. When I was sure it had been fifteen minutes, I stole a quick glance at Dolek, who'd just politely stepped aside to allow other soldiers to enter. He wouldn't abandon our plans. Perhaps my counting was off.

Even a year ago, I could never have imagined being here, ready to attack, eager to attack. Shooting that soldier in the train yard two months ago had deeply affected me. For long nights afterward, I'd lain awake in bed in a cold sweat replaying that moment. Finally, I came to understand that even one less Nazi in Krakow might save the lives of hundreds of Jews.

Esther sidled up next to me, arriving last of all with a freshly knitted scarf around her neck. "Are you ready?" Before I could answer, she quickly added, "Of course, we could never be truly ready. I just wondered if everything is in place. It's almost seven o'clock."

"Are *you* ready?" I asked. "We're all counting on you tonight. Not like—"

"I made a mistake at the train tracks that night, I know." Her expression tightened. "I learned from it. I won't make that mistake again."

I sincerely hoped that was true. The success of this operation balanced on a paper-thin edge. Even the tiniest slip could ruin everything.

"If you don't want any mistakes, then back away from me," I said. The Nazis were suspicious of people in close conversations on the streets. It was not uncommon for them to be stopped and questioned separately about what they had been talking about. If their two stories didn't match exactly, it could be grounds for their arrest.

Only a minute later, the church bells of Krakow rang out, my heart pounding harder with each toll. Seven bells. Seven o'clock.

Still near the café door, Dolek struck first, pulling the pin from his grenade and throwing it through the large front window, which shattered in an ear-piercing crash, followed immediately by an explosion inside the café. Violent shouts of alarm and panic immediately rang from everywhere around me: shoppers rushing into the streets, screaming passersby running in any direction they could away from the café, cars on the street slamming their brakes. Inside the café, all I could see was chaos. Through the thick smoke pouring out the broken windows, furious soldiers began to emerge, many with obvious cuts on their faces or uniforms. They became the target of my first grenade. My second splintered apart the front door. My third went inside the café and exploded with enough force to blow some of the bricks off the building.

Sirens began shrieking toward us, and the bitter smell of dust and smoke and blood irritated my senses. From the corner of my eye, I saw Esther throw her grenades too, though with all the commotion, I wasn't sure where they landed. My ears picked up orders being shouted in German. We needed to go. Now.

Esther pointed down the street to where Dolek was signaling with hand gestures. "We're supposed to run!"

"Get somewhere safe," I shouted to her, already hurrying away. Nazis who had survived the attack were scaling the rubble, their rifles in hand. When they began firing, I saw bodies in civilian clothes fall, but through the smoke, I couldn't tell if any of them were ours. "Run!"

Everyone who could get to the Akiva bunker was supposed to meet there. I tried to get there too, but soldiers were emerging on every street like angry hornets from the hive. Military vehicles with searchlights and sirens roamed every street, forcing me into the alleys, and orders were being shouted through loudspeakers that everyone not indoors would be arrested or shot on sight.

My senses seemed to be on high alert, as if I saw every movement, even the flutter of a lingering autumn leaf in the wind, heard every whisper from apartments above wondering who I was, why I was running. Beneath my feet, I almost had a feel for which way to turn, and which direction would lead me to the Nazis now swarming the city.

I was only a couple of blocks from the safe house where our cell had stored our supplies over the last two months. I'd go there for the night and then make my way to the Akiva bunker as soon as everything calmed down, as soon as *I* calmed down, maybe in another few days. My safe house was on the second floor of a small apartment building. I slid inside it through an alley entrance, barely escaping the notice of a squadron of soldiers who were running through the streets, weapons drawn. I was the first to enter but didn't lock the door, certain that by the end of the night, others would join me.

I stayed awake until dawn, peering out curtains, listening for any faint cries for help, pacing the floor and wondering if everyone else had made it to Dolek's bunker. Were they there now, reviewing what we'd done, celebrating our victory? Did anyone wonder where I was?

Or . . . panic seeped through my entire body . . . was there no one left to wonder about me?

Maybe not.

No one came that night.

Nor the next night, nor the one after that. I snuck out the following day to try to enter our bunker, but the entire building was surrounded by Gestapo officers.

Something terrible must have happened in the aftermath of the attack. I caught my breath in my throat and hurried back toward my safe house, several streets away. If the Nazis had breached the bunker, then they knew about Akiva. We were always careful to keep personal information about ourselves out of the bunker, but traces of every single one of us were there. I tried to think of what I might've left behind. A change of clothes, one of the bags I used for smuggling, full of my grandmother's shawls. What else?

I slammed the safe house door behind me and locked it, then leaned against it, trying not to be sick.

Had I left anything behind that could lead back to me, or my parents? No matter how hard I tried to think, I just wasn't sure.

Did they know about me? What had happened to the rest of Akiva? Was I next?

CHAPTER
TEN

February 13–14, 1943
Akiva Safe house, Krakow

The attack on the Cyganeria Café was well over a month ago, a lifetime ago. Eleven dead, the papers said, and thirteen wounded. For all we lost, it should have been more. Every day that passed seemed years separated from the day before. The raids on German trains and warehouses, our attack on the café, all of that became a memory, a drifting piece of time that felt more like a dream. I had become a shadow of someone I once was, not the actual me.

Gradually, I began venturing out into the city and found myself at the building where our bunker had been. It wasn't guarded anymore, so I cautiously entered, hoping not to see anyone else who lived there because how would I look at them and smile as if all was well? It wasn't.

I got as far as the bunker's front door before I saw the bullet holes. I raised a hand to feel them and could almost hear the exchange of gunfire that must have happened in this very place. Spots of blood were on the wood floor beneath me. Was that our blood or theirs? I wanted to go in, to see our former bunker for myself, but a door slammed on the floor above, startling me so much that I quickly left, retreating to my safe house. A place where I no longer felt safe at all.

It was time to face reality. Those who had made it back to the bunker had probably been killed or arrested. Maybe others had escaped, going to the forests or joining other resistance groups up in Warsaw. As awful as it was to let them go—Rubin, Jakub, Hanusia, and even Esther—I needed to move on and make some decisions of my own.

Beginning with leaving the safe house. Remaining here had become as dangerous as running. Maybe more. I was surrounded by weapons, money, food, and blank identification papers ready to be forged. Everything in this apartment gave my people a chance for life.

And would also guarantee my death. It was only a matter of time before the neighbors began wondering about the teenage girl who rarely went out and never had visitors. About the people who used to come and go at odd hours, often after curfew. Why hadn't they returned ever since the Cyganeria Café was attacked?

Soon after they asked each other these questions, they would ask the Nazis, who would answer with my imprisonment and torture. Then they would kill me.

I wouldn't wait around for that to happen. I had to leave

Krakow, the scene of our crime. More than anything else, I longed to return to the Podgorze Ghetto one last time, to beg my parents to leave with me. But the guards at the ghetto gates would be watching for me, for the blonde girl who threw grenades at the café, then vanished into the night. I wondered if any of my grenades had killed their soldiers.

If they had, I wished I'd had more. The Germans were still here.

So was I, and I'd become more determined than ever. If the Germans took Akiva from me, I would find another resistance group to join and dedicate my life to it. Wherever I went from here, I intended to take with me as much contraband from this safe house as possible.

However, as I began packing the next morning, I found a note under my door. I didn't know how long it had been there, only that it hadn't been there last night.

With my breath caught in my throat, I unfolded the note, signed by someone known only as Antek. My heart leapt. Antek was a code name for an Akiva member who worked closely with our leaders. Maybe he'd seen me near the bunker.

I paced the floor while reading the note over and over. It read, "Despite our losses, we continue to fight. Meet a friend at point B at the usual time tomorrow. Prepare to travel."

Point B was in Krakow's Old Town, an easy walking distance from the train station. The usual time was nine in the morning, two hours after curfew was over, when the streets would already be busy enough for us to avoid any suspicion.

When I'd memorized the note, I immediately flushed it down the toilet. After that, I took time to think through every detail.

Who of our members might still be alive? Jakub's leg was never the same after that bullet, and Esther couldn't have survived while other, stronger people were taken. I liked Rubin, though it would be harder to travel with him than Hanusia. I hoped Hanusia would meet me.

But for now, I was happy just knowing that a spark of life remained within Akiva. No matter who would meet me tomorrow, at least I didn't have to be alone anymore.

At least the resistance continued.

ELEVEN

February 14, 1943
Podgorze Ghetto, Krakow

After a long afternoon of arguing with myself, I decided that I had to return to Podgorze Ghetto and see my parents. I knew it would be dangerous. I knew the soldiers there would still be on alert for any suspected resistance members. But it was also my last chance to say good-bye.

The main entry gate was between two tall archways with the Star of David on top. The concrete walls that stretched out from either side were also arched, designed to look like a series of Jewish gravestones. That was no accident.

The day those walls went up, the people here were buried alive and this place became a graveyard-in-waiting. Like every other ghetto, the people wandered about with vacant eyes, empty stomachs, and a gnawing sense that time was running out.

I studied the ghetto gates from a distance before entering, carefully targeting a soldier who'd be most likely to let me in. I wanted someone who seemed bored, whose attention had wandered back home rather than staying focused on the war.

With the change of a new shift, I finally spotted the guard I wanted. I'd seen him here before and he was kinder than the others. More important, his brain seemed duller than the others. But this didn't mean I could relax. Five other guards were at the same gate, and my timing wasn't as good as usual. I preferred to come when it was busier. When they were more easily distracted and hurried.

Nor would my usual excuses be as effective as before. I couldn't tell them I'd come to sell to the Jews—no one had money left to buy anything, and the Nazis were barely keeping up the ruse of caring whether anyone in the ghetto lived another day.

But I was smuggling in food for whoever might remain. Today, it was canned stew, much heavier than the potatoes I usually brought. I held my posture straight and tall, hoping the Nazi in front of me didn't notice how the cans hidden in my bag were weighing me down.

Normally, if I was discovered, I'd have some chance of talking my way out of any serious trouble. Not with these particular cans. They were supposed to have been issued to German soldiers fighting on the front, but we stole them last fall. If they were found, I'd have no way of explaining myself.

"Why are you coming to Podgorze Ghetto today?" the soldier asked as he examined my papers.

"Bringing supplies to Eagle Pharmacy," I said, a lie that was boosted by the blankets I'd packed near the top and around the sides of my bag.

I followed it with a smile, hoping to look friendly. Eagle Pharmacy was an excuse that usually worked well here. It was run by a Christian man who gave out medicine for free, tended to minor health issues when he could, and most important, managed a secret operation to smuggle children out of the ghetto into safe houses. We loved him for that, but crucially, the Nazis tolerated him. Better he deal with typhus than them.

The Nazi checked the top of my bag but not as thoroughly as he should have, then waved me inside. I released the breath that I was holding and took my first few steps.

"Wait!" This was one of the OD, calling me back. I closed my eyes a moment and steadied myself before turning around. I knew about this man. Before the war he had been a laborer, uneducated and poor. Now he had a blue jacket with lapels and a necktie like the upper class wore, strutting down the streets as if his costume made him something great. When the Nazis asked for volunteers for the Jewish police, he was one of the first to step forward. Now he had power over people who'd barely looked in his direction only a few years ago, and he relished every moment of it.

Some of the Jewish officers had retained their integrity, their loyalty to us, but not this man, who'd chosen cruelty and betrayal as the measure of his worth. If he could not be respected or admired, then he would be feared. It took everything I had to hide my loathing of him, and an extra dose of courage. It was possible he knew me too.

He stared at me far too long, then took a lock of my blonde hair in his hand, twisting it around his fingers. "You are Polish?" he asked. "Catholic?"

"You see the crucifix I wear?" I countered, gesturing to the chain around my neck.

"A Jew would wear a cross if it benefited them. Can you tell me, please, the Hail Mary?"

I smiled. That wasn't even a challenge. "Hail Mary, full of grace. The Lord is with thee. Blessed art thou—"

"Enough." For a moment, I thought he might let me go, but instead he turned me around. He was going to inspect my bag.

"It's only blankets for the children," I said, keeping my voice as calm as possible. "The pharmacy expected them this morning. I—"

"I have children too. It's a cold winter." He reached into the top of my bag and pulled out the first blanket. "For my youngest." He pulled out a second blanket. "For my eldest." I had five blankets with me and was quickly becoming worried that he may have an entire flock of cold children. He pulled out two more blankets. "For my wife and myself."

One blanket remained. I felt him staring at it, wondering what he might get in exchange for a blanket on the black market. It wasn't much. I never brought in anything visible with any real value. That was only an invitation for theft. But apparently, he wanted that last blanket.

He widened the bag and I felt his hand reach down. When he pulled the blanket up, it would disturb the way I'd wrapped the cans of food. I braced myself, barely daring to breathe. As soon as the cans clanked together, my plan was to swing the bag around and hit him with it as hard as I could. Then I'd run. I probably wouldn't get more than five or six steps away, but it'd almost be worth it if I could break his arm.

He tugged on the blanket and because of the cans, it didn't pull out. I began sliding the bag off my shoulder, ready to strike.

Not particularly ready for the consequences.

"Let the girl go!" a Nazi soldier called to the OD. "She's here for the pharmacy."

He grunted at me but immediately obeyed his German masters. "Get going, then, for what little good a single blanket will do."

I nodded back at him, keeping my emotions carefully in check. A part of me regretted not leaving him with the broken arm, though obviously, that would have ended even worse for me. I rounded the first corner I came to, then turned yet another corner until I found myself on a street filled with a long line of people, their ration cards in hand, probably waiting for a wagon with bread or soup. Their children darted about on the streets, the stronger ones building snowmen together while the weaker ones merely sat on the sidewalks, leaning against the buildings, barely looking at me as I passed by. I quietly distributed the cans to them, just as I'd done in other ghettos. Twelve cans. Twelve families that would have a bite of food tonight. The people here were noticeably thinner since the last time I came. Twelve cans of food would save no one.

Worse still, I kept two cans back. Maybe it was selfish. Maybe that made me—even in some small way—like the OD who took those blankets for his family. But I still had a family too. These two cans were for them.

I lowered my eyes as I walked to my parents' apartment. Since the last time I came, the ghetto had been divided between workers and nonworkers. In the next round of deportations, those judged unfit to work would be sent away first. My father should be in the workers' group, but I'd been told he faked an injury during the division of the ghetto, ensuring that he remained with my mother, listed as a nonworker.

If my parents were happy to see me again, there was no sign of it in their expressions. We hugged, and there was a stiff clutch against my back from my father's hands. His strength had kept him alive so far, but it couldn't last much longer.

My mother was alive only in the sense that her heart continued to beat. I wondered if she kept living only out of hope for Yitzchak to return. With each passing day, that hope faded a little, and so did she.

Maybe it wasn't fair for me to judge them this way, not when the same thought nagged at me every time I returned here. Knowing what had happened to Sara was awful, but the uncertainty with Yitzchak was much worse. A question never answered, an itch never scratched.

Mama smiled faintly at me, but although it had only been a short time since I'd last seen her, she seemed to look at me as if I'd become a stranger. Maybe I was a stranger now. My mind was older than my sixteen years, and I carried myself with confidence and purpose. Outside the ghetto, I had enough to eat, so my face wasn't sunken and hollow like too many faces that stared back at me here. Like my parents' faces today.

A hanging sheet now divided this room between my parents and another couple, and three more families had crowded into the other rooms of this tiny apartment. It occurred to me as I looked at their cramped conditions that if the space was divided evenly, each person's share would be roughly the size of a coffin.

I hated thinking that way, but I did. And it took more effort than usual to shake the image from my mind.

At least we were allowed some privacy in the bedroom, but our conversation would have to be brief and meaningless since the others, with nothing better to do, were almost certainly listening. I pulled the two cans of food from my nearly empty backpack and gave one to each of my parents. My father brought the can to his chest in obvious gratitude, but my mother didn't even seem to register what she was holding. He quietly took her can and folded it into his coat, then promised that he would make sure she ate.

"How long can you stay this time?" he asked.

"Not long."

I never stayed long. These were my parents in name and by blood, but they didn't feel like my parents anymore, not as we once were. Certainly, I had changed too.

My father gestured to the same small chair where I usually sat, and he and my mother settled on the wood crates on the floor that served as their bed.

"There are rumors," he said with a hopeful smile. "The Germans have spread themselves out too thin, and their defenses are weakening."

I shook my head. "It's not true, Papa."

"They say the Polish army is preparing to fight again."

"The Polish army remains underground, if it still exists at all." I drew in a breath. "Please don't believe any rumors from inside the ghetto. Where would the people get such news? No letters are allowed here, no newspapers, no radio. Someone wants to believe the war is ending, and that hope turns into rumors, which turn into beliefs that get people killed!"

I watched his smile fade with every harsh word, but this might be his last chance to finally accept the truth and escape this horrid place. Which was why it hurt so terribly when he replied, "We know our fate. We've accepted it."

Anger rose within me above the pain. He was like a man agreeing to drown simply because someone had pushed him in the water. But as much as I wanted to yell at them or shake them back to their senses, all I could do was lower my voice and lean in to my parents, fully aware that my mother was tracing her finger along the folds of the thin sheet below her, only marginally listening.

And as cruel as it was to tell them the truth of what was happening outside the ghetto, knowing it would shatter any hopes of Yitzchak being alive, I needed them to fight for their own lives now. "You must get out now, or the same thing will happen to you that happened to Yitz and Sara. Do you still have the identification papers I brought you a few months ago?"

"We have them, Chaya, but they're no good to us."

"Staying here is no good. You know how things will end if you stay, Papa. You must see that by now!"

"The ghettos are safer," Mama said, still distant. "Out there we were harassed, beaten. Here, at least we are alone with our own people."

I turned to my father. "Papa, please—"

"Chaya, enough. It's more than your mother can take."

His words were gentle, but I didn't want a gentle voice now. I wanted him to be defiant, bold. I wanted my parents to fight for their lives as hard as I was fighting.

Suddenly, I wasn't here as a member of the resistance, or even as a daughter obligated to help her family. I was their little bird again, frightened and lost, desperate to be held in my parents' arms as they whispered words of comfort and promised to make everything better. I was *their* child, and I still needed them. Why couldn't they want to live for *my* sake?

I stifled my tears, but Mama had already lain down on her bed, evidently too tired to continue talking. Papa suggested it might be better if I left and let her sleep. I patted her shoulder and heard her murmur my name. I knew she loved me, just as I would always love her. But looking at her, I silently vowed again never to quit fighting, never to accept defeat. And always to remember that every act of resistance mattered.

Papa walked me to the bedroom door, and after assuring that we were alone, he whispered, "I heard of some Krakow Jews who attacked the Germans at the end of last year, at a café in town. Were you part of that?"

I looked him in the eye, not much different from the way I looked at that Nazi. And I lied to him as fluently as I had at the gates. "Of course not, Papa."

"The Jews were part of that scout group you used to belong to, Akiva. You're not still with them, I hope?" His eyes focused on mine, and for a brief moment he was the stern, protective father I'd always known.

For that one moment.

Then my mother called out and in his distraction, I repeated, "Of course not, Papa."

He should have known I was lying, but he probably needed to believe me. He nodded, assuring himself that his little girl wasn't capable of what had happened at the Cyganeria Café.

Then he gave me a hug, holding tight as if this would be our last time together. I didn't know if that was because of what was coming for him, or for me, but whichever it was, when I said good-bye it felt final. My heart tore all over again, but I had to keep going.

Tomorrow morning, I would meet my contact within the resistance, to hear what Akiva asked of me now. Quite possibly, it would be a mission from which I was not expected to return.

Of course, I was almost never expected to return from any mission, and so far, I always had. Maybe there was only a little hope, but any hope at all was more than I ever dared ask for.

· PART TWO ·

TWELVE

February 15, 1943
Old Town, Krakow

The meeting place was at the base of the ruined statue of
Adam Mickiewicz in Krakow's Old Town district. This
was where we laid the wreath the night we attacked the
Cyganeria Café nearly two months ago. I wondered how
many Poles saw the wreath before it was removed.

Old Town today was nothing like the square where I
used to play as a child. Now enormous red flags with black
swastikas hung from every balcony and topped every flag-
pole. The trumpeter who used to play the first notes of
the Polish anthem every hour from St. Mary's Church had
been silenced. The square was thick with the usual shoppers and businessmen, but now they cautiously mixed with
Nazis and other German officials. I never stared, but I
always looked.

I accidentally bumped into one officer as I was jostled
along with the crowds. He was a tall man with dark blond

hair and a face that might've been handsome if it were not the face of a murderer.

"*Sei vorsichtig!*" he shouted at me.

I mumbled an apology in his language and moved away with my eyes down. There are several ways to warn someone to be careful in German. The meaning he chose was specific—that it was dangerous to have bumped into him.

I smiled despite myself. Perhaps it was dangerous for *him* to have bumped into me. My bag was loaded with weapons, and I knew how to use them all. But that wasn't the purpose for these weapons, nor was this the place where I wanted to make my last stand.

At one time, I would have questioned the wisdom of a public meeting, especially near the heart of where the Germans set up their government. But Akiva had learned that as long as we did nothing to draw attention to ourselves, we were less suspicious meeting beneath the noses of the Germans than in quiet corners on the outskirts of town, where we'd be expected to gather. Where they'd be watching for us.

From a distance, I saw a figure standing near the broken statue, and I blinked a couple of times, certain that could not be my contact. Because even in wartime, facing the extinction of my people, surely fate could not be this cruel. In my mind, I'd felt certain I would see Rubin or Hanusia here, or even someone from another Akiva cell.

Not Esther.

I was glad that she was still alive, of course. I'd be glad

for any of us to be alive, but this was different. This was the person with whom I was supposed to complete a mission, a person I had to trust with my life.

That simply wasn't her. It would never be her.

She approached me as if to offer a hug of greeting, but I stepped back and lowered my eyes. Two seconds into our meeting and she'd already drawn attention our way. We wouldn't hug or speak in hushed tones with our heads huddled together. We wouldn't let our eyes dart around as if expecting to be shot at any minute.

She was dressed in slacks and so was I, which could have been better planned. There would be other teens in slacks, of course, but most girls wore dresses, especially those trying to pass themselves off as respectable middle-class Poles.

Looking around at nothing in particular, and certainly not at her, I asked, "You're here to give me the next assignment?"

She shrugged. "It's our assignment together."

Of course it was. I hoisted the bag on my shoulder again, trying not to show how heavy it was. "Which way are we walking?" If she was coming with me, then we wouldn't talk about the assignment here. I just wanted to get moving.

She was more prepared with an answer than I might have expected. "Train station."

"Taking the train? No, not there. Not with you." Even with my Polish looks, it was dangerous to board the train in Krakow. The Gestapo employed Jews to keep watch for other Jews attempting to leave the city, figuring they could better identify one of their own. Their quota was ten Jews per day, and failing to meet the quota could result in their dismissal. Dismissal often ended in the death camps, so they were well motivated to spot us.

Esther shook her head. "I can get through the train station, Chaya. I can."

We'd see about that. "How far are we going?"

"Lodz."

I drew in a sharp breath and forced myself to release it without visibly panicking. Our leaders had told us never to go to Lodz. It was particularly dangerous to smuggle anything inside the ghetto there, and even if we were successful, the OD was brutal and the Judenrat was corrupt. Lodz was one of the worst.

"You didn't get these orders from anyone within Akiva," I said, my tone accusatory and cold. "Dolek, the Draengers— they always refused us permission to go there."

"Dolek is dead," Esther said flatly. "I don't know how the Gestapo found Akiva's bunker after Cyganeria, but Dolek and a few others refused to be taken alive. Everyone else at the bunker was either shot on site or arrested."

I suspected Dolek's life had ended the way he wanted it to, in a final flash of defiance. But the news settled in me like an unbearable weight. Few men were his equal.

Esther continued, "The Draengers are in Montelupich Prison. Most of the other resistance fighters who survived are there too."

"Montelupich?" My gut twisted. Montelupich Prison was a terrible place, designed and run by sadists. If the Draengers were there, then they had experienced torture worse than anything I could imagine, and even what I could picture turned my stomach. They would be kept at the edge of death in an attempt to make them talk. But I knew the Draengers. The Nazis would get nothing from them. Shimshon cared more for the resistance than his own life. Gusta was tougher than I ever hoped to be. If anyone could survive the prison, it was them.

Esther gave me a moment to absorb her news, then said, "Antek has picked up the reins for Akiva. He's hiding in the forest, trying to reorganize the resistance."

Antek was only a few years older than me but had been high up in Akiva's organization from our earliest days in the resistance. I didn't know him well, but if he had taken over, then orders were orders.

I began walking toward the train station with Esther close by my side. We had already been standing still too long, talking for too long. "How can Antek reorganize with only you and me? Are we all that's left?"

"No, but there aren't many of us. There are other resistance organizations throughout Poland, though. Antek hopes to start one in Lodz. That's our job—to get in and determine if there's any chance to start a group there."

Feeling the weight of eyes on us, I laughed, as if she'd said something funny. She echoed my laugh, though it was forced and false, and much too loud. If we were going to do this mission together, then I'd train her, just as I'd been trained. I'd already begun making a mental list of things to speak to her about when we were alone.

Don't walk with your hands in your pockets. It looks like you're hiding something.

Don't look down or avoid eye contact or stare.

In short, she shouldn't do anything that she'd been doing until now. Except that Esther had survived this long, so she must be doing some things right.

"I've brought a few weapons," I said. "But it's not enough for an uprising in a ghetto as large as the one in Lodz."

"Maybe it's enough for a start."

The walk from Old Town to the train station took only ten minutes, but it was ten minutes of hearing the pounding of my heart and trying to ignore the warning thoughts racing through my head. I often traveled by train to get from one ghetto to another, but I'd traveled alone and I was never comfortable during the journey. Train cars were a space I couldn't control. What if the wrong person sat near me? What if they were suspicious and contacted one of the German soldiers inevitably riding along? I'd jumped off trains a few times during raids, but here, on a passenger train, that sort of behavior tended to look suspicious.

It was harder now with Esther. Instead of the swept-back style that was the current fashion, she wore her hair around her face, hoping to be less visible. But if anyone did look, they'd surely wonder if she might be Jewish. All I could do was hope that my more Polish looks would direct attention away from her.

Since I was older than Esther, no one would think twice if I managed the money and tickets. I also had a pretty face, another weapon in my arsenal, and whenever necessary, I used it as such. If I was the more exuberant, friendlier one, I hoped that Esther would escape the notice of the other passengers.

At one time, Jews and Poles rode the trains as equals, often side by side. Often as friends. Then, as the laws changed, we were charged more than the Poles for the same seats. Then we were banished altogether. If any other Jews managed to sneak aboard this train, they wouldn't want contact with me any more than I did with them.

I'd brought with me most of the cash from the safe house, so it was easy to purchase the tickets. I did leave a little money behind on the slight chance that any other Akiva members returned there, but I saw now that it had been a foolish decision. A pit in my gut became a reminder that nearly all of Akiva was gone. No one would return to that safe house.

"Why are you young ladies going to Lodz today?" The cashier's friendly tone suggested it was a routine question, but I never took that for granted.

"To visit our grandmother," I replied.

At the very same time, Esther said, "It's our home."

"It will be our home *now*," I quickly corrected, giving Esther a small kick to keep her quiet.

Once we were alone, I turned to her and hissed, "From now on, unless the question is specifically directed to you, I will answer. And never tell someone you're headed home to a place you don't know. What if he had asked what street you live on? What if he's from Lodz and asks about your family?"

Her lower lip quivered. "You're right, Chaya. I'm sorry."

I wasn't angry with her, not really. I was angry at myself. I didn't like me this way, cold and harsh. Before the war, I would've taken her hand and told her it doesn't matter if she makes mistakes—we all do, and it can't be all that bad.

But this was wartime, and everything mattered. Even small mistakes could be catastrophic.

"Encourage a resistance movement in Lodz, is that all we're assigned to do?" I asked. She nodded but wouldn't meet my eyes. She was holding something back.

"What else?" I continued. "Tell me and then you can go. I'll do it alone."

My tone was calm, yet she recoiled as if I'd slapped her. "What? No, I'm coming with you."

"You want to come, but we both know you're not up to it. There's no shame in admitting it."

"I won't admit it because it's not true. I can complete this mission."

"So can I, alone. It's safer anyway—sometimes the best thing you can do is get out of the way. What were Antek's exact orders to you?"

She stiffened her spine and pinched her mouth shut,

clearly trying to keep her emotions in check. Finally, she answered. "Our orders are to go to the ghetto in Lodz—together—and see if there is any chance for a resistance movement there. You bought two tickets for the train. One of them is for me."

I groaned and walked with her toward the train platform, carefully looking out for anyone who might be watching us too closely. If anyone seemed like they were, I crossed between them and Esther, blocking their view. Otherwise, we remained separated enough that few people would think of us as traveling companions. I didn't feel like a companion to her anyway, not when she was withholding information from me.

The biggest problem was that I understood why she was doing it: The fewer people who knew a secret, the fewer who could tell it. We were both safer if she told me only what I needed to know. And that would have been enough . . . if I trusted her.

Which I didn't.

"May I help with your bag, miss?" the ticket officer in front of me asked.

I'd shown him my ticket, and all I needed was for him to wave me forward onto the train. Why should he feel the need to have a conversation too? But he did, so I replied as politely as possible.

"Thank you, sir, but I can manage."

I had to manage, because my bag was hiding three Luger

pistols and a pack of bullets. If he lifted it onto the train, he might wonder why it was so heavy—maybe become suspicious. He'd gesture to the Nazi officer at the far end of the platform to come over. Our mission would end before it had begun.

When he reached for the bag anyway, I straightened up and offered a pleasant smile. "Really, sir, I'm fine."

"Very well," he said. Friendly. Oblivious. Completely unaware.

A few minutes later, Esther and I boarded the train. She followed me in silence from one compartment to another. I wanted a space that was more full than empty, because I wanted to choose who my compartment mates were rather than have it be chosen for me after I was seated.

We wouldn't enter the first one, full of Germans, including two women who were chatting about surprising their officer husbands in Lodz. A large Polish man in the second compartment had his eye on me, though I hoped it was because he thought I was pretty and nothing more. The third compartment held an elderly couple, the wife already napping on her husband's shoulder, and a mother with two young children. They'd keep her too busy to notice us.

I hoped.

I pulled open the compartment door and we went inside. The train was already leaving the station. Whatever happened on this journey, we were committed now. There would be no escape.

THIRTEEN

February 15, 1943
Train to Lodz

Before we entered the carriage, I'd done a quick survey to find the nearest exit. If there was trouble, our only choice might be to force the doors open and jump, even onto rocks, rather than be captured. I doubted Esther could make herself leap from a moving train.

Which led to a question I had to ask myself: Would I abandon her if that was the only way to save my life?

I felt terrible even considering that, with Esther right next to me. I felt worse, knowing my answer to that question.

She sat near the window, allowing me to occupy the more visible middle seat. A young girl was at my side, only four or five years old. No doubt she'd felt the effects of war, yet she still looked healthy and happy and had a doll that was entertaining her, at least for now. Across from me were the elderly couple, the mother, and a toddler boy who'd nearly pulled the communication cord at least six times already. In this model of train, a tug on that cord automatically triggered the brakes and would guarantee a visit from an angry engineer to see who had interrupted the trip. Most of the time the cords were covered, but this one was exposed. If I'd noticed that before we sat down, we'd have chosen another compartment.

For her part, Esther was doing exactly what she should, or better. She'd already opened a book from her bag, one with a velvet cover that had a gold cross stamped into it. She immediately bent low to read it. I doubted that she cared a single zloty for the book, though its contents might be useful for her one day. More important, her hair fell over her face as she read, and would probably remain that way for the entire trip. No one would get a good look at her, and no one would question why that was. It was clever enough that I wished I had thought of it too.

I passed the trip staring out the window. Although there was wisdom in keeping my face turned from the rest of the passengers, I also genuinely enjoyed the scenery. In one moment, I saw a rolling hillside with the occasional farmhouse, the winter snow finally beginning to melt on the western slopes, looking completely untouched by war. In the next moment, the war returned, with long, jagged scars in the land where a skirmish might have taken place, or a village with Nazi flags, or rows of freshly dug graves. Then the train pushed on and the scene returned to normal again.

I leaned back and closed my eyes, wondering if I

survived this war, could I ever return to normal again? Could one go back to who one was in an earlier time? That didn't seem possible, which saddened me, yet at the same time energized me. I was stronger now than I ever used to be, more independent and confident.

I was also more cynical and detached, I knew that. It was more of what I didn't like about myself, but it had kept me alive, allowed me to do what I'd had to do. It was why I hadn't spoken a word to Esther, even though we'd been traveling for over an hour by now. Our complete silence must look unnatural to the other passengers.

Reluctantly, I took a deep breath and leaned over to Esther. "Enjoying the ride?"

She looked up with an arched brow, as if she had no idea I could speak. "Er . . . yes," she stammered.

In what appeared to be an attempt at politeness, the older gentleman across from me gestured around our carriage and said, "These rides are better now."

"Oh?" This ride seemed no different from any other, bumpy and loud, but pleasant nonetheless.

"The trains are *Judenfrei* now."

Esther's head shot up. "Why should that matter?" she asked, clearly offended. "What did the Jews ever do but ride here, same as the others?"

I wanted to kick Esther again, hard enough this time to get her head back down in that book. Aside from the fact that this man would perceive her behavior as being uncommonly rude, I also didn't like the darkening of his expression as he looked at Esther. Studying her. Suspicious.

Raising his voice, he added, "The Jews are known to carry disease—typhus and lice and who knows what else? Look at the ghettos for proof of that."

It was true that the ghettos had disease. But we were not the cause of it. No one would be able to live in such close quarters—usually without running water, with no way to rid ourselves of the trash that collected, and with little access to medical care—and not face disease. Disease followed the Jews into the ghettos. We did not bring it.

I smiled, the same smile I wore for the Nazis at the ghetto gates. The same smile that hid the venom pulsing through me. "The trains are less crowded now, that's true."

The man paused while the toddler let out a cry, still upset that his mother wouldn't let him reach for the cord, then said, "Poland is less crowded now. Before long, the Jewish problem will be solved for good."

Beside me, Esther had a white-knuckle grip on her book. She needed to ignore him, or to at least pretend that this conversation held no interest for her.

Desperate for any distraction from managing her children—the boy, who was reaching for the communication cord for at least the thirtieth time that hour, and the girl, who had begun repeatedly throwing her doll on the floor to have an excuse to climb down and pick it up—the mother cut in, saying, "There is no Jewish problem. The problem is with the rest of us who pass beside the ghetto walls with a fresh loaf of bread, knowing the people are starving on the other side, and yet we do nothing." She sat taller. "I throw the loaf over whenever it's safe and pray that it gets found. I pray for those people every day, and so should you. What is happening to the Jews is pure evil."

"I don't wish them harm, of course, but evil is a strong word," the man said, shuffling the weight of his sleeping wife's head on his shoulder. "I'm only saying that the Germans have done us a favor by moving them out of Poland."

"They're still in Poland," Esther said. "Behind the ghetto walls and inside the barbed-wire fences of extermination camps."

"Extermination camps?" The man arched a brow. "There's no such thing. Maybe you are a—"

Anticipating his next word, I opened my mouth to defuse his suspicions, but before I could speak, the train lurched forward as its brakes locked. The mother protectively pulled her toddler boy onto her lap, then her eyes darted meaningfully from me to the train doors.

The boy hadn't pulled the cord.

She had.

I stood, drawing Esther up with me. "I think we're near our stop anyway." My grip on her arm was a merciless pinch, and I intended it that way.

The train slowly ground to a halt, and behind us, I heard

the train's conductor already making his way to each compartment, looking for the person who had pulled the cord. A
quick glance back confirmed that a Nazi soldier was with
him.

We ducked into the closest cove of exit doors, waiting
for them to open. Why hadn't they opened yet?

"You look in these compartments," the Nazi ordered.
"I'll search the rear ones."

The ones directly across from where we were standing.
He'd see us.

I tried to push the doors apart, seeking any gap with my
fingers. But they weren't budging, and the soldier was almost
upon us.

The mother immediately darted into the hallway, making such a fuss that all his attention shifted to her. "Forgive
us, my son pulled the cord. It's my fault."

"There's a heavy fine for stopping a train without an
emergency," the conductor said.

"I can't pay it!" she said. "What happened was only
an accident." Her boy began crying, almost as if on cue, or
perhaps she pinched him to make an even bigger scene.
Other people peeked out of their compartments to see what
was happening.

The woman began crying too, louder than her son.

"Come with me," the Nazi officer said. "We'll settle this
in private."

He took her arm and led her and her children out of the compartment, away from us.

"Will she be in trouble?" Esther asked.

"If she is, it's because of us," I snapped.

As soon as the doors opened, she hurried down the train steps first and I followed. We'd just passed through a farm town and somewhere ahead was a thick patch of woods, but aside from that, I had no idea how far we were from Lodz. I hoisted my heavy bag over my shoulder and led us off the tracks toward the nearest road. We couldn't run, we couldn't look suspicious.

Anger rushed through every vein in my body. We were not leaving because of the communication cord. We were leaving because Esther decided to argue. The communication cord probably saved us from her full declaration of our true identities as proof of how wrong that man was.

When we were far enough from the train, between gritted teeth, I said, "Our job is not to debate the racists, the uninformed. We are here to complete a mission, nothing more."

"But you heard his lies, all that stupidity! How could you sit there like it didn't matter?"

"Because it doesn't matter. Not when compared to the larger picture of what we're doing here. You could've gotten us killed, and for what? Did you think you'd change his mind?"

"No, I—"

"He was wrong and hateful, but he is not our enemy."

"He *is* the enemy, Chaya! The war will end one day and the Germans will go back to their own land. But here we must live alongside thousands of people like that man. If we can't stop his hatred, this will happen again and again and again!"

I stopped there, stunned to see so much force come from someone as small as Esther, and feeling humbled as well. Because Esther was right. This disease, this hatred of Jews, was as old as time itself.

"You're right," I said. "You're right about all of that. But your timing was terrible."

After a heavy pause, Esther asked, "What now?"

I shrugged and looked back toward the tracks. The man in our carriage had undoubtedly reported our sudden exit from the train, and there were no sounds of it starting up again. We had to put as much distance between ourselves and the train as possible.

If we had any chance of escaping this disaster, it was only because that young mother had risked her life to give us time to escape. She knew who we were, and I better understood now the kind of woman she was too.

I began walking roughly parallel to the tracks with Esther at my side. Based on how long we had been on board that train, we were probably about halfway to Lodz. But that still left us a long and miserable walk ahead.

"I knew you wanted me to keep quiet back there," Esther

said as we walked. "I tried, I really did. But isn't that the point of the resistance, to make the world notice us?"

"The point of the resistance is to save lives," I retorted. "Every single day, more Jews are dying. Our fight is to stop that from happening. Nothing else matters."

"I'll do better tomorrow," she mumbled.

"Can you?"

"Yes, I can, and I will!" She crossed in front of me, forcing me to look at her. "Don't you ever make mistakes?"

I sighed heavily, then said, "Every day. But I learn from them and go on."

"That's what I'm doing too. One day, I'll become your equal, Chaya, not your burden."

A gust of wind swirled up around us and I buried my head in my coat for protection. When I looked up again, Esther had already walked on ahead of me. Facing the wind.

Maybe there was hope for her after all.

FOURTEEN

February 15–16, 1943
Lodz

The road to Lodz was even more wooded than it had appeared from the train. The waning sunlight was obscured by tall, thick trees, so strong that they choked out the smaller trees that should have been protected beneath their winter canopy. Between them, small farmhouses could occasionally be seen. I doubted any partisans were here.

"Too bad," I told Esther. "Partisan fighters would have given us shelter for the night, someplace warm."

If it had been cold before, the wind that pushed through the icy trees now was worse, each gust slicing through our coats like knives. It would only get worse when night fell. Esther pulled up the collar of her coat to protect her face, but she never complained. Maybe because she remembered why we were walking. I certainly did.

At least I had the bag on my back for some protection. It felt heavier each minute, but it kept out the wind.

Esther looked over at me. "I never used to lie. I wasn't prepared for the number of lies we'd have to tell as couriers."

"You weren't prepared for anything," I snapped, my tone so sharp that it even surprised me. Softer now, I added, "I'm sorry, I didn't mean—"

"I tried to prepare, Chaya, I really did. I'll bet I'm the only courier in Poland who can recite whole passages of the Torah *and* the Catholic Catechism."

"Every courier can do that."

"I stole apples once and smuggled them—"

"You're not even a courier, Esther."

"After Cyganeria, I was the only one left. Until—"

I stopped and faced her, exhausted and cold and at the edge of my temper. "You're not the only one that anything has happened to. If we're still alive, then it's because we all lie, we all steal, we hide the Star of David on our arms when we can and show it when we must. And we've all lost people we love. We've all lost everything to the point where we have nothing left, so our only choice is to curl up and die, or else to fight back."

"I *am* fighting back. That's why I came!"

"I'm here too, remember that, Esther. You are not the only one affected by the mistakes you make!"

I began walking again and she followed, staying two steps behind me. Finally, she asked, "Well, have you ever made *holishkes* without cabbage?"

A smile nudged at my mouth. "You can't make stuffed cabbage without cabbage."

"Then there is one story that's only mine."

Despite my irritation, I laughed. It wasn't much, but it warmed me for a few steps longer.

Finally, Esther pointed out a home in the distance with overgrown weeds coming up through the snow. No lights were on, and no animals were visible in the gates.

"Abandoned?" she asked.

I shrugged and cautiously led the way toward the home. Whether it was abandoned or not, we wouldn't sleep inside. That was too risky. But the barn might offer us enough shelter to wait out the night.

In fact, when we opened the barn door, I decided it was probably better for us out here than it would have been in the house. Whoever used to live here had obviously left in a hurry. The straw for their animals was still in a large pile, waiting to be pitched to the horses.

Esther and I buried ourselves inside the heap, letting our bodies slowly warm the air pockets around us until the feeling returned to our fingers and toes. Mine ached at first. I hadn't realized on the road how dangerously cold we were. I'd have to be more careful in the future.

"How many?" Esther cleared her throat. "How many lives have you saved?"

My eyes were already closed. "Not enough," I murmured. I remembered the faces of every person I'd helped into hiding, but rarely knew what happened to them afterward. Sometimes the Polish families seemed helpful until the Jewish person was settled into their home, then they would blackmail them or turn them in for rewards from the Gestapo. Sometimes the family couldn't afford to keep the person in hiding. Their allotment of food was rationed too, and every person in hiding forced those rations to stretch further. Or maybe the family simply grew afraid of being discovered, of the brutality their own loved ones would receive if they were found out.

I hoped every single person I'd placed into a safe house truly was safe, and I firmly believed they were better there than remaining in the ghettos, which would eventually force them into harsh labor camps, or worse, the extermination camps. But I didn't know how many were still alive. I only knew that if I kept trying, kept fighting, maybe I could save even one person more.

We stayed in the barn for the night, though I couldn't have slept more than ten minutes at a time. Eventually, I forced myself to get up. When Esther awoke shortly after dawn, her sleepy eyes drifted to the hem of her coat in my hands. I was just finishing up with a needle and bit the thread to finish the knot.

"What are you doing?" Suspicion was thick in her voice.

I showed her the inside hem where I was stitching. "You can't use your Jewish name outside the ghettos. The Kennkarte identifies you as Polish. If anything happens to you, you'll be buried with a false name in a Christian cemetery. I've sewn your identity in here. If something happens . . . well, we have to hope this will be found."

"Do you have one?"

I showed her my stitching inside an arm of my coat. "We all do."

She nodded. "You think of everything, Chaya."

"If I thought of everything, we wouldn't be walking. Now, let's go." We lined our coats with straw for extra insulation, ate as little of our food as we had to, then returned to the road.

Morning should have brought a friendliness to these woods, but nothing here felt friendly. The breaking sunlight was only a stark reminder of how the tiniest trees were dying. The largest ones must be taking too much of the groundwater, too much of the light. It was a rule of nature that the strongest would survive, but that morning, nature seemed unfair and cruel.

Lodz was only a few more kilometers away, so we arrived by midmorning and asked for directions to the train station. The Nazis liked to place their ghettos there. It simplified their transportation to the extermination camps.

Esther commented on this too. "We should have known the Nazis' plans as soon as we saw where they placed the ghettos. We should have known."

I turned to her. "Did you come from the ghettos, Esther? Did you used to live in one?"

She blinked, then turned away from me. "Should we keep moving, find the entrance?"

I agreed, though she was obviously hoping to distract me from my question. That was fine for now, but it pricked my curiosity. Sooner or later, I'd find out the answer.

Unlike most of the other ghettos where I'd been, there were no walls of any sort here, only stark wood fencing with barbed wire stretching between the wide slats. For a place we'd been warned away from until now, it seemed remarkably unthreatening.

"It'd be easy to escape," I whispered to Esther. "Cut the wire, slip between the posts, and they'd be free. Why don't they leave?"

Lines of Jews stood behind the fencing, most of them as still as a photograph, except for the occasional turn of someone's head. They stared at the outside world as if it were a puzzle they couldn't quite work out, a memory encased in fog. A few had hands outstretched, silently begging for a crumb of food. But no one passing by came near enough to the fencing to offer them anything.

"Be patient an hour longer," I muttered to them beneath my breath. "We will get food in to you, somehow."

Beside us on the road, the Poles walked by as if they were unaware of it all. How was that possible? Didn't they care what was happening on the other side of that fence? Couldn't they see it? Or were they afraid to look, terrified that if they stared, someone might wonder if they belonged there too?

Then I noticed a patrol of Polish police walking the perimeter heading north while motorcycles of Gestapo officers circled it southward. That must be why no one offered food, and why the people remained inside a simple fence.

Before long, we found the ghetto entrance, narrow and heavily guarded. A large sign in front read juden, as if there were any question of who might be imprisoned within these walls. It added entry forbidden. Somehow the sign seemed to be speaking to me, but not as a warning. I considered it a challenge, one I intended to win.

"This is a large ghetto," I mumbled, surveying the rows of buildings behind the guards.

"Only Warsaw's ghetto is larger," Esther replied. "A resistance here could make a difference."

Perhaps, but first we had to sneak inside. As eager as I was to defy the Nazi orders to stay out, I didn't like the look of the guards at the gate. There were too many of them to hope to pass through without being questioned. Without being searched.

Esther touched my arm. "The gaps in the ghetto fencing—we can get inside that way."

It was probably the only way we'd get inside, but my stomach was already doing flips at the thought of it. Aside from the patrols on the outside of the fence, the OD would be watching from the inside, and for all we knew, we'd crawl right into their backyard.

"We'll go at night," I said. "In the meantime, let's find a safe place to warm up. A church, perhaps."

Esther began to nod but froze as a truck with Nazi symbols slowly drove on the road beside us. Her eyes darted around and I noticed her hand shaking.

"Stop that." I wouldn't speak gently now. "Stop looking guilty!"

The truck passed and we walked away from the direction it was driving. When all was clear, she said, "I can't help it. Chaya, how can you not be afraid?"

"Because it's not possible to be afraid all the time!" I hissed. "I feel it, but I keep it in the background. You must use fear to sharpen your senses and heighten your instincts. It will drive your determination to stay alive, but it cannot control you. If you give in to the fear, you will die tonight. And you'll probably get me killed too."

Her hand had stopped shaking, but not because of my words. For now, she was only pretending to have her fear under control, pretending that she could face what lay ahead. And for now, that would have to suffice.

If she could pretend well enough, then one day she would feel the churning in her stomach, the sweat on her palms, the pulse in her temples, and know that she was terrified because of what was about to happen. But she would go forward anyway.

Just as I would do tonight.

Because if I was being honest, I'd been fighting the shaking of my own hands for most of the day. I hadn't felt this nervous in two months, since the night we attacked the Cyganeria Café.

Deep in my heart, I knew this was a bad idea. That sole thought occupied my mind as Esther and I stared at the ghetto in Lodz. It was the one place we'd been told never to go, considered the impossible ghetto. And we were going in.

FIFTEEN

February 16, 1943
Lodz Ghetto

I t took most of the day to find the perfect place to sneak into the ghetto, or for that matter, to find any place at all. We chose a spot on the northern boundary with a tall wooden wall that was rarely patrolled, which made me curious. Everywhere else we'd looked showed all the usual sights and noises of overcrowding. Not here.

Esther noticed it too. "Why is it so quiet?" she whispered. "Quiet can't be safe."

I shrugged in response. "Our choice is never between safe and not safe. It's not safe or not alive, that's all we have. This is the best place we've found—the only place we've found." I turned to her. "Do we go in or not?"

Our entry location could be worse. On those occasions when I had to sneak in, I most dreaded the tall apartments just outside the ghetto walls that sometimes hovered overhead. Every window was a spyglass, every occupant a threat, especially at night. Young mothers up late with a baby. The elderly with gout, or even curious onlookers who wondered about life on the streets after curfew. Something as simple as an innocent glance out a window could create enormous problems.

Esther nodded. "We go in."

More concerning now than our location were the snowflakes softly falling around us. It was going to be a cold night. The tips of my fingers were already beginning to throb, but I hoped the weather would work to our advantage.

"This snow is a warning," Esther said, suddenly nervous. "Maybe God is telling us to wait one more evening."

"Maybe God is offering to cover our tracks if we hurry," I replied.

We waited until dark and, wherever possible, walked toward the ghetto fence using well-worn paths in the snow or the footprints of guards who had passed this way before. When the tracks ran out, I glanced up at the new snowfall and whispered, "If you're going to come, then let it be for our good." More than the cold, or the wet layers of my clothing, I cared about not being seen.

Esther was directly behind me, with instructions to step exactly in my tracks, no matter what. If we were followed, I wanted the soldiers to believe there was only one of us to find.

Once we came closer to the area we'd targeted to enter, it became obvious that this spot had been used before as a means for escape. A hole had been dug beneath the wood fence, small enough for the children who are most often used as smugglers by their hungry families. Esther should fit through the gap without too much trouble. It would be more difficult for me, but I was determined to make it through.

"You are the most determined child I've ever seen," my mother used to say, out of exasperation or admiration, I was never sure. If only determination had been enough to heal her pain. I missed her, more than she would ever know.

Esther and I crouched in front of the hole, listening for any signs of people on the other end. There were some sounds, but I couldn't quite identify what might be causing them. Clinking. Shuffling. Very strange. We heard no voices, but no gunfire either. That at least was good news.

"You should go first," Esther said, licking her lips. "You'll know what to do better than me."

It couldn't work that way tonight. I whispered, "You go first, because I'll need your help to pull me through. After you're in, I'll send our bags under and then I'll come last."

She shook her head. "I don't know what to do . . . when we're in there."

"Those are our people inside the walls, Esther. You'll know what to do. Now go."

She took a deep breath and we turned back to the gap, preparing to squeeze her through, when a hand gripped my shoulder, tight and uncompromising, a sign that whoever had grabbed me was comfortable with the idea of causing pain. And he was.

"Isn't this interesting?"

Across from me, Esther's expression darkened from surprise to horror. The man who spoke to me had a Polish accent, but that didn't matter. He could get the immediate attention of a dozen Nazis with little more effort than a casual shout for help.

The guns inside my bag were buried beneath sacks of flour. Even if I could get to one, firing a shot at this man would hardly keep the Germans away.

"Are you Jews?" the man asked. In this darkness, and with my back to him, he wasn't sure.

"We're only bringing the people a bit of food." I kept my body between him and Esther. "A good man like yourself can't object to that."

He chuckled coarsely, as if I'd told a joke. As if this were some sort of game between us. I turned just enough to get my first look at him, and as soon as I did, I knew exactly who this was. What he was.

Szmalec. The Polish word for lard, and he looked every part of it, with a fleshy jawline, baggy eyes, and limp, stringy hair. I immediately calculated what it would take to escape his grip if this went any further. He looked soft, but he'd survived this long, so he must be stronger than he looked. And rotted to the core, no doubt about that.

This man was a *szmalcownik.* It was our name for the treacherous citizens who'd built careers on blackmailing Jews caught outside the ghettos. They might be only one among a group of five thousand other good Polish men and women, but that single individual could do more damage than the other five thousand could ever do to help. Their sense of right or wrong was for sale to the highest bidder, their morality a willow in the wind, blowing this way or that. They'd protect the Jew, or turn him into the Nazis, depending on who offered the better bribe, or the fiercest threat. They were dough, willingly molded, pressed, and plied.

But they existed because blackmail works. Because people like me had no choice but to deal with men like him.

He was here for money. I had some, but needed it to carry us through this mission.

"Ah"—the szmalcownik eyed our bags—"you have food in there. What else?"

"Only a little food for the children of this ghetto," I said. "Please, sir—"

"What children?" He looked genuinely confused, which confused me.

Esther and I exchanged a glance. "What do you mean?" she asked.

He shrugged, completely indifferent. "Ask the Judenrat." His eyes returned to our sacks. "My point is that you don't need all that food. But I'm a fair man. I'll take one bag, and you keep the other."

I firmly shook my head, trying to take control of this moment. "I can't spare that much, sir. One sack of flour, perhaps. And—"

He leaned in close enough that I could smell his fetid breath. How well he must eat off the starvation and suffering of those who were trapped behind these walls. "I'll take your entire bag and let you go. Refuse my generous offer and I'll let the Germans know that I've found a Polish girl and her Jewish friend at the ghetto wall. After they arrest you, I'll take both of your bags."

I tried a threat of my own. "They'll arrest you too. The Germans don't like blackmailers."

"It's all a game, you know that. German soldiers sell food to the black market, you smuggle it in, I catch you, and other Germans punish you for having black market food. Do as I say and the game can end right here."

"Let us go, and the game ends with starving people getting fed tonight." I forced a smile to my face. "Let us help them."

He considered that, then said, "There are hungry Poles too. But I want to be fair. I'll let you choose whose bag I take. You or your Jewish friend's."

Mine had weapons. When he found them, what would he do? Report his discovery to the Gestapo rather than risk being caught with illegal weapons? Or would he keep our secret and not draw the Gestapo's attention to himself?

Esther was clearly thinking the same thing. "My bag, then." She held it forward, too eager, too trusting.

He stroked his chin, his eyes shifting from her again to me, and from one sack to the other. "You want me to take that sack?" He reached for mine. "Then this is the one I want."

He tugged at the handle, but my grip remained firm. I couldn't allow him to take it.

"Something in this sack must be valuable . . . or dangerous." He chuckled again. "Perhaps we'll let the Germans take it from you instead. Let me call them over."

Almost as if on cue, the shadow of a Nazi officer rounded the corner at the end of our street. The szmalcownik may face a few minutes' harassment for being caught after curfew, but it was nothing compared to the consequences we'd get, and we both knew it.

His grin turned as cold as the night. "Well?"

I released my bag, giving up food for dozens of people and every hope to start a resistance movement within Lodz. Worse still, he now held more than enough evidence to have me shot on sight. I was furious with his greed and ruthlessness, but I was angrier with myself for having been caught in the first place.

The instant he was gone, Esther grabbed my arm. "We've got to get in!"

She was right. The Nazi officer would pass by us soon. When Esther slid under the fence, I shoved her bag under.

I was positioning myself to slide under too when she whispered back at me. "Chaya, this might be a mistake. You shouldn't enter."

"Why not?" I asked. But no answer came.

SIXTEEN

February 16, 1943
Lodz Ghetto

I'd become used to hearing Esther sound afraid. By now, the quaver in her tone was almost as familiar as my own voice. But something was different now. As if there were good reasons why her voice had trembled, why I saw the unsteadiness of her feet through the small gap beneath the fence. Something new had unnerved her.

And although I appreciated Esther's attempt to protect me, the fact was, being out here was hardly a safer option. Or if it was, I certainly wouldn't abandon her in there.

"Is it Germans?" I hissed.

Now she answered. "No, but—"

That soldier patrolling this area was still headed my way, so before Esther finished her sentence, I squeezed beneath the fence too. It left a long scrape on my side, one I hoped hadn't ripped my clothes. If it did, there was nothing I could do about it now.

She helped pull me through the fence, and as soon as I was under, we stuffed snow into the gap beneath the fence. Unless that soldier looked carefully, he shouldn't realize we were there.

Of course, there would be footprints in the snow and flattened areas where our bodies had lain, but it was growing dark and I hoped the heavy snowfall would mask that.

I held my breath until I was sure he'd passed, and only then did I look around, taking in the odd sight around me. Now Esther's warning made sense.

A thin blanket of newly fallen snow covered what appeared to be a field of rubbish, layers of empty food jars, broken pieces of furniture, scraps of spoiled food. This must be where the people deposited their garbage since the ghetto was sealed. Most of it must have been frozen; otherwise the odor would have been unbearable.

But it wasn't the reason Esther warned me away.

Almost a dozen women were digging in the trash with sticks or large spoons, depositing whatever they'd managed to collect on old items of clothing beside them. They'd all seen us come in, yet no one had said a word. Perhaps they had no energy for words. Most of them looked like they'd welcome death and yet here they were, continuing to dig because something within them wanted to live.

"What are they doing?" Esther whispered.

"Surviving." One woman appeared to be collecting anything that could burn. I'd seen this before. The only way to

heat the apartments was with fires, but no wood was coming in from outside the ghettos. The people were forced to
find wood anywhere they could get it: breaking up pieces of
furniture, digging into the framing of their walls, or pulling
the slats off stairs. This woman must be hoping to find
enough here to provide heat for the night.

Another woman was wearing a dress too threadbare to
be sewn together again. Every time she found a piece of
clothing, she held it up to herself to check the size. I
had clothing in the bag that blackmailer took. I could have
given it to her.

Most of the other women seemed to be scavenging for
anything that might be eaten, and from what I could see in
their small piles, they weren't picky. Rotted vegetables,
moldy crusts of bread, leftover scrapings from inside a jar.
They were digging for what might amount to a mouthful of
food, and if it was only half that, I was sure they'd still be
grateful.

"We should give them the potatoes." Esther spoke in a
whisper, yet I noticed ears prick up around me. These
women weren't nearly as passive as they pretended to be.

"Let's get deeper into the ghetto and decide how to put
them to the best use," I said, helping her to her feet. "Don't
look at anyone. Just walk on through."

Esther swung her bag over her shoulder, and I led the way
through a sort of trail across piles of picked-over garbage.
My stomach became sick at the thought of anyone eating it.

No, it was sick at the thought of being in a place where this must be eaten.

Ahead of us was a building that looked like it might have been a factory at one time. A few windows were broken out now. If I could get a piece of the glass, it could be used as a crude sort of weapon, if necessary. And if I could find a door, we could spend the night there, out of sight, and then begin distributing Esther's food in the busier daytime hours while we looked for possible contacts, someone here who still had enough spirit to fight, to resist. Enough strength to hold a gun, if I could get another one inside here.

As we left the rubbish pile, Esther cried out behind me and fumbled for my arm, but she was immediately pulled down to the ground. I twisted around and found two women fighting for her bag, even while it was still on her shoulders. They might not have realized—or cared—that her face was down in the snow and she was flailing about for air.

"Chaya!" Her muffled plea for help didn't even register with these starving women.

I dove for Esther, but when the first potato spilled from her bag, the two desperate women suddenly become five, and then all of them fought for anything that was left. To get it off Esther's shoulders, one woman knelt on her back. They were suffocating Esther, but the only thing that seemed to be in their vision was the bag.

"Stop!" I shoved the woman off Esther, then pushed the others away until she could breathe. We were close enough now that I could see their eyes, stricken with horror at what they'd done.

"We meant no harm," a woman mumbled, shamefully covering her face to avoid looking at us.

Esther stood beside me on wobbly legs and I whispered, "Let them have it."

She wriggled free of the bag, which was immediately snatched by the women as they divided the potatoes among themselves.

"They might've killed me," she cried.

I put my hands on her shoulders, steadying her. "It would've been an accident. They only wanted the food. But we are surrounded by soldiers who will kill you deliberately if they get the chance. Never confuse the two."

Esther's reply was cut off by the sound of whistles coming up the street toward us. Gestapo. Someone must've heard the scuffle back there and reported it.

I tried the door of the old factory that I'd eyed earlier, but it was locked and the windows were too high. We'd never get in there. And we couldn't run back toward the rubbish piles—that's surely where the Gestapo officers were headed. If they stopped to question us, it wouldn't be hard to figure out we didn't belong here, or why we had snuck into a ghetto at night. I might withstand their torture, maybe. Esther wouldn't.

"This way!" Esther grabbed my hand and pulled me behind a crumbled wall near the factory. No one had been back here in some time—I could tell because we created new footprints in the snow. Which meant it wouldn't take the officers long to track us.

But for now, we crouched behind the wall and the Germans ran by, shouting orders at the OD, who followed like dogs on their heels to find the cause of this trouble and to stop it. I peeked out to see their guns drawn.

Less than a minute later, a shot was fired.

"Maybe it was a warning shot," Esther whispered. "Maybe they're urging the women to hurry back to their apartments."

"Maybe," I replied.

But I knew better.

With the officers momentarily occupied at the rubbish piles, Esther and I left the wall and ran deeper into the ghetto. The streets were nearly abandoned for curfew and I had no idea where to go for shelter.

"Stop!" a man shouted in Yiddish. A Jewish officer.

The cock of his gun got my attention. It took all my courage to turn around and face this man. Esther had already stopped a few paces behind me and was visibly shaking. I was frightened too, but I couldn't let it show, not if I was going to talk us out of this one, though it'd be more difficult than usual. I knew almost nothing about this ghetto. Not the streets here, nor the names of any residents, nor the Judenrat leadership. It wouldn't take this officer long to realize I was lying.

I would figure out an excuse for why we were here. I had to.

I must.

But nothing came to my mind, and that infuriated me. I would not have my end come at the hands of one of my own people. That was intolerable.

The Jewish officer's face was as long and thin as the szmalcownik's face was plump. His cheekbones protruded at dramatic angles, giving him a harsh appearance. But I didn't think he was. Instead, he looked hungry, much like those women before. His gun was aimed directly at me, but Esther was almost hyperventilating, pulling his attention to her. She needed to stop. Rather than pity us, this man would despise us for weakness.

"Why were you running?" His voice was raspy, sending a shiver up my spine.

"We were going to the rubbish piles to dig," I said. "Then we heard the whistles and thought it might be an Aktion. We ran."

"There have been no Aktions since last fall," he said. "It's proof that the Judenrat's plan was a good one." Then his eyes narrowed. "You two aren't from this ghetto."

In that instant, an excuse entered my mind. I crept forward and put an arm around Esther. "My cousin and I have been in hiding since the war began and were only recently sent here. We don't want any more trouble. May we go?"

He glanced back, toward the rubbish. "We got a report of two girls sneaking into the ghetto. I think it's you two."

He was being coy. He knew it was us, but he hadn't fired

his gun yet. Which meant he wanted something. A bribe? My money would do him no good. Some ghettos had their own currency and I suspected Lodz was one of those places. Offering him Polish money was useless. He was sealed in too.

Esther stepped forward and pulled a small potato from her coat pocket. She must have managed to grab one in the fray. She held it cradled in her palms as if it were a precious diamond. "If we give this to you, may we pass, just this once? It's all we have, sir."

He snatched the potato and stuffed it into his own pocket before anyone else could see it. But his face softened. "Either you snuck in or you're trying to sneak out. One is as bad as the other, so if you are still here when I turn around, I will take you to the Gestapo."

I thanked the man, and we walked in the only direction we had left. Away from him, away from the other officers behind us. And deeper into a ghetto where we had nothing left to offer.

"Where can we possibly go now?" Esther whispered.

"Come with me." A boy near our own age stepped from the shadows. He looked a little like I remembered my brother, Yitzchak, with a thick tousle of dark hair and a pleasant smile. "My name is Avraham. You belong with us."

SEVENTEEN

February 16, 1943
Lodz Ghetto

Esther tugged at my arm, warning against following this complete stranger. But I'd have followed nearly anyone in that moment if it got us off the street. Besides, my instincts about people were usually reliable, and everything within me suggested he could be trusted. There was something in his eyes when he smiled, in the friendly tone of his voice. I immediately liked him.

But Esther and I hadn't come to make friends. We were looking for someone who could create a resistance cell. Was he that kind of person? If we went with him, maybe we'd find out.

With Esther gripping my forearm, we followed Avraham into a dark building with six heavy doors for apartments on the main floor and a wooden staircase up the back. The mottled plaster and dingy paint didn't bother me, but the smell did. It reeked of death in here, an odor that persisted despite the horrible draft. Perhaps the draft brought the smell in, for I'd also noticed it outside, carried like smoke on the breeze.

"This building is scary," Esther whispered to me.

Avraham grinned, having overheard. "It is, which keeps our enemies out."

In a strange way, that made perfect sense, though I wasn't sure it made Esther feel any better.

"Do you live in here?" she asked, trying unsuccessfully to stifle a cough.

He shrugged back at her. "The fact that we live is most important."

"We?" I asked. "Your family?"

"No." He stopped walking to look me directly in the eyes. "Not anymore." A beat passed, maybe only a second, but it felt like hours before he smiled again, with more effort this time. "Two of my friends are upstairs."

It could be the start of a cell, if they were interested and capable. Not everyone was.

What would it take to spread the resistance here? Did Avraham have connections? Could he get money?

Most of all, would he be willing to fight? To steal at every opportunity, attack when possible . . . and kill if necessary? Even a year ago, I wouldn't have believed I was capable of any of that.

Avraham began leading us upstairs, occasionally skipping a stair that looked weak in the center. Esther and I did too.

"We saw you hiding and knew you weren't from Lodz," Avraham said. "Then we heard the shots and figured you two were in trouble."

"If you saw us, then surely you've seen others come through here . . . like us."

Other resistance fighters, that's what I meant. But I didn't want to be the first to say the words, just to be safe.

Avraham glanced back. "No Jews come into Lodz anymore. They only leave."

"How long?" Esther avoided my eyes as she spoke. "How long has it been since any large groups were brought in?"

He considered that a moment. "Not since early last year."

"Are you sure?" She sounded distressed, and her whole body seemed to deflate a little.

"I'm sure. No one comes, and eventually we'll all leave, either on the trains or in the wagons that collect the dead."

I caught up to him on the steps. "It doesn't have to happen to you. There are options—"

"I know." His brisk nod seemed strangely confident, given the situation. "But we don't need them."

I furrowed my brows, confused by his statement. When we had a chance to talk in private, I'd ask what he meant.

The final flight of stairs was missing every other slat. Avraham grinned back at us and demonstrated how to hold on to the railing for balance as we made the steep climb.

"It's scary at first," he said, offering me a hand. "But once you're used to it, it's kind of fun."

My idea of fun didn't involve slipping on a step and falling through to the stairway below, but Esther nimbly jumped from stair to stair, even though her legs were shorter than mine.

The top floor of the building had a dusting of snow from visible holes in the ceiling, and the draft was brutally cold. The layout was similar to the floors below, except only one apartment door still remained in its frame. The rest were missing. When we hesitated, Avraham opened the door and widened it for us to look inside. "Don't worry," he said. "You're safer in here than out."

Don't worry? What a ridiculous phrase these days.

We walked inside and I immediately noticed the other teenagers he'd mentioned, a boy and a girl, huddled next to each other in blankets. Their noses were red and they were shivering; their fireplace was empty.

Remnants of several families who had once filled this apartment were apparent—clothes left behind, someone's teapot, a set of dusty books. Lives had been abandoned here, just as this room had been abandoned. I wouldn't ask what happened to the people who lived here because I already knew the answer. I just hoped they had been strangers to these teens.

Avraham introduced us to Sara, who shared my sister's name but nothing of her appearance: She had a closely shaved head and a wary expression that likely knew terrors about this war that I hoped I never would. The boy, Henryk, had nice eyes. Or would have had nice eyes, before the war. They were hollow now, like what I'd seen in my mother's eyes for far too long. I could only guess at the horrors he'd seen.

"I wish we had something to offer you to eat," Avraham said, sitting cross-legged beside Henryk. A lump formed in my chest. No, I wished *we* had food for them. We owed them that much.

"We're grateful to be here," I said as we sat, although I didn't like that we were facing away from the door or that we were on the third floor of this apartment building. If it became necessary to escape, the front window wasn't an option. I should have checked for a fire escape before we came in the building, but I'd been in too much of a hurry to get off the streets. That was a stupid mistake. "We don't need anything," I added.

"The greater our need, the nearer our God, no?" Sara asked.

"And God is very near now," Henryk said with a smile.

Or rather, he was probably very near to God. My fingers could have fit around his wrist, and I saw every bone in his face, the skin a thin sheath that had become slightly translucent. His ragged clothes hung with such slack on his body that another person could have shared the extra space. He was clearly starving, dying a little bit more each day. All of them were dying.

Sara nodded at me. "Are you Polish?"

"No." Then I saw where her eyes were focused, on my Catholic cross necklace. In all the commotion of getting in here, I'd forgotten to take it off. I fumbled to unfasten it and shoved it in my pocket. "I'm Jewish, the same as you."

"You may be Jewish," Henryk said. "But you're different."

I took a deep breath, then leaned in. "We're couriers for the resistance." Seeing no visible response, I continued, "We can get things into the ghettos that people need. Or we can get people out of the ghettos if that's what they need more."

"You're too late," Sara said, a bitter tone in her voice. "Where were you last fall?"

I shook my head. "What happened last fall?"

The teens looked at each other, nobody wanting to speak first. Esther filled in the silence. "We heard that something happened to the children here. Please tell me they didn't . . ."

Her voice trailed off, and from the heavy silence that fell on the group, I knew she shouldn't have asked. Henryk finally mumbled, "What is it the invaders like to tell us? *Arbeit Macht Frei.*"

German for "Work will make you free." I'd heard that those same words stood over the entrance to the Auschwitz-Birkenau concentration camp, a place that existed for far darker reasons than forced labor.

"Our Judenrat believes work is the key to our survival," Avraham said. "So when the Nazis demand a deportation, anyone who can't work has to go."

Henryk picked up the story. "The elderly, the sick, the disabled were turned over to the Nazis first. We all lost loved ones then, and we still mourn for them. But something worse was coming. Last September, the Nazis wanted another deportation."

My gut twisted, wishing they wouldn't continue the story. I already knew how it would end, and that was hard enough. But once they said the words, I'd have to hear them over and over in my head. I couldn't stand that.

But Sara said, "The Judenrat gathered all the parents together in the square and insisted that they hand over their children. Sacrifice the innocent so that the parents might survive. Naturally, the parents objected, but . . ." Her voice broke.

"But they took the children anyway," Esther mumbled, sealing the words in my memory.

"All of them," Henryk said. "The rest of us are still alive only because we let them take the children."

Another silence followed, and for the first time since becoming a courier, I had no idea what to do or say. My sister's face entered my mind, and no matter how hard I tried to erase it just to be able to breathe again, I could not. Every ghetto I'd entered could describe their individual children who had been taken away since the invasion, but I'd never been to any place where they all were the chosen sacrifice, offered up so that the parents might live. I thought again of my mother, how deeply it had wounded her to lose two of her children. I imagined that same thing had happened to every mother in the Lodz Ghetto on the day their little ones were forced from their arms.

Esther finally broke the silence. "If you want revenge on the Germans, there are ways to do that. Sabotage, for example, maybe in the jobs you do here."

Avraham and Henryk exchanged another look, but Sara only leaned forward. "We will not work for the enemy, not to survive and not if we die."

I arched a brow. "You won't work?"

"That's why you're hiding here," Esther said. "You don't want anyone to know."

"They know," Avraham said. "It's only a matter of time until they come for us."

Henryk tilted his head upward. "We've given our lives to God. Whatever happens to us now is all right."

I blinked hard. "What is that supposed to mean? How can that be all right?"

"We're ready for whatever comes," Avraham added. "We're at peace with our decision."

"At peace?" I nearly leapt from my skin. "We are in a war!"

"Our governments are at war."

"No, the Führer of Germany has declared war on you and me, on all of us!" I sat up straight, determined to make them hear me. "We can get you out of here."

Avraham frowned. "Why?"

"Why?" I struggled to understand such an obvious question. "To give yourself the chance to live!"

"We want to live, of course. But that is in God's hands."

I shook my head, as hard as I wanted to shake him. "Just because God allows something to happen does not mean He wants it to happen!"

Sara touched my arm, two fingers only, again sparking a memory of my little sister. "If we escape, if we hide or fight, how does that honor God?"

"Hasn't He commanded us to choose life?" I asked. "If you stay here, you are choosing death."

"No, we're choosing faith," Avraham said. "The highest honor we can give God is to die in His name."

"Or fight in His name," I countered.

That was the wrong thing to say. Sara leaned forward. "Hiding from the soldiers is one thing. Defending one's life in the moment is allowed. But killing them is different. That's murder!"

I paused, wondering again how many Nazis I killed the night we attacked the Cyganeria Café. Or about the man I shot in that train yard. Were those murders, or a defense of innocent Jews?

Esther took over. "Chaya and I believe that God wants us to save ourselves. And we'll save you, if you'll come with us."

The group stared back at us like we were speaking a foreign tongue, and maybe we were. Finally, Avraham said, "I'm sorry, but we cannot leave. Faith will sustain us."

I hoped that worked, because they certainly weren't being sustained by food or fuel, or even the comfort of their families.

"You will die here," I said. "Avraham, listen to me, you will—"

"And when we do, we will take our place in history among God's chosen people," he replied. "We will die with honor."

His words echoed in my ears.

My parents would die from fear, and their love for each other.

Others would die from a stubborn refusal to see the truth.

The teens in this apartment would die for God, to honor Him.

But they all would die.

And there was nothing I could do about any of it.

Esther and I whispered about it later that night as we lay beside each other in a corner of the apartment while the others slept. "You were too hard on them," she said.

"Because they've given up!" I replied.

"No, Chaya. As much as the Nazis want to take our lives, they want to take our faith too. We fight for one, Avraham's friends fight for the other."

"What good is faith if you're dead?"

"What good is life without faith?" A soft sigh escaped her lips, but she remained more patient with me than I ever was with her. "We'll all die one day—no one escapes that fate. Our only decision is how we live before that day comes. Our path requires courage, but so does theirs. Both paths are ways to resist."

"What was your path?" I asked Esther. "Where were you before you came to Krakow?"

In the quiet darkness, I could almost hear the moment her breath lodged in her throat before she stammered, "It's . . . complicated."

"I've got time to listen."

But after a long pause, all she said was "Good night, Chaya."

EIGHTEEN

February 16, 1943
Lodz Ghetto

Sometime in the middle of the night, shots were fired in the street. I bolted upright, immediately wide awake, as were Esther and the other teens of this apartment. Sara must have been acting as a lookout while we slept, for she burst into the room and shut the door behind her. "It's a raid!"

Her eyes shifted to me and something pinched in my chest. They had to be looking for me and Esther. Either the szmalcownik who took my sack turned it in, or the OD reported us. Patrolling soldiers would have found the gap beneath the fence where we entered the ghetto. They knew we were here, somewhere.

"We need to leave the ghetto," I said, looking around the room. "Help us."

"There are no ways out," Avraham said. "It's amazing you got in, but they'll be even more vigilant now at the gates."

"There's always a way out," I insisted. "Weak places where the wood has decayed or the brick has been chipped away. Gaps where the children sneak in and out to smuggle food, or—"

"Lodz doesn't have those places anymore. That's why it's amazing you're here. There's no smuggling in Lodz, no sneaking. There are no holes."

More shots were fired out in the street. If we could not escape, then we had to hide, but I wouldn't ask Avraham for help. His punishment for hiding us would extend beyond cruelty.

While Esther scrambled to put her boots back on, I asked, "Is there any way out of this apartment other than the door?"

"There's a fire escape, out the back window," Sara offered.

"I'll show them." Henryk led us out of the apartment, into the hallway, across a rickety floor, and around a corner. At the end of that hallway, I lifted the back window to access the fire escape. He whispered, "I know a way out of the ghetto, but it will be very dangerous."

"Where?"

"There's a munitions factory a few blocks from here, on the south end of the ghetto. If you can find a way into the basement, a window straight ahead will take you outside the ghetto walls."

"Come with us," I offered. "Please. If two of us can get out, then three of us can get out."

His brows pressed together as if he was considering my words. I felt desperate for him to accept my offer, for there to have been one good thing about us coming here. But then he glanced back at the apartment where his other friends remained. "No, I—"

"God expects us to have faith." I wasn't giving up yet. "But doesn't He also expect us to act according to our faith?"

Footsteps pounded the floor below us. They were coming up the stairs.

"That's what I'm doing," Henryk whispered. "Go. I'll distract them for as long as I can."

Esther went out the window first and I followed, but Henryk hadn't yet shut the window before a bullet caught him from behind. He fell forward across the windowsill, and I pulled Esther with me against the building's wall, where we wouldn't be seen. She had covered her mouth with her hands to keep from screaming.

"Don't look," I whispered, trying to block her view from Henryk's still body. A second later, we heard Avraham's apartment door being forced open, banging against the back wall. Heavy footsteps followed.

"No," Esther whispered. "Chaya, no."

The words had barely fallen from her lips when Avraham and Sara shouted, *"Shema Yisrael!"* The first two words of our daily prayer, meaning "Hear, O Israel." They got no further before gunfire echoed in the apartment.

I let out a silent scream of my own, pain rippling through me. Avraham, Sara, and Henryk had taken those bullets as proof of their devotion to God, and so that we could escape.

I hoped God would hear their words. I certainly heard them. I just didn't understand them anymore.

Tears blinded me as I followed Esther down the fire escape. We had to be quiet, but it was equally important to be quick. We were far too visible up here.

The only thing masking the sound of our feet upon the metal was the one thing I wished it wasn't: gunfire on the streets, followed inevitably by wails of pain and suffering. The next shots ended with silence, which meant something far worse.

This kind of escape was new for me, and horrible. The gunshots and loud cries for mercy were saving my life. The silence threatened it. I was surviving only because others were dying. A choking sob rose in me, but I couldn't let it out, not here, and not in front of Esther. I shoved it down, all of it.

Ignoring the guilt, for trying to live while others around me were dying.

The pain, for coming here in the first place and inciting tonight's Aktion.

The confusion. Because I wanted to kill the people who were killing my people, and I didn't understand how anyone could say that was wrong or that it dishonored God. But maybe it did.

We reached the ground and immediately hid within the shadows of night. The snow had mostly stopped falling, but dark clouds covered what might have been a bright moon.

If only it were too dark to see the violence spreading like a cancer across this ghetto. People were being herded onto the street right in front of us, ordered to stand in lines.

We'd run on by then, keeping to the shadows. But I still heard the shots, each echo like a fist to my gut. And the inevitable, awful silence.

"This is the factory!" Esther grabbed my arm, bringing me back into the moment. Somehow, she'd kept her senses together to find this building, even as my own attention wandered into despair and hopelessness. I'd needed her help just now.

I had needed her.

Still needed her.

And she needed me to pay attention.

Hearing footsteps back on the street, I pulled Esther against the wall of the munitions factory and hoped that whoever was coming didn't aim their flashlights in our direction. Lights bounced in rhythm with their run, waving back and forth. They were still searching. And they'd continue searching until they found something to justify this Aktion.

I took Esther's hand and realized that hers was shaking again. In a strange way, this comforted me because it was familiar, and because I knew Esther needed me to be strong and brave and bold enough to guide us through that factory.

The flashlights were coming closer, but just when it seemed they might swing toward us, a call was barked out and the men holding them turned down a different street.

This was our chance.

As quietly as possible, we trudged through the snow toward the back of the brick building, looking for any way in, a door we could test, or a window. We found a couple of each, but everything was locked or closed.

"Up there!"

Esther pointed to a window over our heads, slightly open but too high to reach on our own. A tree was nearby, sturdy at its base but the branches looked brittle, as if the slightest pressure might cause them to collapse.

"They'll hold my weight," Esther whispered.

"I don't know if you—"

Esther spoke more firmly. "I can get into that window, Chaya. Help me, then wait by that last door we passed."

I wasn't sure if she was right, but I was absolutely sure what would happen if we didn't at least try. I locked my fingers together to make her a step, and then when I had her foot, I lifted it as high as I could. The branches would be cold and slippery with ice, but there was nothing I could do for her once she was in the tree. She shinnied along the limbs, moving from the thicker ones to the thinner branches above, and the thinner ones still that were near the open window.

She gripped one branch with her right hand while with her left she pried the window open wider. It moved, but only a little. Even if I had climbed the tree, I'd never have made it through the window's narrow gap. She released her right hand and I gasped, certain she was falling. But she held on to the frame with both hands and wiggled her body inside.

Just in time too. More soldiers ran down the street, passing me on their way to another part of the ghetto. My mind raced. If they came back this way, *when* they came back, their lights would aim toward my side of the building. I needed to be inside before then. I tried to estimate how far to the factory floor Esther would have to drop after she was inside. Could she manage that distance? Would there be any light inside to help her navigate the fall? What if she was injured in there?

I glanced down at my hands, clasped together near my chest. They were shaking violently. This level of fear was so unfamiliar to me that I didn't entirely understand it anymore. I'd spent so long accepting my death that I'd forgotten how very much I wanted to live.

I wanted to live. And for now I was still here, as was Esther, and I wanted it to remain that way.

After the soldiers passed, I retraced my steps to the door. I gave it another gentle tug, in case Esther had already opened it, but it was still locked.

A minute passed, and nothing happened.

Another minute passed.

And another.

Was I at the right door? Had she gotten disoriented inside the factory?

I tried the door again. It was still locked.

Where was she?

The shooting resumed, somewhere in the distance. The cries of the victims were dimming.

Where was Esther?

NINETEEN

February 16, 1943
Lodz Ghetto

After several minutes, I remembered a pin in my hair. I'd never picked a lock before, but I needed to try. It was better than waiting out here, increasingly anxious for what was happening to Esther inside that factory.

I pulled it out and straightened it, but before I could stick it into the keyhole, the handle twisted and Esther was at the other side of the opened door.

"Get in, quick!" she whispered.

As soon as she closed the door behind us, I asked, "Are we alone here?"

"I think so."

"Are you hurt?"

"No."

Then I was free to get angry. "I imagined all sorts of horrible things happening to you. What took so long? Look! I ruined a hairpin!"

She stared at it for a moment, trying very hard to care about the pin. Trying too hard. A smile tugged at her mouth and soon I was smiling too. Forgetting how furious I was and only overwhelmed with relief that she was okay.

But gunfire echoed outside the factory again, and I remembered there was nothing to smile about in here. Esther and I locked eyes. Then she said, "I looked around before I opened the door. I wanted to make sure I wasn't leading you into a trap. I found the stairs into the basement."

"Then what are we waiting for?"

She led me through a maze of long metal tables covered with tools and parts of weapons, and large wooden crates between them. My eyes weren't fully adjusted to the darkness in here, but I saw enough to know we were surrounded by a whole arsenal of weapons.

For a while, Akiva had focused on breaking into munitions factories near Krakow to sabotage the weapons ready for shipment. The cell assigned to that task would bend the firing pins or stuff salt into the barrels, or do whatever it took to ensure the weapons would be useless on the lines. But their mission was eventually changed. It turned out those who were forced to labor in the munitions factories were already doing plenty to sabotage the weapons when they could.

Another form of resistance.

But I doubted that was happening here. The Judenrat had its thumb too firmly on these people. Anyone cruel enough to send an entire ghetto's children away to their deaths certainly would not hesitate to quash even the smallest of rebellions.

"Stop!" I grabbed Esther's arm and we froze at a clicking sound at the front of the factory. The main doors were flung open and flashlight beams began scouring the room.

We ducked low, but the flashlights offered enough light to see the distance we still needed to cross to get to the stairs, and how little cover we had for it. Also, for the first time, I saw that Esther had found another bag here, one that she now wore over one shoulder and crossways on her body. It was empty, but it was ours now, and I hoped we'd get the chance to make good use of it.

"The doors were locked," an officer said. I instantly recognized his raspy voice as the same OD who stopped us before. "Why should we search a place those girls couldn't go?"

"Because it keeps us away from the Aktion outside." His companion's accent sounded Russian. "Why did you have to tell the Germans about those girls?"

The two officers were moving deeper into the factory, so this wouldn't be a cursory search, as I'd hoped. They'd spend as much time as they could here because the alternative being outside—was worse.

"The Aktion is a mercy compared to what's coming," the raspy-voiced man continued, still trying to justify reporting us. "The lists are already being prepared for the next deportation."

"More lists!" The officer cursed in Russian and moved

to a far wall to search there. Another few steps forward and he'd be parallel to Esther and me. "The Judenrat can speak of how they're tortured by having to choose who gets sent away, but those lists are power. If the people knew how well they live off bribes and favors to keep certain names from deportation, they would revolt."

"Well, I'm not saying anything. No one in my family has been on a list yet, and I'll do what I'm told if it remains that way."

"It's only a matter of time for us. Eventually, there won't be anyone left to add to the lists but us."

If they made it that long. Quietly, I lifted my hand to the nearby bench and located a gun that looked assembled, except it wasn't loaded. Not yet. Ammunition must be in here somewhere.

I brought my arm down and saw Esther shaking her head at me, eyes widened in horror. "No," she mouthed.

It was my plan if everything else failed, and we were closer to that than I wanted to think about. Hoping for another chance, Esther raised up just enough to throw something into the far corner of the room. It landed hard and heavy, like a bullet or scrap metal from a gun. If it was a bullet, I'd have liked to use it in a very different way, but her plan worked. The two officers ran to the corner. As soon as their flashlights were ahead of us, we tiptoed to the stairs and hurried down them as quickly and quietly as we could.

It was easy to find the window Henryk had described to

us, though it was high up, nearly to the ceiling. One crate was already against the wall, but we quietly carried another over to stack on top, making it high enough to get out.

Esther clambered up first and pried open the window. While she wiggled through the opening, I climbed onto the crate, but I'd only barely secured my footing when the voice with a Russian accent ordered, "Stop!"

I lowered my gun before turning around. I didn't want to tempt him to shoot, not when my gun was empty. His flashlight was so bright in my eyes, I couldn't get a good look at him, but I spoke slowly and with a calm voice. "I'm Jewish, trying to live, just like you are."

"Not like me," he said. "You're escaping, after sneaking in here with who knows what contraband."

"The 'contraband' was food, sir. I came to help these people here. Your people. Our people."

"You can't help the dead. And if you want to live, then you should have known better than to come to Lodz."

"We're both survivors, both of us doing what it takes to get through this war. Both of us trying to do the right thing whenever possible." He lowered his light enough for me to see a tuft of black hair beneath his OD cap with a red hatband. Lower still, and I saw his eyes, darting from me to where his partner was still upstairs searching. I shook my head at him, trying to keep his attention. "You won't shoot me."

"No, but I must bring you to the Gestapo for questioning."

"You know what they'll do to me. Can you live with that?"

He shifted his weight, clearly uncomfortable with the question. I was sure the answer bothered me even more.

His partner called from upstairs, his raspy voice brushing like sandpaper across my already brittle nerves. "I heard you say something. Everything okay down there?"

"It's nothing," he replied. "Rats, I think."

I smiled, relieved that he hadn't turned me in . . . yet. If he wanted to consider me a rat, I could live with that.

If I could live.

"Let me go," I said. "I'll never return here, and no one ever has to know."

After a brief hesitation, he said, "On one condition. My mother is up in Warsaw. I've had no word from her. If . . . if you ever meet a woman named Rosa Kats, will you tell her that her son loves her and that she was right? I never should have joined the OD."

"I doubt I'll ever get to Warsaw," I said, "but if I do, you have my promise. If she is there, I will find her."

"She would admire your courage," he said. "So do I. Now go."

Without another glance back, I climbed to the upper crate, then squeezed through the window. Together, Esther and I pulled it shut and then we ran a safe distance away from the ghetto walls, and just in time too. This was a well-patrolled area.

"I've never been more relieved to get away from a place in my entire life," I said to Esther. "Going there was a mistake."

"I know," she whispered. "I'm sorry, Chaya. I'm so terribly sorry."

"We were following orders. And at least our mission is over. There's no chance of a resistance here."

She licked her lips, and her shoulders returned to their familiar hunch. "I heard what that OD was saying to you down there."

"His mother won't be alive still," I said. "And it doesn't matter because we're not going to—"

"We are going to Warsaw," Esther said. "Lodz was only the start. There's a delivery we need to make in the ghetto there, one that Akiva promised to send in the event of an uprising."

"What delivery?" Other than what was in our pockets, a little cash, our identification papers, and the weapon I grabbed on our way out of the building, we had nothing.

Unless Esther had been secretly carrying something all this time.

"Last month, the Germans entered Warsaw's ghetto for a major deportation," she said. "The resistance there is led by a man named Mordecai Anielewicz. He ordered his fighters to fire, forcing the Germans out of the ghetto. They haven't come back yet, but—"

"But they will," I said. "They'll come back with the intention of destroying the ghetto and everyone in it."

"Yes. The people there are trapped, Chaya. And the Germans are coming for them."

My eyes narrowed. "Antek is sending us there so you can deliver some sort of package to Mordecai Anielewicz, which will save everyone in that ghetto?"

Esther slowly nodded her head. "It won't save everyone, but it is important that we get there before the Germans return."

"What's the delivery?" I asked.

Her brows pressed together, but she kept her gaze steadily on mine. "I'm supposed to discuss it only with the resistance in Warsaw. Please trust me, Chaya."

I bit my lip and studied her for any clues, then reminded myself that if I was captured, I wouldn't want that information forced out of me. It was better if I didn't know.

"Promise me that this package can help our people in Warsaw," I said.

"It will, if we get there in time."

I closed my eyes and thought of what would happen to the thousands of people in the Warsaw Ghetto when the Germans returned. If we were going to Warsaw, it would make our experience here in Lodz seem like a summertime picnic.

Then I opened my eyes, gave Esther a slight smile, and said, "Well then, let's go."

CHAPTER

TWENTY

February 17, 1943
Lodz

y initial plan was for Esther and me to return to the train station, to get out of Lodz as quickly as possible. But the dense clusters of Nazi soldiers at the station that next morning immediately shut down that plan.

"Do you think they're looking for us?" Esther asked as we watched from well over a block away.

"It's possible." And certainly not worth the risk of finding out, though my fists were clenched in frustration, and the morning had only just begun. Warsaw was over a hundred and thirty kilometers away, and if Esther was right in what she'd told me, any day now the Nazis would return to that ghetto to finish what they'd failed to do a month ago. No, they would return to finish off the ghetto entirely, a liquidation. I couldn't be here, uselessly creeping forward one footstep at a time along snow-covered, German-monitored roads. I had hoped to get to Warsaw today by train, to deliver Esther's package and offer the resistance any help they needed.

We backed away from the train station because we had to. Because it was only a matter of time before a soldier noticed us and compared us to the description of two girls who had entered the ghetto in the moonlight and vanished by dawn.

"Now what?" Esther asked.

"How long do you think it'll take us to walk to Warsaw?" I mused. "We'll have to move at night and hope for places to hide during the day. How fast can you go?"

Esther's eyes rolled upward while she did the calculations. "Realistically, it'll probably take us a week."

I cursed under my breath. I knew Esther heard it and that she was probably shocked, but she could add that to the list of my personal failures. She probably didn't know the full extent of crimes I'd committed over the past year. Endless lies, bribes, thefts from Polish shops, or the occasional ambush of a Nazi soldier. I could spend hours describing my growing eagerness to repeat what we had done at the Cyganeria Café, to take a bigger bite from the Nazi occupation. Passive resistance wasn't enough anymore. It wouldn't stop the ghetto liquidations, the deportations to death camps. It wouldn't shut down the showers at Auschwitz-Birkenau that rained down poison and genocide.

If I was going to make a difference, then I needed to fight.

But instead, I was facing a week of walking and hiding and cursing the cold weather for its relentless chill, just as this war was relentless and death was relentless. Just as my frustration constantly gnawed at me like a slow-moving drill, burrowing deeper every day.

In fact, the only thing that I was certain would end was the luck that had carried us through Lodz. I couldn't expect it to follow us all the way to Warsaw. I shouldn't even hope for it to last until curfew tonight.

Half of our remaining day was taken up with buying better wintertime clothes for our journey, which we put into Esther's shoulder bag. Except the bag must also hide the gun I stole, so I agreed to carry it. By the time we were finished, most of our money was gone, adding to my irritation. I had hoped to enter the Warsaw ghetto with supplies to help the resistance fighters.

Our goal was to escape the city before curfew and then find a place to rest until it was quiet enough to walk through the night. And for the most part, we left Lodz with no one giving us a second glance. There seemed to be an assumption here that every Jew was already behind the walls, so we weren't worth a second look. For those who did look, I smiled back as if we were friends. And maybe at one time, we might have been.

Esther had been studying me all morning, though she hadn't said much. Finally, she asked, "How do you do it?"

"Do what?"

"Mix in with these people like you're Polish, and then with ours as a Jew? It's like you have two separate personalities."

"I'm only me. But I don't go about with my eyes on the ground, as if I'm ashamed, or as if I expect to be hurt. Why should I? I'm proud of who I am, what I am."

"But you wear the crucifix," she said softly. "You lose the Jewish accent out here and present yourself as one of them."

I sighed and looked away. "Out here, I have to survive. And so do you. One day this war will end, and then I will walk these streets again as myself."

"Will you?" Esther shrugged, her shoulders as rounded over as usual. "I wonder if this will ever end."

"The war?"

"The hatred. I remember my father saying that he'd finally come to believe the world had moved past its hatred of Jews, and then this happened."

"Maybe when the world opens its eyes to what has been done to us, they will realize how destructive hate can be."

Esther shrugged again. "Maybe. But they'll forget again, in time. And when they forget, this will all start once more."

I put an arm around her and used it to straighten her posture. "Enough of us must survive the war to tell our stories, and every story will matter. When they remember our stories, they will forget their hatred."

She smiled and began walking taller. "Thank you, Chaya."

"For what?"

"For being patient with me, and teaching me, and . . . for helping me get through this. I know I've made a lot of mistakes."

I brushed that off, like it was nothing. Like it was what anyone else would've done too.

But that just bothered me more. Because I hadn't been at all patient with her, and I was teaching her only because her mistakes threatened my safety too. Worst of all was that despite my poor treatment, she'd been helping me far more than I'd helped her. For as little experience as she had, she was learning fast.

Or . . . did she truly have so little experience?

"Where were you before you joined Akiva?" I asked.

"I joined Akiva when I was twelve. Just not your group in Krakow."

"Then where?"

"Farther north."

Considering that Krakow was in the southern part of Poland, nearly anywhere would be farther north. And maybe around others, I had to let her get away with avoiding any talk about her past, but now it was only the two of us. I had the right to know who I'd been partnered with, who I was trusting with my life. I had to be careful, though. I didn't want to ask about her family, not yet. Because chances were, she didn't have a family anymore, just as it was possible that I didn't have a family anymore.

"Tell me about yourself, then. What were you like before the war?"

She considered that a moment, tilting her head as if deep in thought. This in itself was interesting. To answer, she had to compare herself to who she was now, how the war had changed her. I knew how I would answer such a question, because I'd thought about it many times. I *could* answer it—I just didn't want to.

"I guess I was . . . I don't know . . . before the war I was . . . happy."

The simplicity of her answer left me speechless. How often I once took that for granted, as if life would always be as innocent as it used to be.

Esther broke the silence with a question of her own. "Chaya, do you believe in God?"

I paused in my walk. "What do you mean? Do I believe He exists? Of course."

"No, I mean, do you believe in God's words? His promises to our people?"

I knew where she was going with these questions, and I tried to find any excuse to change the subject. But the earnestness of her expression deserved an honest response.

"I believe in God's promises," I said. "But I've run out of patience waiting for them. I believe in God's laws, but—"

"What about God's law not to murder?" Esther was ahead of me, but when she looked back, her face had become deadly pale. Suddenly, I realized those questions weren't for me. She asked because she needed the answers for herself. "Avraham and his friends believed that what we've done . . . what we're doing is murder. Are they right?"

I drew in a slow breath. "Last fall, after I shot that soldier in the train yard, I was upset one night and Rubin found me. He believed that God has given us the right to defend ourselves."

"Were we defending ourselves the night we attacked that café? Because it seems like we started that fight. And did any of it matter? We didn't stop the war or get the Nazis to leave Krakow. We can't even say that lives were saved because of what we did." Her voice rose in pitch. "What about in Lodz? All we did there was make things worse. I only wanted to get some answers, but instead we stole a weapon, lost food that could have saved lives, and ended up being the cause of an Aktion. Maybe what we're doing is just as bad as the enemy!"

"Stop it!" It's a good thing we were outside of town because I heard myself yelling. "Don't ever say that again. Don't ever think like that again. We are *not* like them!"

She instantly cowered. "No, of course not. I didn't mean—"

"What happened in Lodz was murder, every single shooting. The Aktion might've started because they were looking for us, but—" I stopped there, the words choking my throat. Until this moment, I hadn't had to think too much about this, that the consequences of entering the ghettos weren't always good. But I'd never been part of anything that awful. "The Aktion started because they were looking for us. They were looking for *us*."

This was never what I had joined the resistance to do. I became a courier to save lives, to offer help and a chance for survival. I was never supposed to be the reason people died.

"Chaya, I'm sorry. It's all my fault."

"No more talking." Tears welled in my own eyes, but I didn't want them. I didn't want to think about Lodz anymore, about the people who were being buried today, including three brave teens I would have considered friends, had they lived.

Would it be the same story in Warsaw? Would it be the same story until the last of our people were gone?

Off to the side of the road was a small woodshed. It had a narrow window facing the road that we could use to see out, if necessary, and it was guarded by a blackthorn tree bare of leaves. I could see the thorns sticking out along every branch, hopefully a deterrent for anyone else approaching the woodshed. It should provide us a decent place to rest until dark. A safe place to cry away the memories of Lodz.

TWENTY-ONE

February 18, 1943
Road near Brzeziny

I awoke with a start to the rattling sound of a car driving by. Morning light streamed in uneven streaks through the dirty window, where patches of bright sunlight blended with splotches of shadow. Esther yawned beside me, but it took her a moment to realize the same thing that had me already shaking my head.

We had overslept.

This little shed must have been gathering heat all day, so when we climbed in here, feeling secure from being discovered, it had been too easy to nest ourselves on the round logs, curl up near each other, and sleep. Truly sleep.

Maybe we needed it, but now we were facing a full day ahead in which walking was unsafe and hiding was unbearable.

"We'll just have to be careful," I told Esther. "We're not staying here."

"But if we're seen, if we're questioned—"

"Who gave you this assignment, to go to Warsaw?" I asked.

"Antek did, I told you that already."

"And when did he explain that your safety was the top priority? That at all costs, you were to protect yourself?"

Esther lowered her eyes. "He never did. We're to get to Warsaw as quickly as possible."

"Then gather your things. Let's go."

The problem was, we had very few "things," the exact opposite position I wanted to be in at this point in our journey. I had the stolen gun hidden in Esther's sack, but not a single bullet. Thanks to yesterday's purchases, we also had warmer coats where our identification papers were now, but we hadn't had enough left to buy any food. Our last meal had been a full day ago, but I tried not to think of that.

To avoid entanglements with the Nazis, we kept to the back roads, but they still showed tire tracks from cars and wagons, and prints from horse and foot traffic.

I doubted we'd see anything today beyond scattered farmhouses and the occasional shop, but that was hardly reason to relax. The neighbors in this small community would be familiar with one another. Anyone who did see us would know we weren't from here.

Which was why I immediately raised my guard when I spotted a woman headed toward us with a basket in her arms. She waved, then realized we were strangers and lowered her hand. This was wartime, and she knew she must be cautious too. She came closer and I saw her basket filled with eggs, perhaps on her way to a market.

I wanted those eggs, even a single one. It had been a long time since I'd had a fresh egg and my mouth watered for it. Don't stare at the basket, I reminded myself. Don't give her a reason to be suspicious.

She greeted me in Polish and I responded in Polish, as polite and friendly as possible.

"Where are you going?" she asked. "There's nothing around here."

"Our grandmother lives up the road," I casually replied. "Our parents sent us out of the city to stay with her."

"Who's your grandmother?" Her tone was marginally friendly, though her eye was almost constantly on Esther. That worried me.

"Maria Nowak." It was a good Polish name, matched my papers, and was common enough that it wouldn't surprise me if there actually was a woman nearby with that name. Lying had become second nature to me now. Half the time, I had to stop myself from lying when it wasn't necessary, just because I could.

The woman shrugged. "I don't know her. But we've had many new people come in from the city over the last couple of years." She looked at Esther again, too long, too earnestly. In response, Esther looked down at her feet, all but admitting guilt. "Where are you girls from?"

"Lodz." Although I'd told Esther not to claim having come from anywhere she was unfamiliar with, in this case, we had to. There was no other big city close enough to justify why we were here on foot.

"I go into Lodz every week to sell eggs." She lifted her basket, igniting my hunger again. "Maybe I've seen you there before, because you look familiar." That was addressed to Esther. "Perhaps on Bracka Street?"

Esther drew in a breath and looked down again. Bracka Street was one of the few roads in Lodz that we did know. It was inside the ghetto, the very road where we stood before Avraham brought us into his apartment. The road where Avraham and his friends were shot.

I laughed that away, each chuckle choking on my feelings of guilt and shame. "Bracka Street?"

The woman didn't laugh, and any friendliness in her smile vanished. She addressed me first. "I don't know about you, girl, whether you're one of those Jews or whether you're one of these fool Poles trying to hide them." Her eye turned to Esther. "But you are definitely one of them. And if you've come from Lodz, then you escaped from Lodz."

It was time to be aggressive. I pulled my Kennkarte from my pocket and held it out for the woman. "See this? I'm Polish, same as you." By then, Esther had her identification out as well. "And same as my cousin. How dare you make such accusations?"

"Identification papers can be forged. I've seen—" She

paused at the sound of a wagon headed up the road. In it was a large man driving a pair of horses. His face seemed kind and grandfatherly, but then, so had the man's face on our train to Lodz. I wasn't foolish enough to judge anyone based on appearances.

My mind raced. In a small community such as this, these two surely knew each other. She would tell him her suspicions, and if he tried to grab us, I'd have only one choice.

The gun. It was still unloaded, but they didn't know that. I'd use it to steal this man's wagon and we'd get as far as we could with it before we found another place to hide. I had no idea what we'd do after that.

"Dzien dobry!" The man greeted us in Polish and stopped his wagon, but his friendly smile quickly evaporated. Perhaps he sensed the tension in the air. Or perhaps he also suspected Esther and me. Why wasn't she looking up? Why didn't she defend her identity—her false identity?

"These girls and I were talking," the woman said. "I think they are—"

"Visitors to our little village," he said. "Welcome!"

"We're on our way to visit our grandmother." Digging in with the lie was my only option, short of waving my unloaded gun around. "Maria Nowak. Do you know her?"

He smiled. "As a matter of fact, I do. My name is Wit Golinski. I can take you there."

Esther and I looked at each other. Could we trust him? And what were we supposed to do when he dropped us off at this woman's home? Go to the door and have her shoo us away as strangers, right in front of this man?

"Look at that one," the woman said, pointing a crooked finger at Esther. "She's obviously—"

"Cold, how right you are," Wit said, finishing the woman's sentence again. "Your concern for the health of these two girls does you credit, ma'am. Thank you for your kindness, but I'll make sure they get to their grandmother's."

I didn't think he was nearly as naïve as the woman clearly believed. But I hadn't decided yet what that meant for us.

"Thank you, sir, we'd appreciate the ride," I said, heading to the back of the wagon. When the opportunity came, we'd jump out and run.

Even that would be impossible. Wit patted the seat beside him. "Ride up here where we can pass the trip with some good conversation. Your—"

I took Esther's hand. "She's my cousin."

He smiled. "Your cousin can sit behind us. There's plenty of room."

We didn't have any choice. I certainly wouldn't stay another minute in this woman's company. I disliked her enough by now that I didn't want her eggs anymore.

Well, yes, I did. But if I ate them, I wouldn't enjoy them nearly as much as I would have before.

The bigger question was, would getting into this man's wagon save us from the woman, or prove more dangerous than she ever could have been?

TWENTY-TWO

February 18, 1943
Road near Kolacin

From what I'd seen, there were three kinds of Polish citizens in the country these days. The first were those who endeared themselves to the invaders, who proudly allowed their homes to be assimilated into the German territory and their lives into the Nazi culture. They helped in the war effort, either because it benefited them or because it kept them from harm. The woman with the eggs probably belonged in this category, but I was glad we weren't there long enough to find out for sure. These were like the men who had stopped Yitzchak and my father on the street and harassed them or even beat them, knowing they wouldn't fight back because the persecution would only get worse if they did. Or the women who rode the trolleys through the ghetto to laugh at the Jews and shout that we had finally gotten what we deserved. I considered them traitors to Poland, and certainly traitors to their fellow citizens who were being crushed beneath the boots of the Nazis. When this war ended, I suspected many of these people would meet their end just as the Nazis eventually would, with shame and cowardice, having been betrayed themselves. And I wouldn't shed a single tear when they did.

The second group of Poles, the largest group, were merely surviving, trying to blend into the background. They might've moved into the homes abandoned by Jews who were sent to the ghettos, and might've taken over our shops and our possessions, but they felt little joy in it. They didn't help us, but they believed that at least ignoring our situation caused no harm. They were wrong. If there was any difference between causing a man to drown and failing to throw him a rope, it certainly didn't matter to the man in the water.

Although a small minority, the third group of Poles was different. They helped. They snuck close to the ghetto at night and tossed bread over the walls. They looked the other way when a Jewish child stole food from their shops to take back to his family. Or they took Jewish people into their lives, into their homes, and offered them a place to hide, a chance to escape the fate that tens of thousands of us had already suffered. They did this knowing what would happen to them and their family if they were caught. I would love these people for as long as I lived, and fight for them as hard as I would fight for any of my own.

And now I was sitting beside a man on a wagon, trying very hard to figure out which of these three types of Poles he was. I couldn't make any assumptions, and I couldn't give away anything until I knew for sure. But this was always the most dangerous moment in a first contact. How could we get his help unless I gave up some information about myself?

Everything I'd told Wit so far was a lie. That my name was Helena, and Esther was my cousin. He seemed to believe we were looking for our grandmother's house, though I'd not had to give him an address since he claimed to already know where she lived. And so far, he was speaking to me as if I was Polish, as if I was like him. I wanted to keep it that way.

"Where are your families?" he asked.

"Still in Lodz. But they felt we'd be safer out here in the countryside."

"Nowhere is safe." Wit sighed. "The partisans often move through this area, which brings the Germans in to search for them. It's only a matter of time before we feel the full effects of the war out here." He looked over at me kindly, perhaps with sympathy. "I suspect you two have already felt far too much of the war."

"The war is everywhere," I replied. Keep the lies simple, general. Give up nothing.

"Why was that woman giving you trouble back on the road?" he asked.

"She meant no harm. She just doesn't know us."

"Ah. Well, I know her. She is delivering those eggs to a German officer today."

"He buys them?"

"He buys the information she brings along with the eggs and pays her well. She tells him about any partisan activity here, about anything suspicious she might have seen. It's possible she will tell him about you and your cousin."

Behind me, Esther drew in a sharp breath. The possibility that we'd have German soldiers tracking us toward Warsaw was a terrible threat, one that twisted my gut into knots too.

But I couldn't let it show, so I shrugged it off. "She has nothing interesting to say about us."

"We both know what she'll tell that officer. You have no grandmother anywhere near here."

"I do. Her name is—"

"What is your real name, child? It's not Helena, and I doubt that's your cousin."

My hand slipped into the bag with the gun. I wrapped my fingers tight around the metal, though I wouldn't bring it out unless I had to. He seemed so nice. *Had* seemed nice. Now I wasn't sure what to think, though I was fully willing to believe the worst, if necessary.

Before it came to that, I'd try to quell his suspicions. "My name is Helena—"

"No, it's not, and that's fine." Wit sighed. "It's all you can say. I understand. I need you to know . . . Helena, it took a long time for me to realize what was happening to the Jews, and there are still far too many of us who don't understand it, because it's not happening *to us*. Does that make sense?"

I shook my head. And it wasn't because I missed his

point—I knew far too well what he meant. The animal who wanders free has no idea what is happening to the one caught in the trap. But I wanted to keep this man talking as long as possible. Better him than me.

Wit took a slow breath, then said, "There will come a time when everyone must account for their actions during this war. Some will be judged as evil, others as complacent. But I suspect the greatest number of us will fall to our knees and weep when we discover the full extent of the crimes being committed here."

"Will that be you, sir?" I asked. "Do you mourn for those who have died here?"

"I mourn for those I could not help." He eyed Esther, who had been facing sideways as much as possible. "You girls need a place to hide, I think."

I didn't know what to say. To admit that we needed a hiding place was to admit our identities. If this was a trap, if he was only a gentler, kinder version of that woman we met on the road, or a clever szmalcownik, then with a single nod of admission, I would walk us directly into it. But if I refused his help, doubled down on my lies, perhaps he would make us leave this wagon, and I'd rather be here . . . if he was safe.

Esther sat forward. "Offering to help anyone hide is a serious crime these days."

"And refusing to help is a serious sin." He shrugged. "That's what my wife believes. Last September she was in Lodz when she heard screams coming from within the ghetto, women begging for their children. She followed the cries to the train station and saw what was happening, the children being taken away. When the soldiers weren't looking, she grabbed two of the children from the train and hid them in this very wagon. We're raising them as our own now, along with a Jewish man who helps on our farm and keeps an eye out for any passing SS men. I'll bring you girls in as my orphaned nieces, should anyone ask. But we'll try to keep you out of sight if possible. There's a false floor in my barn. I can't promise you safety forever, but I can promise that no one in my family will ever betray your trust in us."

Silence followed, and I was surprised to find myself considering his offer. After months of fighting and running and lying, I was exhausted. What if he really was offering a place where we could hide and wait out the war? A place to forget all about the resistance.

But I never could do that, even if I wanted to. If Esther was right, then at this very moment, there were hundreds of fighters in Warsaw, trapped in the ghetto, scrambling to figure out how to defend thousands of Jewish civilians. Nazi tanks could roll in there any day. Esther had some sort of package to deliver. They needed our help.

Tears filled my eyes, but I blinked them away and blamed it on the sting of the cold wind when he noticed. "I think you're a good man, Wit. Full of courage and honor, and may you be rewarded for what you're doing for . . . those people. But my cousin and I need to find our grandmother, and we will. When you come to the turn in the road between your farm and the road ahead, please drop us off there."

"If you stay in this wagon, I can save your life," he said. "Leave, and you will almost certainly lose it."

Hadn't those been almost my very words to Avraham and his friends? I'd begged them to come with me, to save themselves. They had refused because they believed their lives had a higher purpose.

As I had to refuse this man, for a similar reason.

When I told him so, he nodded, seeming genuinely sad, but so was I. I didn't dare look back to see how Esther was feeling because I was sure she was equally tempted to accept his offer, and I didn't want to see that. My decision was made.

Little was said between us as we continued the ride. He knew who we were, but that was all right, because now I understood who he was too.

When he did stop the wagon at a turn in the road several kilometers ahead, he pointed to the right. "Stay on this road for as long as you can. If the Germans come looking for you, they are less likely to go that way."

I smiled, hoping to lighten the heaviness in my own chest. "What a coincidence. I'm sure our grandmother is just ahead on this very road."

Wit's expression back at me remained serious. "Your grandmother must be a good woman to be a part of your family. I hope you will stay safe with her until this terrible war is over."

My eyes felt hot and I didn't know what to say. I hoisted the bag higher on my shoulder and gave him a nod of thanks. It was time for us to go.

"Wait." He reached into his pocket and pulled out some money, which he offered to me. "It's all I have here, but I want you to take it."

"No, sir, I can't—"

"Wherever you're going, you need this more than I do. One more thing. I was out delivering some bread for my wife, but I think we can spare a little." He opened a bag at his feet and offered us an entire loaf of bread. It smelled so good I wanted to dive for it, but I held my composure until he placed it in my hands.

With sincere thanks, I accepted both the money and the bread, then Esther and I climbed out of the wagon with heavy hearts. We said nothing to each other as he drove away. We turned and silently continued down the road. The money he'd given us would help a little with replacing the items we had lost in Lodz, and I was determined to save as much of it as possible for ammunition, when I found any to purchase.

"I think Wit was being honest," Esther finally said. "I think he would have hidden us."

"He was one of the good ones," I said, to myself more than to her. I intended to remember Wit Golinski for as long as I lived, to remind myself that wherever there was evil, good men and women would also rise up to fight it.

For the first time in weeks, I felt hope for the future.

TWENTY-THREE

February 18, 1943
Road to Warsaw

The road we were walking on was as beautiful as any place in Poland. Vast acres of farmland reached to the horizon on every side of us, covered in untouched snow with patches of trees laced with ice. The sun was sinking fast, coloring the snow in a sea of reds and deep purple.

But the open beauty also made this area very dangerous. There was nowhere to hide here. Even the trees, barren of leaves, became cruel teases for safety. From one viewpoint, we might be impossible to spot from the road, but if the angle changed, we'd be betrayed. As beautiful as the sunset was, tonight we needed the darkness.

"What now?" Beside me, Esther walked slower and slower, and she'd begun shivering. I was sure her feet had as many blisters as mine, each step sending prickles of pain up my calves. We'd been going almost nonstop since Wit dropped us off earlier this morning. I didn't know how far we'd come, only that my mind had become numb to distance. No matter how much road we left behind, it continued to unfold endlessly ahead.

A dog began barking from a farmhouse we were passing. Maybe the owner would invite us in for warm cider and something to eat. Maybe not.

Probably not.

Shadows of a large man crossed in front of the home's candlelit window and we hurried away from its glow, taking comfort in the shadows and the safety of approaching darkness.

"I feel like a criminal," Esther said, glancing back at the light. "I suppose that's what we are."

"These days, it is a crime to be Jewish, to have been born." I barely felt the weight of my own words. What did right and wrong matter in a world that had been turned upside down? One in which the murder of innocents was the law, and defense of those same innocents was punishable by death.

I smiled over at Esther, adding, "If we have no other choice, then let us be proud criminals, honorable criminals, and criminals who will die one day knowing that we did everything we could to disrupt the peace."

She laughed, though it started the dog barking again. She quickly muffled her laughter, and we picked up our pace, getting as far as we could from anyone who might see us out here.

Just like criminals.

"Tell me a story," I said. "Something from before the war."

"I don't want to—"

"Something pleasant. We need the distraction; please, Esther."

It took her a long minute of thinking before she finally began. "All right. Well, when I was eight years old, my school had a large oak tree in the yard. An enormous, beautiful tree that begged to be climbed. The branches were perfectly placed—if you could get to the lowest one."

"They'd let children climb this tree?"

"Of course not! But the more the teachers said no, the more I wanted to do it. And it was the last day before summer break, so I knew I'd never get another chance. I came to school early, carrying a step stool along. It boosted me up to the first branch, where I could see the whole schoolyard. From there it was a simple thing to get higher. I climbed above the top of the school. Then higher, where I could see homes all around."

"That must have been incredible."

"It was . . . until I fell." Ignoring my gasp, she quickly added, "I didn't fall far, but what saved me was a branch that got caught on my bloomers."

"Your bloomers? You were—"

"Hanging facedown with my dress halfway over my head and my bloomers caught on a tree branch. I didn't dare move. If the branch broke, I'd go straight to the ground. I just had to wait until someone came who could help me."

I giggled, hoping she didn't think it was rude. "How long was that?"

She rolled her eyes. "Well, that's the problem. I was too embarrassed to call down to anyone, and they never looked up. They walked right beneath me, going about their business. Finally, after a few close calls, I thought I'd at least better get my dress off my head. But I wiggled too much. And I fell . . ."

"Oh no!"

She started to laugh. "Oh yes! Right as I fell, a grounds-keeper was passing below, hauling a wagon of fresh dirt. I fell right into it! Face-first! The only thing sticking up out of the wagon were my bloomers, still perfectly white!"

I laughed too, enjoying the fact that because we were finally far enough from any homes, it was safe to be a little loud. Safe to enjoy being a pair of ordinary teenage girls, even if only for that one small moment.

But in wartime, laughter never lasted long. Only a half kilometer down the road, we came to a field that must have been the site of a terrible battle. Ditches had been dug through cornfields. Small pits to drop seeds into were now whole chunks of earth blown apart by exploded shells. It took little imagination to visualize where bodies might have fallen. Some of their soldiers, more of ours.

But the Polish army must have had some luck in the battle. At the far end of the field, I saw a German tank. It was camouflage green with a tank number and black Iron Cross on each side; the scrapes and dents on it looked like it ran over its fair share of obstacles to get here. But it was clearly damaged. The gears were off its track and its turret was bent.

Another smile widened on my face.

Esther noticed, and her tone immediately sharpened. "No, Chaya. What if—"

"No one's in it. It's obviously been abandoned."

"We can't sleep in a German tank! It's wrong!"

"It's perfect. Think of what a great story this will make for your children and grandchildren one day, of the night we hid inside a weapon designed to kill us."

"That's not funny."

I grinned over at her. "Well, it's not funny in the same way that you falling into that wagon was funny. But this comes close. Let's go."

Careful to avoid making tracks where possible, I led the way toward the tank. I paused long enough to examine the exterior damage.

"What could have done this?" I asked.

Esther stood several meters behind me, reluctant to come any closer. "A single mosquito carrying malaria can end a human life. It's small but deadly. I suppose if you hit the tank just right, even with something small, this can be destroyed too. But we don't need to know how to stop a tank."

"Maybe we will one day." My expression became stern. "We have to go inside, Esther, purely for research purposes."

Ignoring her protests, I turned my attention back to the

tank. My first concern was how we'd get inside, but a glint of reflected moonlight showed a gap between a hatch on top and the rest of the tank. It was open.

I climbed onto the track wheels in the front using the tank's gun turret as a brace. How cold the metal was now, though it must've been as hot as fire during its final battle here. When I was balanced on the platform, I leaned down to help Esther, but her arms were folded and she looked ready to run.

"I can't. If there's someone inside—"

"If there's someone inside, we've already woken him up by coming this far, and on your best day, you'll never outrun his gun."

She sighed, gave me a miserable half-smile, then reluctantly took my hand. I did her the favor of checking inside the hatch first. I wasn't worried about a live body down here; that wouldn't make sense on a battlefield that must've been a couple of years old. I was worried about a dead body, which the Germans sometimes left behind as a trap, with a device that would explode if anyone tried to move it. I couldn't see anything from here; it was pitch-black down below. Grinning again at Esther, I took a deep breath, then sank myself into the darkness. Almost instantly, I landed on a metal floor contained in the upper, rotating half of the tank. The lower half would have belonged to the commander and driver. They'd have more comfortable seats than these, but up here, we were surrounded by leftover weapons, an entirely different kind of comfort.

I called up to Esther. "It's empty."

"No soldiers?"

"That's what empty means, Esther." Once she descended beside me, I sealed the hatch, allowing only a small pistol hole nearby for our air, ensuring that other than us, it would remain empty.

Esther began feeling around for anything that might provide light but found nothing.

"It's better this way," I told her. "A light would make us a lantern out here. It'll be morning soon, then we'll have plenty of light."

"I can't sleep," she said. "Not closed up inside this terrible place."

"I can sleep just fine," I replied with a yawn. "Get some rest. We still have a long walk ahead."

TWENTY-FOUR

February 19, 1943
Road to Warsaw

My eyes opened earlier than I wished they had, partially from the discomfort of the cramped space within the tank, but mostly because sunlight was peeking in through the pistol hole directly onto my face. Aside from being impossibly tired, I was eager to explore my surroundings. I'd never been inside a tank before, but I knew they were manned by a well-armed crew. At our strongest, Esther and I couldn't carry any of the larger munition shells with us, nor would I know what to do with one if I could, but if there was a pistol hole, then there had to be pistols here too, or at least ammunition. Since we had climbed into the gunner's hatch, we were in the most likely place to find any remaining weapons if they were left behind.

I stole a quick peek at Esther, who was curled up almost into a protective ball. I knew it frightened her to be in here, but it frightened her to be nearly anywhere, and besides, we were probably safer here than out in the open. The tank wasn't foolproof; that was obvious now that I'd seen the inside of one. If someone wanted to flush us out or kill us, a gas bomb or grenade rolled into the tank's muzzle should do the trick. But I wouldn't tell Esther that. Besides, a gas bomb or grenade wouldn't be friendly no matter where we were. At least here, we were surrounded by thick metal and a hatch with an interior lock.

I began searching quietly so as not to disturb her. Very quickly, I found a compartment containing German army rations. I hoped this food wasn't packaged by any resistance members determined to add a dose of food poisoning to the German diet, but we were going to take the risk—and take the food—anyway.

The markings on the food packages were in German, but I knew enough of the language to recognize the crackers, tinned meat, and most exciting of all, squares of chocolate! Unable to stop myself, I tore into one package and broke off half a piece for myself, then leaned back in the chair and smiled, letting it melt in my mouth. I hadn't had chocolate since the war began and had forgotten until this moment how much I missed it.

With that thought, the guilt returned, this time like a lead weight inside my stomach. I hadn't needed that piece, I'd only wanted it, and I wasn't out here to satisfy my wants. I had responsibilities to literally thousands of people who would trade a limb from their bodies for that bite of food.

"What do I smell?" Esther opened her eyes with a smile and her eye zeroed in on the chocolate. I could hardly deny her what I'd just given myself, so I offered her the other half of the piece I'd eaten. Except that where I popped the entire thing into my mouth, she only nibbled at it from the corner, determined to make the half square last as long as possible.

"Can I hate the Nazis and love their chocolate?" she asked.

I grinned. "Chocolate does not take sides in a war, and that is a good thing."

Now that Esther was awake, we began a thorough search of the tank, opening every hatch and searching every gap inside this metal monster. Some of what we found was disgusting, a reminder that the soldiers who once operated this tank didn't get out as often as five grown men should have. But we found a half-used package of unused rags that we gratefully used to clean ourselves, bottles of clean water, and more food than we'd be able to carry.

I wanted the food, but I was still searching for ammunition. The gun I brought out of Lodz was fine for waving around if I wanted to look threatening, but it might also start a fight I couldn't finish. I needed bullets.

Since Esther was smaller, she maneuvered herself into the lower section of the tank. The driver would have been on the left, but she slid right, to where the commander would sit. Almost immediately after she shifted into position, she called up, "A radio!"

Radios were almost impossible to come by these days, and even those who had one hidden were reluctant to bring them out. But Esther switched it on, her eyes wide with hope and expectation. Finding an Allied or resistance station would be invaluable.

However, the radio was already tuned to a German military news broadcast, the only reception she could get after scanning through the entire dial. For now, it would have to be enough. Esther looked to me for the translations, so when I could understand the broadcaster, I passed on information while we continued our search of the tank.

"Mostly they're describing different battles that are taking place," I said. "It sounds like the war is reaching all over the world."

"Who's winning?"

I shrugged. "This station will say that the Germans are winning, even if they're not."

Her eyes widened as she looked back at me. "What if they truly are winning, Chaya? What happens then?"

I'd asked myself that same question countless times. If they won, the extermination that began with us would extend to anyone they viewed as a threat to their twisted ideals. If there was any chance of them winning, then the resistance mattered more than ever.

But all I said to Esther was "I never let myself believe in a future where evil wins. Because if I do, then everything I've done, everything you and I are still doing, is for nothing.

We need to believe in a future where love is stronger than hate. Where peace is normal. Where this"—I gestured around the tank—"is just a page from the history books."

She nodded and we returned to our search. I found a few well-made winter hats, but they'd have to be left behind. As nice as they would be over the next few weeks, spring was coming, and besides, we could use the space in our bags more efficiently.

Meanwhile, the radio announcer kept speaking, little more than a German backdrop to our exploration of the tank. Until—

"Oh no," I mumbled, almost unconsciously.

Esther's voice registered alarm. "Is that the news? What did they say?" When I hesitated, she said, "I can handle the truth, Chaya. Tell me!"

I took a deep breath, then said, "There's a student resistance movement in Germany that calls itself the White Rose. Akiva wanted to prove that not all Jews went like lambs to the slaughter, right? Well, the White Rose members hoped to prove that there were good Germans who disagreed with the Nazis and Hitler's war."

Her voice faltered a bit. "What happened to them?"

"Their leadership was arrested last night, and they'll be executed before it's over." I leaned back and closed my eyes. One group at a time, the Nazis were shutting down anyone who resisted. Every whisper of freedom was being silenced. Every chance of escape was being snuffed out.

I still believed that Germany would lose the war, but I believed it less than I did five minutes ago.

After a long moment, Esther began exploring her area again. "Bullets!" She dragged a metal box from beneath her seat, and it looked heavy.

"What caliber?" I yanked the pistol from our bag and opened the chamber. When she held up a bullet, I let out a disappointed sigh. They didn't match. In addition to a gun with no bullets, I now had bullets with no gun. If it came to a standoff, I'd have to throw the bullets at the Nazis and hope one poked out an eye. That'd be the worst I could do.

But surely, once we reached Warsaw, someone there would want this ammunition. We had to bring the box with us. I stuffed the gun, bullets, and radio into a knapsack I'd found behind my seat, along with as much food as I could fit inside. Esther loaded her bag as well. With our overstuffed bags, one of which had German colors, we'd look more suspicious than usual should anyone see us on the road, but it was a necessary risk. We'd just have to be extra careful while we were out in the open. As always.

We emerged from the tank with caution, but the field was quiet, the late-afternoon sun bathing the field in a final hour of daylight. I hoped we could make a lot of progress before it was gone. We moved too slowly at night, and now that Esther had told me about Warsaw, all I wanted was to get there before the Nazis crushed yet another resistance group.

Esther began the conversation today. "You're always

asking about me, but what about your family? Are any of them . . . still with us?"

I was surprised by the boldness of her question. It was more than I'd dared ask her, despite my intense curiosity. But perhaps if I shared a bit of my story, she'd share more of hers.

"I have a grandmother in a safe house near Krakow," I began. "My parents . . . I don't know. I'm not sure if my mother cares anymore whether she lives or dies, and I don't know how long my dad will go on if she doesn't . . . If they haven't already begun liquidating the Krakow Ghetto, they will soon."

"Why . . ." She was being more cautious now. "Why doesn't your mother care anymore?"

I wondered if there would ever be a time in my life when I could answer that question without a swell of pain rising inside my chest. "My sister used to sneak out of the ghetto to smuggle food for my family. She knew of a hole in the concrete walls that wasn't well guarded, and like me, she had a look that wouldn't draw a lot of suspicion on the Polish side. But one day she was caught by an OD when sneaking back into the ghetto. He demanded her food and she refused, then ran away, thinking she had gotten away with it. But when the Gestapo demanded a list of names soon after, her name was there. My parents didn't know at the time what it meant to have your name on a list like that. They figured maybe she'd be sent to the countryside, same as what happened to me. So when they demanded everyone on the list show themselves on the street, they sent her out. She—" My voice broke and I stopped there. I'd said enough.

"I'm sorry, Chaya."

I sucked in a deep breath. Strangely, it felt good to be telling her all this. Like an infection that needed to be drained. It hurt to talk about it too, but for the first time since that day last summer, it wasn't a wound I had to carry alone.

"There's more," I added. "I have a brother—had a brother—named Yitzchak. He disappeared around the same time. He was probably either taken away with my sister or killed. But maybe not. Maybe he's still alive. No one knows. No one will ever . . ." My voice trailed off.

"That's why you became a courier," she said. "Every ghetto you enter, you look for his face. Every bite of food you distribute, you think, maybe if he's there, maybe he'll get it."

"Or, at least, maybe I'll find someone who can tell me what happened to him." I tried pushing his face from my mind again. It never worked.

"I understand," Esther said. "My family is . . . was—" She clamped her mouth shut again, and I knew she wanted to tell me about them too, but something still held her back.

"Where's your family, Esther?"

She shook her head and pushed on at a faster pace. "Never stop hoping, right? That's what keeps us alive, to never stop hoping for a happy ending."

TWENTY-FIVE

February 19, 1943
Road to Warsaw

We had a particularly bright moon tonight, and it was a little warmer than before, a whisper of spring in the air. We walked farther and faster than usual before we finally decided to take shelter in a barn similar to the one where we stayed days ago. The nearby home looked abandoned, and no animals were in or around the barn. It should be a good shelter. As always, I checked for all possible exits before settling in for the night. There were doors on both the front and back of the barn, and in the loft above, a rope dangled from a hook and extended almost to the ground.

"Let's sleep up there," Esther suggested. "There's more hay for warmth and then if we need to look out and see if anyone is coming, we'll have a better view."

It was a good suggestion, though by now, I was beyond exhausted. I would've gladly slept on thorns if that was all we had.

Once we were folded beneath warm layers of hay, we faced each other with the radio between us and turned the volume low. The broadcast hissed out the same propaganda as before, all the victories the Axis powers were enjoying, how their areas of control were expanding, and how the Allied forces were certain to crumble any day now. I didn't know how much of it was true, and I was careful to explain that to Esther as I translated.

Then my ears pricked up as Warsaw was mentioned. I stopped translating.

The broadcaster said, "German forces are preparing for a massive assault on the Jewish Quarter in Warsaw, following resistance during a resettlement campaign last month. Military leaders have promised a fierce response to the Jewish bandits and have assured the Führer that all resistance movements within the General Government will be crushed. The White Rose Movement . . ."

"What are they saying?" Esther asked. "I heard them mention Warsaw."

I switched off the radio. "It's nothing we don't already know. Let's go to sleep."

"What aren't you telling me?"

"What aren't you telling me?" I was tired after a long day of walking, and irritable after hearing news about the deathtrap I'd walk into within the next few days. Still, I softened my voice to add, "Where'd you come from before joining us in Krakow? What's your story?"

She opened her mouth, then closed it, then rolled away from me. "You're right, Chaya. Let's go to sleep."

Truly irritated now, I rolled away too and fell asleep immediately, only waking up an hour or two later when I heard noises from below. "Esther?"

She called up. "I needed a bathroom break. Everything's . . . wait!"

The sounds were coming from outside the barn. A crunch of snow, spaced evenly apart. Calculated, timed steps.

Faint light seeped in through the barn slats, though I thought it was still predawn. It might be an animal. I hoped it was an animal.

But I didn't think so.

I wanted to tell Esther to hide, but as quiet as this early morning was, I didn't dare make another sound. I hoped she understood that she needed to move. Before bedding down, we had found places that would work in an emergency. Did she remember where they were? Could she hide without making too much noise?

Up here, we'd already buried our bags deep inside a storage bin, beneath some filthy burlap bags and animal harnesses. I silently climbed in there now, getting as deep inside as I could so that if they lifted the lid, they shouldn't see me.

But even as I burrowed in, I was terrified for Esther. I'd heard no movement from her. She needed to hide.

Finally, her footsteps crunched onto the hay scattered on the floor below. If I heard that from here, then anyone outside would have heard it too. She stopped walking, and I heard her sniff. Even that was too loud.

The barn doors burst open, and in the same instant someone shouted, *"Auf Knien!"* The German order to kneel. Esther screamed but quickly stifled it, and they didn't repeat the order. She must have understood their words or their intentions, and obeyed.

"Kennkarte?" Based on their efficiency, I thought this had to be the Gestapo.

Her papers were up here in the bag, with me. If she told the Gestapo where they were, I'd need a reason for why I was hiding here. If I was truly a Polish citizen, why should I hide? My mind raced.

But with a trembling voice, Esther said, "There are no papers." She spoke in Yiddish, which was far more devastating than her actual words.

An officer shouted, *"Jude!"* which was immediately followed by a slapping sound, then Esther's cry of pain.

I was trying to figure out how many of them there were. At least three men, and maybe a fourth. My unloaded gun wouldn't bluff our way past them all.

What should I do?

There was nothing I could do.

What was the right thing to do?

In Yiddish, another officer asked, "Who else is here?"

"I'm alone," Esther said. "I ran away from the family that was hiding me. They beat me—"

"After tonight, you'll wish you were back with them."

Esther was hit again and probably knocked unconscious, because she made no other sounds. The order was given to carry her to the truck on the road.

"Burn this place to the ground." The order was given by a new voice, and seconds later I heard the first whoosh of fire. Whatever he used for ignition caused the flames to burn hot and rise fast.

I had to escape the fire, but that wasn't my biggest problem. Not even close. In the distance, a truck's motor started. They were taking Esther away.

TWENTY-SIX

February 20, 1943
Road to Skierniewice

The first rule of the resistance was loyalty to the resistance. We all made vows that under no condition would we reveal the name of our leaders or fellow fighters, or even our missions. Not under threat of torture or death, to us or to our loved ones.

I gave my promise without hesitation, because I understood the reason it had to exist. The resistance was bigger than any of us individually. Not even our leaders could consider themselves important enough to betray the others.

The second rule of the resistance was that if we could save ourselves without breaking the first rule, we should. That thought forced me out of the storage bin, hoisting Esther's bag across one shoulder and the German knapsack slung over the other. That left my hands free to open the loft door, now my only option for escape. Flames licked at the floorboards beneath me; I felt through my boots how hot they were already getting. It was likely only seconds before the upper floor collapsed. The rope dangled from a hook at the widow's peak a little over a meter away. With twice the usual weight on my back, I didn't dare lean out to grab it. I had to jump.

Smoke filled the loft and poured out the doors around me, choking me, blinding me. A piece of the floor behind me collapsed, taking part of the barn wall with it.

There was no time to think or plan. I got a running start and leapt for the rope. I caught it, though the weight of my bags nearly made me fall, and rope burns stung my hands. I dropped the knapsack to lighten my load and then shinnied down as quickly as possible. It's a good thing I did, because when I was nearly to the ground, the rope itself caught fire and landed in a heap beside me.

The Gestapo officers were gone, but very soon, the farmers along this road would be waking up for their morning chores. They'd see the smoke and flames and come here to investigate. I needed to go now.

I did my best to balance the weight of the bags on my back, but I hadn't realized before that even though I had the weapon and ammunition, Esther's bag was as heavy as mine, since it was much larger than the knapsack.

That thought immediately stuck in my head. For all my feelings of annoyance, Esther was carrying the same weight as me and yet she almost never complained. She would've been as cold as me, as tired as me, but she kept pace at my side without fail.

I had to get her back.

I had no idea how to get her back.

The tracks from the Gestapo truck were still visible and should remain that way as long as it stayed on these dirt roads. But if the truck reached a main road, paved and cleared of snow, I'd never find Esther.

Then the realization hit: the woman with the eggs who we met two days ago. She must have reported us to that officer in Lodz, who sent out word for the Gestapo to look for us. I wondered if the day would ever come when she would realize what she had done. If she would ever know the price Esther was about to pay for the woman's bigotry.

Esther was unconscious when they carried her to the truck, or I thought she was. I hoped she'd remain that way for some time. They wouldn't do anything to her until she was awake. Did she know that? Would she think to fake sleep if she did wake up?

I needed to keep myself awake. We couldn't have slept for more than an hour or two since we first entered that barn. I was exhausted, moving as quickly as I could to follow the tire tracks and wearing out even faster with the bags on my shoulders. They seemed to get heavier with each step.

Inside my head, a voice whispered to drop the bags, but I couldn't allow myself to do that. Whether I found Esther or not, I still had to go to Warsaw.

That thought burrowed into me, a new weight that proved heavier than ten bags combined. If I couldn't find Esther, there would come a point when I would have to refocus on the mission and get to Warsaw.

I didn't think I'd be capable of that. Never knowing what happened to Yitzchak had hollowed out my parents' lives. Mine too, in many ways. I couldn't wonder about Esther too. I would not leave without her.

As I feared, after about ten kilometers, the truck turned onto a main road and the tracks quickly faded. No, this wasn't good. What was happening to Esther now? I knew too many of the possibilities, each one worse than the last.

I had to think. I had to control my scattered emotions and just think.

My options on the main road were to go left, toward Warsaw, or right. If they were taking her to Warsaw, I'd never find her again. If the truck went right, I had a chance.

I walked to the right, solely because I needed the truck to have turned that way. I knew that was foolish reasoning. But I had nothing else left.

Eventually, a small town rose ahead but I couldn't find a sign to tell me its name. I'd never been here, and I wasn't aware of any ghettos nearby. Likely, any Jews who'd once lived here were deported to larger cities long ago. I noticed a small military presence, perhaps a single company of soldiers, but nothing that would ordinarily concern me.

However, this was hardly an ordinary time for me, starting with the German knapsack and ending with Esther's overstuffed shoulder bag, both of which practically screamed for me to be stopped and searched. I couldn't carry these through town.

So before entering, I cleared a spot of snow in the field and put both bags on the ground. Then I rolled enough snow to create the base of a wide snowman. I added a snowball trunk and head and even put two pebbles in place for eyes. It cost me a half hour to build it, but if it worked, it was time well spent.

Unless it became the reason I never found Esther. Maybe she was a half hour farther from here by now.

Keeping hold of my last vestiges of hope, I walked on, trying my best to fit in. Trying to look like I wasn't in a full-fledged panic over what could be happening to Esther right now, if she was even still alive.

The Gestapo frequently took over local jails for its own use, and jails were often located in the center of a small town like this, so that was the direction I took. I saw soldiers here and there, but the townspeople were going about their business, so I did too. I knew this routine. I'd done this a hundred times.

But it had never felt like this before, like I was a walking advertisement for the resistance movement. Every step I took, every turn of my head, every false smile seemed to scream my true identity.

I had to stay calm. I had to do better than this. For Esther's sake. For my own sake.

Several Nazi *Kübelwagens* were parked all over the city, but I was looking for a truck, and I began to notice how many of them were here too. How could I know which one carried her away? I couldn't know. Even if I'd seen it, they all looked alike.

"Dein ist mein ganzes Herz!"

It took a moment to realize the young soldier was speaking to me, telling me his heart is mine. If only he knew how literally I believed that. I turned and offered a brief wave, nothing flirtatious, but friendly enough for him to let me pass without thinking I was interested.

But it didn't work this time. He ordered me to stop, and I did, immediately readying my papers for his inspection.

"You don't need those," he said, brushing them away. "What's your name?"

"Helena Nowak."

"I haven't seen you here before."

My smile was tepid and I began walking again, thoroughly bothered that he followed alongside. "I don't leave home very often."

"Well, I'm glad you left it today. I've just finished with my duties."

How nice for him.

"Perhaps we can get a coffee together, no?"

No. Still walking, I said, "I've got some shopping to do, then I'm expected back at home to help with chores."

"I can walk you to the shops. I'll be good company."

On a normal day, I could get rid of this boy like he was dust to be wiped from a shelf. But I was exhausted, cold from being out in this wintery weather for so many days, and increasingly worried about Esther. I was also out of excuses. All I could think of was to say, "I was headed to the town square."

He took that as permission to come along and fell in beside me, thinking he'd set himself up on some kind of date. Later in his barracks, he'd brag to his bunkmates about the pretty Polish girl who likes him.

If only he knew.

"I started out at the bottom, but I'm working hard to get noticed. I might be a *Soldat* today, but one day, I'll lead this army."

"You and Hitler together." I smiled sideways at him, mostly at the idea of this ignorant schlump aspiring to lead anything more complicated than a line of schoolchildren out to play.

Perhaps my joke was lost in translation because he only nodded. "Perhaps not today. But watch me tomorrow, and the day after that. You'll see."

I wouldn't, because I wouldn't be here tomorrow. By then, I'd have to be as far from this place as possible. With or without Esther.

I couldn't leave without Esther.

I might have to leave without Esther.

My breath became shallow, but I tried to force that away before he noticed.

"What are your duties?" I didn't care how he answered, but as always, the conversation needed to be about him, not me.

"If a report comes in about a person in hiding—a Jew or Gypsy or partisan, perhaps—I'm part of the team to go and find them."

"You're with the Gestapo?" My heart pounded, but I couldn't let my sudden interest in his work show. I casually threw out a hand and hoped he didn't notice the sweat on my palm. "There can't be many places to hide around here."

"You'd be surprised. Just last night, we found a Jewish girl who'd been hiding in a barn. Tiny little thing near your age, I'd guess, like a scared kitten. We were all surprised she'd managed to hide this long."

It occurred to me that the woman who reported us surely had mentioned two girls, one with my description. If she had told them that I was Polish, hopefully the Gestapo wouldn't be as interested in finding me.

Or maybe this ambitious young man suspected that I was the second girl and was hoping to trap me.

Swallowing the new wave of panic, I asked, "What happens to those you find?"

He pointed to a building down the street. "We keep

them there until we can ship them to a labor camp. But you're in no danger. The cells are well guarded."

My gut twisted. Of course they were. How could I possibly get Esther out?

He continued, "We had to make an exception for the girl from last night, though. She claims to have typhus. So we couldn't keep her in the cell with the others."

"Oh?" It was nearly impossible to hide the concern in my voice. "What was done with her?"

"For now, we've got her tied up in back like a dog." He chuckled until he realized I was not. "We'll bring a doctor in from the town to examine her. If she's only pretending to be sick, then we'll return her for questioning—"

"Questioning? Why?"

"My superiors believe she knows more than she's telling. Why else would she refuse to give us any information, even her name?"

"And if she is sick?"

He shrugged again. "Obviously, we can't allow disease to spread. You understand, I'm sure."

I did understand. One way or another, Esther was going to be killed.

TWENTY-SEVEN

February 20, 1943
Skierniewice

I got rid of the young soldier only when I ducked into a shop that sold women's undergarments, explaining I was shopping for my mother. His face turned a hundred shades of red.

"I may be in here for some time," I explained, "but perhaps I'll see you tomorrow, or the day after that." Or when it rained pigs.

He promised to watch for me, and I definitely watched him from the corner shop window until I was sure he was gone. I asked the store clerk for directions to find the town doctor and then hurried that way.

Except when I arrived at his office, breathless from running and ready to offer any bribe necessary to get a quarantine order for Esther, his nurse informed me that he was out on visits on behalf of the "occupiers."

That word caught my attention. A Nazi-friendly office would never refer to them that way. I didn't know if she was speaking for herself, or if that was also the way the doctor thought of the soldiers, but it gave me a glimmer of hope. Was there any chance he'd find a way to get Esther out?

I couldn't risk asking, but it didn't matter anyway because the nurse informed me the doctor wasn't expected back in the office for several hours. When it would be too late for Esther. I thanked the nurse and retraced my steps back to the Gestapo building the young soldier had pointed out to me.

It was right on the road, which ordinarily would have allowed me to study it from the window of a small café across the square, except that as the day wore on, more and more military vehicles parked between us.

If I had a grenade, I could make quick work of many of those soldiers, but I doubted I'd actually use it. Not if it endangered any of the prisoners inside. Or Esther, in the back.

After another hour of watching, a man exited the building with a doctor's bag. I immediately left the café and hurried to catch up with him.

"Doctor!"

He turned, wearing a courteous smile, grandfatherly wrinkles, and eyes that struck me as sincere. "Yes?"

I'd rehearsed in my mind what I was going to say, but now that I was looking at him, the larger lies vanished. Instead, I said, "There's a prisoner inside . . . a girl I know. I think she's out back."

His expression softened. "A friend?"

"What can I do for her?"

He sighed. "I'm afraid there's nothing any of us can do, for her or for any of the people caught up in these atrocities. I wrapped her wrist—"

"Why?"

"It looks fractured, but I can't be sure. And I told them that while she has some sort of illness, it's not typhus, and that I'd return tomorrow to check on her. My hope is that it will buy her some time, but that's all I can do. Frankly, if they leave her outside tonight, by morning she truly will be sick, or dead from exposure."

I shifted my weight from one foot to the other, unsteady and unsure of what to do. Desperate and quickly running out of time, I had to risk more than I usually ever would. "There must be a reason to quarantine her, sir, any reason."

He shook his head. "I'd need evidence."

"Then find evidence, please. Fake it if you have to." He started to walk away, but I touched his arm. "I'll pay you, sir. Whatever amount you ask."

He stopped, his expression full of sympathy, but his tone was uncompromising. "What happens to me when they discover the truth? I'm sorry for what happened to your friend, but take my advice and stay out of it, or I'll be treating you in there next."

I quietly thanked him, then returned to the café. My hope was to be alone with my thoughts there, but instead, the café was beginning to fill with soldiers who were off duty after a change in shifts.

I sat among them, ignoring their flirtatious calls to join their tables, and trying to keep my emotions in check. Was the man who broke Esther's wrist in here? Because none of these soldiers seemed to feel any guilt for having done such a cruel thing.

Instead, they reclined in their chairs, laughing as they tossed around a pack of matches for everyone to light up their cigarettes.

The pack eventually fell onto the floor near me. It looked empty, but I'd been keeping count. If they started with a full pack, there were two matches left. I put my foot over it, then pretended to drop my gloves. When I picked them up, the matchbook came with it, and I left. My cup of coffee also disappeared with me, but I hoped the café owners wouldn't notice my theft.

Once I was alone again, I checked the matchbook and rolled my eyes. My counting was off by one. Only a single match remained. I'd have to put it to good use, testing a theory I'd overheard Jakub and Rubin discussing months ago in planning one of our raids.

Three jeeps and two trucks were parked in a line on the road between the town square and the Gestapo building. Soon there would be fewer of them.

I had one last purchase to make, a small kitchen knife

from a market in the minutes before it closed for curfew. And as I walked back, I noticed a bicycle casually left in front of an apartment.

I stared at it a moment, wondering whose it was. Did a mother use it to get to work each day, her only way to feed her family? Was it a schoolboy's, one of the lucky few to still be getting an education? Or did it belong to a Nazi sympathizer? Did its owner laugh when he heard rumors of what was happening to my people, or was he the kind to hide someone in his home?

Whoever he was, he had just donated this bicycle to the cause of the resistance. May God bless him for his generosity, however unintended.

Then I waited until dark, until the streets were quiet. Until my heart was about to burst with worry. Two soldiers patrolled the front of the Gestapo building, but I was already in place beneath one of the trucks. I nicked the fuel line, though not much because I didn't want them to hear the gas dripping into the coffee cup. When it was full, I scooted out from beneath the truck, leaving a small trail of gasoline behind, the thinnest line I could manage with my cold, nearly numb hands. That got me as far as the second truck, farther from the Gestapo station, where I repeated the same action until I was at the jeep with a full cup of fuel. I had to leave the relative safety of the vehicles then, and the same moon that I was grateful for last night now offered far more light than I wished it did.

I kept to a low crouch and moved slowly, though I had to watch for the soldiers, so my thin line of fuel was getting poured out too fast. It'd run out long before I was far enough away from them. I'd have to move quickly.

When the last of the fuel was gone, I pulled out the matchbook. The slight breeze in the air was another problem. I had hoped to light the match and toss it down but now I had to get close to the gas with the flame. This was incredibly foolish, impossibly dangerous. I could just as easily blow myself up.

Using my body to guard against the wind, I lit the match and immediately used it to light the book itself. As soon as the cardboard shell was burning, I threw it onto the fuel.

Everything happened in mere seconds. The line flared up, then traveled like lightning to the truck, where the fuel had been collecting. It immediately ignited a booming fire that popped the truck's hood open and set the engine aflame. Heat rushed back at me just as quickly, fierce enough to be felt even with my arms in front of my face. The line of fire continued almost instantly to the second and third trucks, where the fuel had been collecting the longest. The last truck exploded into the air with a booming sound that would be heard for kilometers around.

I didn't see it land, because the explosion knocked me to the ground, and I immediately launched back onto my feet, racing away from the crime scene. I tried keeping my body directly in line with the flames, which I hoped would prevent the soldiers from seeing me, but it probably wasn't necessary. The entire square was in commotion with soldiers and civilians rushing from their shops and buildings, bumping into one another in their rush to get away from whatever happened next.

I reached an alleyway near the café and followed it to a street that I'd already explored earlier. I knew the route to the back of the Gestapo building: a high-fenced yard where I hoped Esther was still being kept.

Soldiers were shouting and a siren was going off in the town, which helped me more than the Nazis could have known. Moreover, I heard a second explosion. The fire must be spreading. Good.

I was prepared for the tall brick fence back here too. A tree on this side had long tentacle-like branches that would carry me into the yard. I scaled up the trunk and shinnied out across one of the thick lower branches, momentarily reminded of Esther's story about the tree in the school yard. Then I saw her, and my heart sank.

Esther hadn't noticed me yet, though I certainly took in her disheveled appearance. The dark bruise on one side of her face. Her bandaged wrist. How very small she looked against the tree. Her attention was focused on the wailing sirens and shouting soldiers. A third explosion went off in the street, giving me a great amount of satisfaction. I hadn't expected the plan to work so well. Perhaps the trucks contained some fire-sensitive equipment.

When I dropped into the yard and called Esther's name, she jumped, and shook her head in disapproval. "Chaya? Did you . . . out there, did you do that?"

Both arms were tied around the tree's trunk, which must have caused her wrist considerable pain. Up close, I noticed the bruise was even worse than it appeared from a distance. There was a cut on her cheek too, and other smaller bruises on her neck and probably elsewhere that I couldn't see. Without a word, I used my knife to cut through the ropes and then led her by her good hand back toward the wall.

"We can't climb this." She held out her wrapped wrist. "I can't—"

"I'm going to push you to the top, and then you've got to help me get up too." She started to protest, but I added, "You've got to do it, Esther. I don't care if it hurts."

I did care, but that couldn't be an excuse. Not now. It wouldn't be long before a soldier was sent to check on the prisoners. Including the one left outside to freeze in the winter air.

I clasped my fingers together to boost her up. Then she grabbed on to the top of the brick wall with her good hand and gasped in pain as she braced herself with her injured arm.

"I can't, Chaya."

I'd already climbed as high as I could on my own, but I lifted my hand to hers. "Take it." I wasn't offering sympathy now, or even mercy. "Now, Esther!"

She squirmed around until the weight of her body kept her balanced on top of the wall, and propped her wrapped arm in front of the brick. Then she reached down with her good hand and took mine. She wasn't strong enough to lift me, and I worried that I'd pull her down instead. But she was pressing into the wall with her injured arm, although I heard her stifled yelp of pain as she did.

I climbed as fast as I could, skinning my elbows on the brick as I dug in to find every possible grip with my other hand. Then I reached the top of the wall and hoisted myself over. As soon as I let go of her, she let go of the wall and fell to the ground.

"Esther!"

I jumped down and found her on her back, clutching her injured arm against her chest. The bandage on her wrist had become twisted and was probably useless now. Wrapping my arms around her, I pulled her to her feet and led her down a side street. That was where I'd left the bike.

It wouldn't be a comfortable ride, but she could sit on the handlebars, keeping her balance with her good hand, if I drove carefully.

Unfortunately, careful driving was not the priority. I needed to go fast, regardless of the pain it caused her.

"I'm truly sorry," I whispered. And then we were off. I pretended not to hear her gasps or pleas for me to slow down, and only pedaled faster. I had to.

TWENTY-EIGHT

February 20, 1943
Bolimowski Park

Four separate times on our way out of town, we had to hurry off the bike to hide from Nazi vehicles that screamed past us, sirens blaring or with loudspeakers ordering every citizen into their homes. Every time we crouched in hiding, Esther began crying again, but I only scolded her, as sharply as I'd ever spoken to her before. It felt cruel to be so harsh— it *was* cruel —and I understood the tears, but we couldn't allow anyone to hear it. After all we'd gone through, getting caught now was unacceptable.

Finally, we were on the edge of town, and when I stopped in front of the snowman, Esther looked at me as if I'd gone crazy.

"What are you . . . ? Oh."

By then, I'd kicked away at the snow, revealing our two bags, still intact, if a little more frozen.

I started to sling her bag over my shoulder, but she said, "No, I can carry it."

"You're hurt."

"My shoulder isn't. Just help me."

So I did, remembering once again that Esther's burden was every bit as heavy as mine. She was the one with the injury. She was the one who'd been kept in an open yard for a full day, tortured, terrorized, and almost certainly expecting to be dead by morning. Through all of that, according to the young soldier I met, she never told them a word.

At the nearest crossroad, we abandoned the bicycle near a river. I tilted it visibly against a tree near the road. Then Esther and I planted tracks through the snow down to the river, suggesting we were moving in a direction leading away from Warsaw. I hoped that if we were followed, and we surely would be, this was where we'd part ways with the soldiers.

I expected her to protest getting in the water. I saw how she was shivering already, and knew how chilled she must have been after so many hours outside. I hated that I had to make her do it anyway.

And she seemed to understand that. With a flat voice nearly empty of emotion, she said, "I need help with my boots and socks."

I took mine off first, giving her as much time as possible before I knelt down and removed hers, tying the laces together for the boots to dangle from her shoulders. Then she followed me into the icy waters.

It came up past my knees, but the cold enveloped me entirely, instantly sucking the breath from my lungs. I began shivering, and had taken only a few steps before my feet were too numb to feel the river rocks below. With every stumble and slip, I warned Esther to be careful, but seconds later, I'd slip again, making myself wet even above the water level. Ice seemed to have moved inside my veins, requiring more effort with each step. All I wanted was to give up this ridiculous plan and return to land, but it wasn't safe. Not yet. I tried to tell Esther it'd be okay, but my teeth were chattering, and I couldn't form the words.

And maybe it wouldn't be okay, because we had a lot farther to go until I was sure they'd have quit tracking us. Every time I looked for an exit point, I saw where we'd leave footprints in the snow, or crush the first tender grass blades of the new season, or drip onto rock. We couldn't get out until I was sure we were far enough away.

A few minutes later, Esther mumbled, "P-p-please, Ch-chaya."

I glanced back and her lips were almost blue. I suspected mine were the same. Whether they'd follow us this far or not, we had to get out now, or we never would.

I stepped onto a frozen bank and helped her from the water, where we stood on a fallen tree branch to let our feet dry. While they did, I pulled her toward me, holding her in the same way my mother used to hold me when I'd wake up from nightmares.

Esther had spent the past day living a nightmare, no doubt. I folded one hand around her back and with the other, I brushed her hair, letting her bury her head against my shoulder. She sniffed, drew in a sharp breath, then began sobbing. This time, I didn't stop her.

"Think of warm things," I whispered after a few minutes. "Apple tea, fresh-baked bread. Matzo ball soup."

"Warm baths," she replied, calmer now. "Wool blankets. Reading with my family in the evenings in front of a fire."

That wasn't what I'd meant for her to remember, and those same memories left me feeling emptier than before. But at least she wasn't shivering as much.

I took the boots from around her shoulders. "Your feet should be dry. The sooner we start walking, the sooner we get our blood moving again."

Walking might stave off the hypothermia. It might get us another few kilometers closer to Warsaw. It wouldn't erase the last twenty-four hours from Esther's mind. She wouldn't look at me directly, and when I did catch her eyes, swollen and red from crying, a haunted glaze took over before she turned away and shuddered. I couldn't begin to imagine what she'd gone through back there.

Or worse . . . I *could* imagine it.

We walked for a couple of hours, at a brisk pace to keep our blood moving. The road wound into a forested area, thick enough with trees that the moonlight became filtered with long, dark shadows. As quiet as it always was at night, this place made me feel closed in. My instinct to find routes for escape was stronger than usual.

Maybe for good reason. Although the trees offered countless places to hide, the snow was deep around them. We'd never wade through it in time to dodge a passing car. Even if we did, we'd leave tracks.

"Walking upriver won't fool them for long." Esther had clearly been sharing my thoughts. "We need to get out of here as soon as possible."

"The partisans hide in forests like these," I said. "So the Germans avoid them. We're safer here than we were before."

The first part was true. Poland was dotted with thick patches of forest, areas that the locals knew well. It was a natural hiding place for partisan fighters, and, I'd heard, even for members of the Polish army who continued to fight despite being abandoned by their government.

The second part was based on hope more than fact. I'd heard stories of German patrols who were ambushed in the forests, so I couldn't imagine anyone relished orders to search the woods. But Esther was right that they would look for her—and whoever helped her to escape. Soldiers would be ordered in this direction.

I tried to pick up the pace, but no matter how tired and cold I was, Esther was worse. She hadn't stopped shivering all night, and she was holding her injured arm against her chest, bracing it with her good arm. The bandage that dangled from her wrist was useless, but she wouldn't stop and take the time to let me rewrap it.

"Want to talk about it?" My voice was gentle, urging her to talk.

"No."

"I know you didn't tell them anything," I continued. "That must've made them angry."

"Angry?" She snorted. "Angry is where they started, before putting me in a dark room where everyone was yelling and if I looked away, someone slapped me or hit me to get my attention, and they were telling me what would happen if I didn't talk. But I kept reminding myself that even if I did talk, they'd still hurt me, maybe even kill me. I really believed that, Chaya. I believed that I'd never get out of that room."

She went silent for a while, long enough that I wondered if I ought to say something. But I figured if it was me, I'd need time to work through all that had happened, at my own pace. So I stayed silent.

Finally, she continued. "After an hour, I started to think that it'd be all right if they did kill me. Maybe it'd be better. Then they . . . did this." She nodded at her arm. "It hurt so much that I screamed, loud enough to scare them. Suddenly, I wasn't afraid anymore. I was the angry one, more than any of them. I said, 'You want me to talk, then I'll tell you this! The reason I ran away is because I have typhus and I didn't want to infect anyone. But I'll gladly infect all of you!'"

Esther straightened her posture, clearly proud of herself. "Then I sneezed on them. A big, wet, slobbering sneeze."

I respected the courage it must have taken to do that, and the cleverness for having thought of it in the first place. No doubt that had ended the questioning. "That's when they brought you outside?"

She went quiet again, and I didn't think she'd say anything more. Then, in a whisper, "One of the Gestapo raised his gun and I closed my eyes for what was coming. I knew it was coming and that it'd hurt, but maybe not as much as the pain I was already in. I know that's cowardly, Chaya, but it's how I felt."

"Nothing you're describing to me is cowardly."

She sniffed, then added, "Someone told him something in German. I couldn't understand it, but he hit me with his gun and I realized he'd been ordered not to shoot. I sneezed again and again until I could see them getting nervous. Finally, they ordered me to be tied up outside while they figured out what to do next. I knew that I had to be patient out there, and not fall asleep in the cold. And I knew that you'd come."

"I would have come sooner, if I could have."

"But you did come." With her good hand, she squeezed mine. "And at least it's over."

I kept hold of her hand, to warm her frozen fingers, to offer what comfort I could. In the gentlest way possible, I said, "It's not over, Esther. We still have to get to Warsaw."

She must have forgotten that, because her shoulders slumped and she shook her head. "I don't want to go anymore. I can't."

We stopped walking and I turned to her, wishing I could take her pain away. "It's all right, you've done enough. I'll find a safe house for you in the next town, a place where you can stay until this war is over. Do you still have the package they wanted you to deliver? Give it to me. I'll get it there safely."

She nodded and a single tear rolled down her cheek. Then she swallowed her emotions and looked up at me. "I have to be the one to deliver it. I promised I would, and I'll keep that promise."

"Then I'll keep my promise too," I replied. "I'll get us to Warsaw."

Her eyes brightened a little. "I'm glad you were the one chosen for this mission."

I smiled back at her, surprised to hear my own answer. "Me too. I'm glad it was me."

TWENTY-NINE

February 20, 1943
Bolimowski Park

No matter how tired we had become, the night crawled on, as endless as this road, yet there hadn't been a single place safe enough to stop and rest. With no shelter and such deep snow, I worried that eventually we'd lean against a tree, promising ourselves not to sleep, and never open our eyes again.

Hoping it would keep us going, I turned on the radio, keeping the volume as low as possible. Since it was after midnight, it played mostly popular German music, although the upbeat songs were interspersed with newsbreaks.

The Germans claimed a major victory over the Americans in Tunisia. I vaguely knew where Tunisia was, and I didn't particularly care. Why couldn't they report any losses, just once?

During the next newsbreak, we learned that a high-ranking Nazi named Joseph Goebbels called for "total war" against the Allies. Esther looked over at me and frowned. "What does he think has been happening for the past two and a half years?"

I held her thoughts inside me for some time. If the Nazis had been holding back on their full power, then I couldn't imagine what total war would look like. That bothered me far more than I could ever let on, but it left my stomach in knots.

As the first hints of dawn finally began to peek through the trees, a new announcement came over the radio. "Amon Goeth has been assigned as commandant of a new labor camp now under construction in Krakow." My ears pricked up. I'd heard that name before, associated with other concentration camps in Poland. This man had been trained in death, trained in murder, and if he was being sent to this new camp, then he was one of their "best."

That was where my parents would undoubtedly be sent, as soon as the camp was completed.

I snapped off the radio and we walked in silence until my thoughts were so flooded with images of my father and mother that I could hardly stand it anymore.

It was a relief when Esther said, "We missed Shabbat last night."

"I was busy rescuing you last night."

"I've never missed a Sabbath before. Never."

"God will understand, Esther! He understands why we missed Shabbat, and why I wear the crucifix. He understands the gun inside my bag, and if I have to use it again, then I hope He will understand that too, because every single day, my first thought is how to keep us alive until I have the very same thought again the next day."

She fell silent, then said, "We'll celebrate next week."

We might. I expected by then we'd be in Warsaw, possibly in a fight for our lives with the other resistance members. I hoped God would understand that too.

"What would your plans have been if there had been no war?" I asked.

Esther shrugged. "I would have wanted to get married, perhaps, in a few years. There was a boy who went to the same synagogue as me. He was handsome." A beat passed, then, "He was sent to Belzec. I'm sure he's gone by now."

"You don't know that."

She looked over at me, barely able to keep her eyes open, yet the sadness registered clearly in them. "I can't have hope for everyone, Chaya."

If this was a chance to find out more about her past, then I had to ask. "Who do you have hope for, then?" She looked away, tightening her lips. I added, "I hope to one day know for sure what happened to my brother. Even if it's terrible, I need to know his fate."

She took that in with a quiet nod, but her thoughts had drifted away from me, until she said, "I had a brother too, once."

Had.

Once.

"Are they all gone?" I asked. "All your family?"

"My brother fought in the Polish forces when the Germans attacked. As for my parents . . ." She drew in a tense breath. "The Nazis murder us many times over. They take our ability to worship properly—a spiritual death. They separate our families—another death there. They kill our dignity, our will to live, and finally they take our lives. The question isn't whether my family is gone. It's only a matter of how many deaths they've suffered so far."

After the effort she'd made to avoid discussing her family with me, she'd just revealed more than she might have intended. Sometime since the war began, Esther became separated from her family, but she did not know their fates. Just as I didn't know about my brother.

I thought of my parents again, trying to picture them on their wood crates in that apartment, side by side. I wanted to have hope for them, I really did. But I thought of the way Esther described the many deaths of our people. I wondered if my parents had suffered too many of them for their hearts to continue beating.

"What about you?" Esther asked. "If there had been no war, what would you have done?"

"I'd have tried to enroll in a university," I said. "There is so much about the world I want to understand. I would have liked to spend the rest of my life learning."

"Maybe you still can, when this is over. What would you study?"

I opened my mouth, but nothing came to mind. I wanted to answer, to tell her everything I could be if the world would only give me a chance. But for as hard as I thought, my mind remained empty.

How could that be? I did have plans before the war, grand and ambitious plans, hopes and dreams that seemed too bold to be spoken aloud.

And now, I couldn't even think of a single specific subject I would want to study.

Worse still, I knew why.

It was because joining the resistance had required me to accept the likelihood of my death.

Chances were that I wouldn't survive this war. Which meant there was no point in making plans for the future, or even thinking about it.

I spoke to Esther of hope for our loved ones, yet I didn't even have hope for myself.

To cover my silence, she said, "Well, if I outlast the war, then—"

"Shh." I grabbed Esther's arm and pulled her close, certain that I heard a noise off in the woods, to our right.

"What is—" Then she heard it too. The crunch of snow and the fallen leaves beneath it. The crack of a branch against a body in motion.

It was the very same sound as we had heard last night. Except this time, we didn't have the barn to hide in. We didn't have anywhere to hide.

And we were definitely not alone.

"Keep walking," I whispered. "Don't look around. Just walk, like we have every right to be here."

"Should we get out your gun?" she asked.

"I won't brandish a weapon that I can't use." But the kitchen knife was in my coat pocket and I wrapped my hand tightly around it. I didn't know why. The only way this knife would help me was if I had to fight someone up close, and whoever was in the woods could shoot us before I'd even seen their face. Nor was it just one person. Now that I was attuned to it, I felt the weight of many eyes on us. It was still too dark to see them where they hid in the undergrowth. However, Esther and I were out in the open and plenty visible. Plenty exposed.

"It might be deer," she offered.

It wasn't deer. The hairs on the back of my neck were raised, an instinctive warning of an approaching threat.

If it was German soldiers, then they'd been tracking us since our escape last night. What were they waiting for?

Esther pressed at the back of my arm, pushing me to walk faster, but I couldn't do that. We couldn't let on that we knew we were being watched. That might prompt a confrontation sooner than I wanted it. I needed time to plan. To think of something—anything—to do.

The sounds were moving closer. From the corner of my eye, a glint of metal reflected in the moonlight. A rifle barrel was aimed directly at us.

"Stop where you are," a man's voice ordered. "Drop your bags or we'll shoot."

We obeyed, though my legs were shaking so much that I didn't trust them to keep walking. I clasped Esther's good hand in mine and was surprised at how hard she gripped my fingers. The rest of her body had gone rigid and her eyes were closed, but I intended to look. I wanted to see the face of the man who shouted that order. If he was going to shoot, I wanted him to remember me.

CHAPTER
THIRTY

February 20, 1943
Bolimowski Park

Seconds passed and no one emerged from the woods. Esther and I both remained exactly where we were, though I hated feeling that the delay was only giving the people in the woods more time to position themselves for what would be an entirely one-sided fight.

Finally, I'd had enough. "Show yourselves, cowards!" I shouted.

Esther opened her eyes long enough to send me a scalding glare, but I ignored it. Whatever was about to happen wouldn't change whether I insulted them or fell on my knees to beg for mercy. And I had no plans to do that.

"Wait, I know her!" a voice called from the woods. "Don't shoot—that's Chaya Lindner."

Esther and I exchanged another look, a different one this time. No one should know me up here. No one should really know me anywhere.

But when a familiar face emerged from the woods, I let out a shriek of joy and surprise. "Rubin?"

I hadn't seen him since the night of the Cyganeria attack two months ago. Had he really survived?

He pulled me into a hug, then, as we parted, his eyes settled on Esther. Somehow, he must not have recognized her before this. His mouth hung half-open when he looked back at me. I'm sure this was the last person he would have expected to see within a kilometer of me.

"You're alive too?" he asked Esther. "I had no idea—either of you."

Questions rushed through my mind, but then three other people emerged from the woods, two men and a woman. One man wore a Polish military uniform, but the other two were in thick winter overalls, belted at the waist, and with rifles slung over each shoulder.

"Who are they?" Esther whispered.

"It's all right." Rubin gestured back to them. "They're friends."

The woman reached out, taking my hands in hers and pulling me closer. "And we're friends to you. My name is Mindla. You helped get me out of the Krakow Ghetto. You saved my life."

I remembered her now. We'd smuggled her out in a wagon built with a false floor that could fit two or three people between the two layers of wood. She was not as thin as before and had a fire in her eyes that I never saw back in the ghetto.

Slowly, at least a dozen more men and women joined us on the road. One or two were about my age, and some were much older, perhaps in their forties. A couple of others were in military uniform, but everyone was armed.

Rubin widened his arms with a goofy smile. "We always said we'd join the partisans one day. Well, you made it here too!"

I was so relieved to be in friendly company, to see Rubin, I hardly knew how to respond. I only smiled back at him and gladly let him take my bag and then Esther's to carry.

"Let's get off the road," one man said, then turned to me. "We have some hot coffee back at camp, and a warm place you can rest."

"Is it safe?" Esther whispered.

"Safer than out here," Rubin assured us.

As we followed the others back into the woods, Rubin stayed close by my side. "Where were you going?"

"Warsaw."

He touched my arm. "No, Chaya. You must know what is happening there."

I stared back at his widened eyes and his mouth pressed into a tight frown. Maybe the conditions in Warsaw were worse than I'd heard.

"I know the Germans tried to carry out a deportation a month ago, but the resistance fought them off," I said. "Which means the Germans will return with a far greater show of force."

"And what do you think they'll do when they return?"

"We both know. The resistance will need as much help as they can get!" I nudged his arm and gave him a slight smile. "I'm sure they'd welcome the help of the partisans."

"Their uprising will fail; every ghetto skirmish does," said the uniformed man ahead of us. Based on his look and accent, he must be from the Polish army. Maybe he wouldn't care if hundreds more Jews were killed.

"It's not *our* uprising or *their* uprising," I countered. "We must think of ourselves as one organization. If we join together, we'll be stronger."

"Mordecai Anielewicz has united all the resistance groups in Warsaw," Rubin said. "They're now known as ZOB. We're helping them acquire food and weapons as best we can, but fighting from within a ghetto is a position of weakness. Ultimately, the people there are trapped, backed into a corner."

I shook my head. "If the partisans were to attack from behind, when the Nazis move into the ghetto, *they*'d be the ones trapped—"

"You think like one of us," the uniformed man said. "Stop with this nonsense about going to Warsaw. Join us, Chaya. You can do far more good here."

"We have a package to deliver in Warsaw," Esther said. "If it's true that the Germans will return to destroy the ghetto, then the people there will need this package."

"A *package*?" Rubin stopped walking to look at both of

us. "Almost a year ago, the Germans lined up fifty-two members of the resistance and shot them in public, hoping that would stop the uprisings. Mordecai vowed to fight harder. I don't care what package you have. It won't stop the Germans when they return this time."

Esther glanced at me but said nothing more. I pushed past Rubin to follow the others, saying, "We're not going there to stop the Germans. We're going because we belong there."

The partisan camp was a half kilometer off the road, built in a ravine that gave it cover from any casual sightings. In the summer and autumn months, their canvas tents and motorbikes would be harder to find, but I wished they had better ways to hide the dark colors against the snow. Spring would be coming soon. If the partisans lasted that long, they might be able to continue hiding here for some time.

Esther and I were taken into a tent with handmade wooden chairs settled around some large rocks that emanated a heat I longed to wrap my frozen body around. Instead, I scooted my chair as close as possible to a larger rock and held my hands even closer, letting them thaw. Rubin explained this technique. The rocks had been warmed in a fire earlier tonight and would hold their heat for several hours. On top of them was a steaming coffeepot, and cups were poured for everyone who followed us in.

We still had our bags with us and we set them between our chairs. Rubin took a seat to my right.

"You went back to our old safe house, after Cyganeria," he said. "You must have."

"I thought others would come there too, but no one did."

"Most of the people who weren't arrested near the café collected at Dolek's bunker." His eyes flickered with sadness. "We were betrayed that night, Chaya. Two Akiva members told the Gestapo where Dolek would be. Everyone there was killed or arrested, including the two who betrayed us, hoping to gain favors from the Nazis. The only favor those traitors received was a one-way trip on the trains."

"You survived."

"I'd left the bunker an hour earlier, looking for you. But when I heard about the arrests, I got scared and left Krakow." His eyes softened. "I wanted to go to our safe house, but I thought if the Gestapo knew about the bunker, they probably knew about the safe house too."

I shrugged away any need for him to apologize and only asked, "What about Hanusia and Jakub?" The other two members of our cell.

"Jakub was killed in some cross fire at Cyganeria. Hanusia was arrested I don't know if she's still alive."

I closed my eyes and vowed not to remember them that way. Only to think of my friends as we had been, courageous and strong, back when we raided the warehouses and trains, when we believed anything was possible if we just dared enough. It was odd to consider that those were the good memories, but they were.

"What's in your bags?" Rubin asked.

I dragged mine closer to me, almost subconsciously. "Supplies, for Warsaw."

Rubin hesitated a moment, then gestured at Esther's wrist. "We have a doctor here. He can look at that."

"Come with me." A woman who had been sitting near us stood and smiled down at Esther. "I'll take you to him."

Rubin whispered to Esther that it was okay and she followed the woman out. Now he turned his chair to face me, and everyone else around us seemed to melt into the background. I looked into his eyes and felt myself genuinely smile, one of the few times I'd done that in weeks. I'd missed Rubin's counsel, his ability to plan and to console. I'd missed Rubin.

He said, "It's better that we talk without Esther. She seems more . . . fragile than before."

"She's not, I was wrong about her." Still, now we'd get to the more serious business. "What do we need to talk about?"

"Warsaw. Last fall, the Nazis sent over three hundred thousand people from there to the death camps. The Allies did nothing then, and they won't come now."

"Then the people of Poland—"

"They won't help either. Seventy thousand Jews remain in Warsaw. ZOB posted warnings inside the ghetto not to willingly get on the trains, not to believe the lies. The Nazi response was to post warnings outside the ghetto, telling the Poles that anyone caught hiding a Jew, or helping them in even the smallest way, would be put to death. The people inside that ghetto are entirely on their own."

I straightened my back. "Then it's even more important for me to go! Because they have no other help."

"ZOB has no chance of winning."

"It's not about winning. It's about fighting, about proving to the world—"

"At some point it has to be about winning, about surviving. Dolek talked about three lines of history. Well, someone must be around to write those lines!"

"Maybe they could be, if the partisans would help them!"

"We have! We are, but it's not enough, it's never enough. You must understand, Warsaw has become a pressure cooker, and it's ready to burst. Mordecai wants a fight, and as soon as the Germans put their first toe inside the ghetto, he'll get it." Rubin took my hand and leaned in. "You are a good courier, Chaya, and have more courage than most people I've ever known. But none of that will save you in Warsaw."

I bit my lip and took my final sip of coffee. "When my brother and sister disappeared, you supported me. When I promised to honor them with my life, you supported me again. Can't you support me now?"

The light in his eyes dimmed. I felt the same sadness, but my resolve remained. After a heavy pause, he nodded, then said, "Try to rest. When it's safe to move, we'll get you as close to Warsaw as we can."

I didn't know exactly how he intended to do that, but I liked the idea of someone else being in charge, and once I was offered a bedroll near the warm rocks, I wrapped the blanket tightly around me and quickly fell into a deep sleep.

I didn't dream this time. Or if I did, I remembered nothing but dark before my eyes. And I hoped that wasn't a sign for my future. Because everything I knew about Warsaw warned me that what was coming would be worse than any nightmare.

· PART THREE ·

February 21, 1943
Road to Warsaw

We slept late the next morning, but I was finally warm, comfortable, and felt reasonably safe. I didn't even pretend to care about what time it was.

The partisans were preparing a midday meal when I ducked out of my tent. Esther had been kept in a nearby medical tent for evaluation, but she was already up and helping with the food. Her face brightened when she saw me, and she showed off her newly wrapped wrist.

Breakfast was simple, a thick slice of bread and a little dried meat and hot coffee, but it tasted like a feast to me. Life as a partisan wasn't easy, but at least they had a chance to live free out here, beyond the ghetto walls.

After we'd eaten, our bags were returned to us, but with one difference. "We loaded your gun and packed you some extra ammunition," Rubin told me. "If you're going to Warsaw, you'll need it."

"I'll use it well," I replied, a promise I fully intended to keep.

The partisans had a sidecar motorcycle, which they offered to take us in to Warsaw. Esther chose the sidecar while I rode behind Rubin. The roads were good, and the weather looked promising. Assuming we weren't forced to detour around any Nazi patrols, we should reach Warsaw in a little over an hour.

"I'll get you into the city," Rubin said, "but not into the ghetto. I hope you understand."

I understood why the partisans discouraged us from joining a fight that was sure to fail. But if they joined the fight too, it might offer enough of a boost for the ghetto fighters to succeed. Why couldn't they understand that?

Due to its central placement in Europe, Warsaw had been erased from the map many times over in its history, each time returning stronger and more beautiful than before. It boasted the nickname "Paris of the North," and had been my favorite place to go as a child. I would accompany Papa when he had to travel there to get supplies for his shoe repair shop. I particularly loved walking the gardens near the Saxon Palace, or touring the art museum, or sneaking away with my mother for a bit of shopping. On our last trip together before the war, Warsaw was a bustling, vibrant city of over one million citizens, a third of them Jews.

Warsaw would be a very different place now.

Our ride into the city was remarkably easy, especially

considering all the trouble we'd had since leaving Krakow. Still, once we entered the city limits, a lump formed in my throat. Suddenly, Esther's and my mission felt far too real. The city looked as if it was on the brink of being erased from the map yet again.

We passed whole buildings that had been leveled to the ground during the Blitzkrieg, some of the back streets still impassable with debris. Polish citizens walked with their eyes down, avoiding the Nazi soldiers who roamed nearly every corner. Esther saw them too and ducked so low into the sidecar that unless someone looked down on us from above, they probably wouldn't notice she was in there.

She still hadn't said much about what she'd endured the other night, but I suspected it was worse than what she had described. Fear lingered on her face with every change of expression. Not her usual dread of the unknown, but the terror that came with knowing how far the Nazis would go to get what they wanted.

Rubin turned onto a quiet street and offered me a grim smile. "Is there any way I can persuade you to return with me to the forest?"

I wished we could, truly. It seemed cruel to discover Rubin was still alive, only to have to say good-bye already. But I climbed off the back of his motorbike and gave him a hug. "I'm afraid not. We have to see our mission through to the end."

He nodded at Esther, who was stepping onto the street.

"You say you have a package to deliver to the ghetto. What is it? What could be so valuable that you have risked all of this to be here—"

Before she could answer, if she would have, I cut off his question with a warm "Thank you." If it wasn't my business to ask about the package, it certainly wasn't his. And he seemed to understand. He gave my hand a squeeze, though this time there was money in his palm. "It's all I have," he said. "Use it well."

"Thank you," I whispered. "We will."

Rubin frowned at me, and I felt his heart tug at mine, begging me to reconsider. I gave him one last hug, though it had to be brief; it couldn't look as permanent as it was.

Nor did I look back when he drove off. I couldn't, but not because it'd raise suspicions. My reasons for avoiding a last look at him were far more personal.

"How do we get into the ghetto itself?" I needed conversation again, as a distraction.

"We'll find a way." Esther faced steadfastly forward as we walked. She was different from the girl I first met last fall. Somewhere amid her fears, a new confidence had emerged, a determination to finish what the Nazis had started.

"We should get as much as we can bring in," I said. "Once we're in, that's probably our last stop."

Ever.

She looked over at me and nodded. A gesture given with

finality because there was nothing more to say. We both knew what we were walking into.

Esther hid with the bags inside a bathroom stall of a small restaurant. Hopefully, that would keep her safe while I took the rest of our money to buy provisions. There were only two things I wanted: food and medical supplies. Because of rations, I couldn't buy much of either without raising suspicions, but with enough trips to various markets and a small stack of forged ration cards, I gradually obtained a good stockpile. I imagined the ghetto had very few bandages or bottles of aspirin and rubbing alcohol. For food, I concentrated on what could be eaten quickly, assuming that a fight was coming and no one would have time to prepare a meal. I bought dried meats that I hoped were kosher, although I could hardly ask about them, pierogis, and even some pastries that might raise the spirits of fighters who could only see a bleak future. A jelly-filled *paczki* might go a long way toward reminding them that life still offered good things.

Or I hoped it would. And not because life was easy or happiness was guaranteed, or because we had any chance of waking up to find all our problems were over. No, life offered good things because life itself is good. And whether I had days left, or months, or years, I wanted to make the most of every moment.

And with that thought, I couldn't return to Esther fast enough, ready to join the fight.

Together, we stepped out of the restaurant, but almost instantly she froze, her eyes locked on a woman ahead of us. The woman became equally still, her face a virtual beacon of fear. My first thought was a question, wondering why these two should be wary of each other, as strangers.

But that was my answer. They weren't strangers at all.

The woman must be Jewish, attempting to disguise herself as Polish, much like I did. But she clearly was not prepared to see someone she knew, nor was Esther.

Their standoff was already drawing attention our way. People even moved around them, no doubt whispering to one another about this uneasy exchange.

The woman broke from her trance with a start and marched over to Esther with her hands on her hips. "How dare you?" she hissed. "How dare you show your face back here? Your parents got what they deserved. So will you!"

I put my body between the woman and Esther, keeping my eyes fierce and locked on the woman's face. "Walk away now, or we're all dead." I refused to look away until she finally took a step back.

But she added, "You wouldn't defend her if you knew the truth."

"I'll defend her until my last breath because she's my friend. Now go."

The woman smiled and stepped back. "Stick with her, and your last breath will come soon enough."

Once I was sure the woman was gone, I turned and

pushed Esther into an alley behind the restaurant. Tears welled in her eyes, but I had no sympathy this time. "You're from Warsaw?" I tried to keep my voice low, but anger seeped through every syllable. "Why didn't you tell me?"

"I was going to . . . I didn't know how."

"That was a fine way to find out! Who was that woman?"

"What did she mean, that my parents got what they deserved? Are they dead, then?"

"Who is she, Esther? Who are your parents?"

Esther looked back, then tilted her head toward the right. "About five blocks that direction was my home, where I grew up. It was lost in the Blitzkrieg, on the same day my brother was killed. Suddenly, it was just me and my parents. We had nothing else in the world."

My voice softened. "I can't imagine what that felt like."

She offered a grim smile. "Yes, you can. I'm not the only one anything has happened to, remember? My father was offered a position on the Judenrat." She quickly added, "I know you don't trust any of them, Chaya, and I understand why, but my father believed it was the only chance we had to survive."

I did understand that much. "If he's Judenrat, shouldn't you have been protected?"

"We were, until the Aktion last summer. The head of the Judenrat killed himself rather than provide the Germans with a list for deportations. The responsibility of creating the lists passed to my father, but he made two agreements first. The first was with ZOB. My father would keep resistance members off the list if they agreed to smuggle me out of the ghetto."

"That's how you met Dolek," I said. "Then he brought you to Krakow."

"Yes. I asked to join the resistance, to thank the people who helped me escape the ghetto. And to make up for the names my father put on the list instead. Such as the family of that woman we just saw." Her voice broke. "I'm only alive because . . . because . . ."

"Because that woman's family was on the list." A beat passed. Then, "Your father made two bargains."

"The second was made with the Germans. He refused to provide names for a death camp, so they agreed to deport the people to another ghetto, to help with the overcrowding here."

"Lodz." I barely breathed out the word, then shook my head in disbelief. "That's why you apologized after we left. We never had orders to go there. You took us to Lodz to see if the Germans had kept their promise. *You* decided we'd go there. Esther, you lied to me!"

"I had to know! A few days ago, you told me how much worse Yitzchak's disappearance is because you'll never know what happened to him. That's how I felt, only instead of one person, it was thousands."

"And how many more died in the Aktion we started because you wanted to settle your conscience?"

"I didn't know that would happen, and I sincerely hoped we could help whoever was there. I'm sorry, Chaya."

"What about here? Did we ever have orders to come here?"

"Yes, we do, I swear it!"

I turned away, furious and failing in my attempts not to let it show.

Barely under her breath, she whispered, "I think my parents are dead."

Her lower lip quivered, but she couldn't cry here. Our hushed conversation was already getting second looks from passersby. I was angry with her, and heartbroken for her, and completely unsure of what to do now except to get us both off the streets. I hoisted my bag again, keeping my tone firm. "Can you get us into the ghetto?"

She nodded, brushing away a single escaped tear. "I can."

"Then nothing else matters right now. Get us inside."

The ghetto was located near the center of Warsaw close to the Vistula River, but with no access to the water. It encompassed a three-and-a-half-kilometer area with a foot-bridge connecting two halves, allowing a streetcar to pass underneath.

The ghetto's brick walls were three meters tall and lined on top with barbed wire. As we approached, I saw where holes might've once been dug beneath the walls for children to escape and return with their smuggled food. These children knew which market owners left old fruit in an easily stolen pile behind their shops, or which housewives pretended to cool bread beneath an unwatched windowsill. But these holes were filled now and the bricks replaced.

"What if your way in doesn't exist anymore?" I asked Esther.

"It does. At about the time I left, they began shrinking the ghetto boundaries. Some of the former area was given back to the Poles, for their occupation. The rest is supposed to be abandoned, uninhabited."

"What do you mean, 'supposed to be'?"

"They're considered the wild areas. No one is allowed there, but there are plenty of places for people to hide."

"How do they survive?"

She shrugged. "How do any of us survive these days? We should be able to get into the wild after it's dark, then make our way through the buildings until we cross into the ghetto."

I didn't understand how that was possible, but she was asking me to trust her. Given what I'd just learned about her history, I knew how foolhardy that was, but what other choice did I have?

"Tonight," she said. "We go in tonight. For the last time."

THIRTY TWO

February 22, 1943
Warsaw Ghetto

We entered the wild shortly after midnight, sneaking in near the cemeteries, a detail I noticed with a particularly grim scowl. German patrols still crossed our path, but they were on vehicles, making it easy to time our entrance.

As awful as it ever was to enter an overcrowded ghetto full of starvation and disease, the wild was somehow worse. Building after building stood vacant—or at least, that was the impression those in hiding wanted to give. Scavenged pieces of luggage lay open on the streets, as those who were herded from here had been forced to leave their belongings behind. Nothing edible remained, and certainly nothing with any monetary value. But I saw a photo album lying open on the snow, the pictures blurred from the moisture, and nearby a single hand-knitted baby's bootie. These were someone's treasures, someone's memories. Stories of someone's life.

Once.

It was haunted here. Anyone could feel that. Death permeated the night air, carried on the wind like a vulture's hiss. I smelled the blood, bitter to my senses, and seemed to hear echoes of despair from those who'd discovered their fallen loved ones on these streets.

Esther gestured that we should move quietly, not out of concern for the soldiers, but because she didn't want to alarm anyone hiding here. Perhaps she remembered the way the women attacked her in Lodz for those potatoes.

Eventually, Esther and I would have to discuss her deception. I understood why she had wanted to know what had happened to those thousands of people, many of whom must have been her friends or acquaintances. But she couldn't ask for my trust one moment and betray it the next.

And she'd need time to properly mourn for her family. But not yet. Not while we needed to focus on getting through the wild.

We crept up a rickety staircase to the second floor of a building. Even in the darkness of night, Esther moved with confidence, secure in each step. From her lithe movements, I was sure she'd been here before, likely had traveled this very hallway before. For all I knew, this apartment was once hers, or had belonged to a close friend.

She raised a finger to her lips again and then pointed to a closed door on our left. Listening carefully, I could hear movement inside the room. Someone was awake and aware of our presence, probably slipping inside a hidden compartment, terrified that we might be soldiers or looters or thieves. I wanted to tell them not to be afraid, that we were friends. But I didn't. I couldn't.

Even more, I wanted to offer them some of the food Esther and I were carrying. We had enough to provide the people here in the wild another week or two of life. But our supplies had to get to the resistance members. Their lives were no more valuable, but their fight was.

At the far end of the building, Esther knelt beside a framed and broken mirror hung on the wall. It looked nailed down, but the lower nails easily pulled free from the plaster walls, revealing a tunnel. Esther put her bag in first and scooted in after it. I followed, though I had to crawl on my elbows to fit through the small space, especially with the German pack still on my back and pushing the medical bag ahead of me. When the mirror rolled back into place behind us, the tunnel went black. I closed my eyes and listened for Esther ahead. For the first time since we met, she consoled me, quietly whispering that everything was okay.

We emerged through a closet in a new apartment, and probably in an entirely new building, one that was closer to the new ghetto boundaries. Obviously, these aboveground passages had been designed to move people from one part of the ghetto to another without having to go onto the street. It was brilliant. If I ever returned to courier work, I'd tell other ghettos about this too.

Esther carefully peeked out a cracked open door of this apartment before declaring it safe to leave. Then we repeated the process from before, making the long walk to the far end of the building, entering this time through a hole that was disguised as a heating vent and exiting in a new building through the cupboard beneath a kitchen sink.

Yet this time, as we tiptoed through the dark apartment, I tripped and fell to my hands and knees. My breath caught in my throat when the object I'd tripped over sat up and let out a small cry.

Not an object at all: It was a child, a little girl with wide eyes and dark hair in need of combing. She grabbed her blanket and backed into the corner, clearly terrified and looking like she was about to scream.

We couldn't have that.

"It's all right," Esther quietly said, then slowly crouched low to the girl's level. She offered a smile and smoothed her hand over the girl's hair. "We're your friends."

I followed her lead, speaking as softly and kindly as I would've spoken to my own sister. "Are you hungry?" For her, I could spare a little food. I gave her some of the German army rations we'd taken from the tank, and an entire loaf of bread. If she was careful, it would last for some time. There was one more gift I wanted to offer her: the rest of the chocolate bar Esther and I had opened. I held it out and she cautiously took it, but her eyes flicked almost nonstop between me, Esther, and the chocolate.

"Shh," Esther said. "Be safe."

The girl remained in place until we left, though as soon as we closed the apartment door behind her, I heard the foil of the chocolate bar being torn off. I doubted she'd eat it all right away, maybe allow herself only a tiny piece. But I pictured a smile spreading across her face, and that warmed me.

We crossed from this apartment safely into another, where Esther turned and said, "This is our last crossing. After this next tunnel, we'll be inside the ghetto."

It was so simple, I almost couldn't believe it. "Why hasn't everyone left this way?" I knew the question sounded naïve, especially given all I'd seen as a courier, but I wanted to understand. It was one thing to have to be smuggled out of a ghetto. That could be expensive and required the help of a smuggler. But here, the people could get themselves out. Why would they stay?

Esther shrugged. "These tunnels were built by the resistance."

"Did your father know about them? Does the Judenrat know? Because if they did, then the Germans know too."

"I was involved with smuggling before I left," she said. "My father didn't know that, nor about these tunnels. Obviously, the resistance had to keep this secret. Otherwise, word would spread, eventually someone would be caught, and then these passages would be shut down. But even most of those who do know about the tunnels haven't used them for escape. They'd need friends on the outside to have any hope of survival, and as you already know, the Jews have a short supply of friends in Poland these days."

Yes, that I knew far too well.

By now, we had entered the final tunnel, a hole drilled through the shared brick wall of the neighboring building and hidden by a chest of drawers. We exited through a hole at the back of a mostly empty wardrobe, and a deep sigh escaped from me. It was a relief to be out of the wild.

Or perhaps it was a sigh of worry, because we were officially inside the Warsaw Ghetto. And the clock was ticking.

Esther suggested we wait until daylight before going out in the open. "I'm sure the people here are extra watchful for strangers," she said as we sat in a corner of the abandoned room. "You're a stranger, and I'm—"

"—the daughter of the Judenrat." I bundled my coat around me, blocking her out.

"Chaya, I said I'm—"

"Good night, Esther." I wasn't ready to talk about that, not yet.

When morning broke a few hours later, we slipped out onto the streets. In appearance, it was similar to other ghettos, a place where seven people had to share every available room. The problem of such severe overcrowding had taken its toll on the streets and buildings. Most of the trees had been felled for their wood, and the ghetto walls were a constant reminder that this place was, and always had been, a kind of prison.

Despite all that, I was immediately struck by how diffcrent the people of this ghetto were from any other I'd seen so far.

No one wandered here. No one sat idly by, watching the world turn. Those who were on the streets moved with purpose. They knew what was coming, the same as I did. They were preparing.

Within only a few blocks, our presence was noticed. A hand tapped me on the shoulder and the voice was sharp, accusatory. "I don't know you girls."

I turned to see a square-built man in his early thirties with a distinct scar on the side of his face. It looked recent. Forcing myself not to stare at it, I gestured at Esther. "This is Esther Karolinski, and I'm Chaya Lindner. We're with Akiva, from Krakow. We were sent here to help."

"Hmm." His expression remained cautious as he looked me over first; then his eyes rested longer on Esther and her shoulders hunched. She was looking anywhere but at him. I wondered how this man was affected by her father's lists.

He nodded at our bags. "What do you have there?"

We opened them for his inspection. He checked carefully through everything before looking up at us again, now with a wide smile on his face.

"Krakow?" he asked. "We heard the resistance there was crushed."

"Akiva is broken, that's true," I replied. "But some of us remain, and we want to fight here."

His eyes returned to Esther. He must know who she was, or her father. He was suspicious of her, and I worried he might not allow us to remain.

"My name is Tamir," he said. "I fight for ZOB under the direction of—"

"Mordecai Anielewicz," Esther finished. "So will we, if you'll have us."

"Will we have you?" Tamir laughed, a surprisingly booming laugh. "My dear, we would take a blind man with two minutes to live if he knew which way to point his weapon! Come with me."

And so our morning began. This was one of the rare times when I was able to receive thanks for what I'd brought into the ghetto and I wasn't prepared for the hugs and offerings of gratitude. We handed over everything, with one exception: my gun. I knew I'd need it, and I'd worked too hard to give it up now. By the end of the day, we belonged to one of twenty-two ZOB units inside the ghetto and were given the assignment to dig bunkers.

I didn't know how to dig a bunker, and other than Esther, I didn't know anyone else in my cell. But I was where I belonged, and I intended to learn as fast as I could.

So when a shovel was put in my hands, I smiled and began to dig.

THIRTY-THREE

March 1, 1943
Warsaw Ghetto

After a week of working within the ghetto, Tamir found me again, asking if I would come speak to him and other leaders of ZOB.

"What about Esther?" She wasn't far from me amid a pile of sticks smuggled in from the forest. We'd been carving them into crude pikes, weapons that would take little more training than "Stab with the sharp end." The word passing through the bunkers was that our leaders expected face-to-face fighting with the Nazis. A sharpened stick wouldn't stop a bullet, but it was better than nothing, and we had plenty of nothing here already.

Tamir eyed Esther, then said to me, "We only need to speak with you."

With a glance back and a shrug, I followed him from our half-constructed bunker, down Mila Street to another larger bunker that served as the headquarters for ZOB's leadership. Mordecai wasn't here, nor had I met him yet, but much as I would have relished the honor, I was sure he had far more important things demanding his attention.

Instead, for this meeting, only one other person was here, a woman who introduced herself as Rachel. She had a pretty face with thick brows, and dark hair pulled into a bun, and wore what appeared to be a mechanic's uniform. She'd belted it and created a holster at her side for a gun, and I had no doubts about her aim. Tamir sat beside her and invited me to sit in a chair across from them. Their formality unnerved me. Was this a conversation or an interrogation?

Rachel began, "I'm told you were a courier for Akiva."

"I still am," I replied. "Though there isn't much left of Akiva anymore."

She glanced over at Tamir, then said, "Nor will there be much left of ZOB after the Germans are through with us."

"I understand that." Why did she think I had come all this way, risked everything I had left in the world?

Tamir shifted the conversation. "How old are you, Chaya?"

"Sixteen."

"Only four years younger than Mordecai Anielewicz was when the war began. Like your Akiva leaders, he had no military training, no real leadership experience, and yet we follow him. Do you know why?"

I shrugged.

Rachel cut in. "Mordecai escaped Poland at the beginning of the war and could have remained free. But he cared more about the youth he left behind. He cared more about helping us than about his own life. Now we fight for him." She leaned forward. "Will you?"

"We have one enemy," I said. "So as far as I'm concerned, there is only one resistance, and he leads it."

Rachel smiled. "You've been involved with the resistance for several months, correct? We've heard your name, we know your work. Why did Akiva fail in Krakow?"

"What does it mean to fail? We never expected to defeat the Nazis. But we wanted to meet our deaths in an honorable way, to bring attention to our cause from those who are strong enough to win."

"Yes, yes, that is true of all our resistance groups." Rachel was becoming impatient. "But we want to know what lessons you learned from Akiva that we can use here. Help us avoid the same mistakes."

Oh.

I drew in another breath, then began, "We spent most of our time just trying to convince people of what was happening, both inside the ghettos and out. When we began to fight, it was too late."

Tamir and Rachel exchanged looks. I thought of last fall's deportations in Warsaw, hundreds of thousands of Jews sent to their deaths on the trains. And I'd seen more of the ghetto now. Yes, there were many who were working and planning and preparing, but they were doing it all for the thousands who remained, some too weak to offer any assistance and others so broken that they welcomed their deaths. We needed more workers, more fighters, anyone who wanted to live enough that they would die for it.

But maybe it really was too late for all of them. For all of us.

Before the Nazis could kill the Jews, they had to break us down. To save the Jews, we had to build them up again. Was that still possible here?

I gestured around us. "This is headquarters for all the leadership, correct? I think it's a mistake. We had only one bunker for our leaders, which made it easy for the Nazis to find them. And it's the only reason I'm still here—I had somewhere else to go. If this place is compromised—and it will be sooner or later—you must give the people another place to go. The Germans believe taking out the leaders' bunker is like removing the heart."

Rachel nodded. "Anything else?"

I shrugged. "I'm not telling you anything you don't already know. The fact is, we made many more mistakes than that. Most of us are young, none of us are trained to fight against an army such as this, and we're operating with few resources, limited movement, and a world that has almost entirely ignored what is happening to us. The only thing we really wanted, to trigger other uprisings elsewhere in Poland, never happened."

"It's happening here, as you hoped." Rachel tilted her head. "Do you believe there is any chance of uprisings from the other ghettos?"

I shrugged again. "Krakow won't fight back again. Nor will Lodz, though I'm sure there are people in both districts who would if they could. But I think there is hope for Bialystok, and Sobibor or Tarnow, and if we are very lucky, the Polish army will see what a handful of Jews can do with a small cache of weapons and less than a mouthful of bread. If we can fight, then they can too."

Now Tamir and Rachel were smiling. Tamir said, "Where did you get this fire, Chaya? This desire to stand against Hitler's armies?"

My cheeks warmed, and I didn't know what to say. Was it fire within me, or foolishness? But the question evaporated when Rachel continued, "What about your friend Esther—"

"I know she looks timid, but she's stronger than people know."

"We do know her," Rachel said. "Or, we knew her father. Esther must leave the ghetto, for her own good. Other fighters won't risk their lives for her, nor will they trust her to help them."

My fists tightened. Maybe Esther and I hadn't fully resolved the issue of trust between us, but that was no reason to send her away. "Esther is as much a part of the resistance as I am!"

"It's not about her beliefs, only her background. A lot of people here lost family members, thanks to her father."

"And those same people need her help now." I looked at Tamir. "You said that we need every person we can get."

"Not if that person gets in our way. We won't send her out on her own, of course. We're looking for a safe house that will accept a girl of her age and with her looks. That isn't easy, certainly not with tensions so high throughout Warsaw, but we are trying. We didn't want to surprise you, just in case she isn't here one day."

I stood. "You're wrong, both of you. Esther risked her life to come back here to deliver a package. Did she give it to you yet?"

They looked at each other, confused. They had no idea what I was talking about. Did Esther lie about the package too? I felt stupid, uncommonly naïve. Of course she'd lied. She couldn't have hidden any sort of package from the Nazis when they captured her.

I wouldn't say any of that to Tamir and Rachel, though, not until I found out what she was up to now. Instead, I said, "Esther must stay. You've asked for my opinion about how to best carry out your fight. Well, it's my opinion that you need Esther here. She won't make the difference between a victory or a loss, but she will carry out her orders as well as anyone else, or die trying."

After a brief pause, Rachel said, "Thank you for that. We'll consider your words."

"We have one last thing to tell you," Tamir said. "Or, rather, to show you. There's someone who asked to be here when our meeting was finished."

My brows pressed together as I tried to make sense of his vague words. But I turned when Rachel stood and opened the bunker door, mumbling, "Come in."

It took me a moment to recognize the person who walked inside. He was older now, several centimeters taller, and clearly was fighting back tears.

It was Yitzchak. My brother.

THIRTY-FOUR

March 1, 1943
Warsaw Ghetto

In my mind, I had often pictured finding Yitzchak again one day, but it was always imagined as a dream, a fantastical story that could never exist within the harsh realities of life.

Yet here he was, standing in the doorway, looking every bit as hesitant to approach me as I was him. Had he ever wondered if I was still alive? Did he take a second glance at every girl he passed who was about my age and had my color of hair? I'd certainly done that with every boy in every ghetto who looked about fourteen, with dark brown hair. They were always missing the mole on the right cheek, like Yitzchak had.

Like Yitzchak still has. This was my brother!

I took one step toward him, then two, and then he closed the gap and folded me into a hug. Immediately, every memory of my little brother flooded back into my life. He used to walk around our home in my shoes, which were too big for him, and scribble on my schoolwork. He had a sweet tooth for rugelach and a lifelong aversion to peas. And he took great care of our younger sister, Sara. We would never be complete without her, but seeing Yitzchak again lifted my spirits in a way that nothing ever could.

Rachel suggested we take our reunion to a more private place. Yitzchak led the way back onto the street, and we became oblivious to everyone else around us, firing questions at each other almost faster than the other could answer.

At first, it was easy. "How have you been? When did you get so tall? How did you know I was here?"

He smiled, the same impish smile he used to have many years ago when he nestled under my arm and begged me to read to him. "I saw you and another girl walking across the street yesterday. I called out, but you must not have heard and I couldn't get away in time to catch up. But I started asking around until someone knew who you were and how to find you."

"I'm glad they did," I said. "Though I wish we could have met again somewhere else, in another time."

Or better yet, I wished we'd never been separated at all.

Then the questions became harder. With his eyes as bright as ever, Yitzchak asked, "How are our parents?"

My mouth went dry. There was too much anticipation in his voice, too much hope. I slowly exhaled, stalling until I could find the right words, or any words at all. It left an ache in my lungs that made it even harder to say, "Last I heard, they were still in Krakow. But I don't"—I swallowed hard—"I don't think we'll see them again. Losing Sara was hard on Mama especially. And then you . . ."

He nodded and glanced away, maybe so I wouldn't see the emotion suddenly etched into his face. He wiped his eyes with the back of his hand and sniffed, but once he'd steadied himself, he said, "I went after Sara when she was taken. I know how foolish that sounds, given that I was only twelve years old. But I thought I was small enough to sneak her off the train. I didn't make it in time, but I did see her before the train left. A woman was holding her, taking care of her. Whatever her last hours were, Chaya, I believe she felt love at the end, not fear."

My heart had been wrung out a thousand times over, yet I still had more tears for Sara. At least Yitzchak gave me a final memory to picture whenever I thought of Sara again, which I would do every remaining day of my life. It was also the way I wanted to live my last moments. At the end, I hoped to feel love.

We cried there together, for Sara and our parents and for all our family had lost. Then we cried because in a war that had done nothing but scatter and destroy and kill, somehow we had found each other again.

Eventually, Yitzchak added, "After Sara was gone, I had no idea how to get back into the ghetto and I didn't want to be caught and put on the trains either, so I ran into the woods. A Polish couple took me in. They cared for me as long as they could, until their neighbors became suspicious. Then they sent me to other family members farther north, where the same thing happened and I had to be moved yet again. On my third family, I was simply turned over to the Gestapo and ended up here. But I'm glad to be here, Chaya. I'm glad to be able to fight."

"Me too." I squeezed his hand, and then suddenly we had nothing to say. And not because there was so little, but because so much had happened that it couldn't all be explained in these first few minutes. We'd each lived a life-time over the past two and a half years, and we were at once the closest of siblings, all the other had left in this world, and still somehow total strangers.

He seemed to recognize this too and released my hand, leaning back against a building. He began to hum a tune, one we used to sing together as children, although I rarely hit the right notes. Yitzchak still had his beautiful voice, though.

After a moment of listening, I asked, "Do you still sing?"

"Every week," he replied. "When we celebrate Shabbat. And before the last Aktion, we often held concerts in homes. An older man here had a violin he managed to keep hidden from the Germans, but he smashed it over the head of a soldier when they tried to take him in January. Others used to recite poetry or perform in small plays, and anyone who had painted something could put it on display for people to view afterward." His eyes became wistful. "There should be more singing now, not less."

I tilted my head, curious. "They were still holding concerts here? Performing while all this tragedy was happening around them?"

"It had to be that way." Yitzchak stood straight again. "Why do the Nazis feel they can commit such violence against us? How do they justify it?"

I shrugged. "Because they believe we are less than human. Like animals."

"Exactly! They herd us into train cars like cattle, give our rabbis and scholars the work of oxen, feed us less than what is given to their dogs. And they kill us with no more regard than they'd give to slaughtering a farm animal. But there is something a human can do that an animal never can."

"Create art." I considered that for a moment. "So you sing because—"

"It's proof of my humanity. It allows me, just for the length of that song, to remember who I really am, no matter what surrounds me."

I looked at him again, really looked at him for the first time since the beginning of our reunion. He sounded like our father. He'd even begun to look like our father. In any other time or place, Yitzchak would have become a great man one day.

But then, he was already great. Our parents would be so proud of him. If only they knew. If only I could walk him back into that ghetto in Krakow, back into their arms. Mama had been right all along. Yitzchak had survived!

He gestured at the gun at my side. "Are you a good shot?"

I stared down at it. "Sometimes. I wish I didn't need it."

"I never would've pictured you doing what . . . what they say you've done. Is it all true, Chaya?"

"Remember what Mama always used to say? To never believe the best of what anyone says about a person, nor the worst."

"I believe the best about you," he said. "I know you've saved lives."

"Never enough, Yitz. It's never enough." I sighed. "And maybe none of it matters. We're trying to empty an ocean with a teaspoon."

"It matters to those you've saved," he said. "It matters that you've stayed on your feet until the end."

"It's not the end yet. There's more to be done."

"And I'm ready to do it," he added. "But now, I'll be fighting for my family. For you, Chaya."

"Come with me." I took his hand again. "I want to introduce you to my friend Esther. She's family now too."

THIRTY-FIVE

March 13, 1943
Warsaw Ghetto

The radio I brought into the ghetto was one of the few that existed here, but every night, if I wasn't assigned elsewhere, I sat with Yitzchak and Esther and Tamir and anyone else who could crowd together to listen for news from the larger world. If nothing else was available, we tuned in to the German propaganda reports, although little of what they said could be believed. More often, we listened to an underground broadcast from London that originated with a Polish woman somewhere here in Warsaw.

Not everything that came through her broadcasts could be believed either. Much of what she said was clearly designed to mislead the Germans, who obviously must monitor this station, though what we heard tonight seemed far too accurate.

"Our network in Krakow confirms the liquidation of the Podgorze Ghetto is under way," the woman said. "Two thousand Jews deemed unfit for work were ordered onto the street and shot."

My mother was unfit for work. And my father refused to leave her side.

Two thousand Jews had been shot.

My vision blurred and time slowed as if the universe knew I needed to absorb every word.

Two thousand.

How could I possibly take that in? I couldn't even think. Beside me, Esther held my hand, and maybe she was squeezing it, maybe speaking to me, I didn't know. On my right, Yitzchak was frozen in place. I wasn't sure if he was even breathing. Was I?

The announcer continued, "The remaining eight thousand Jews are being sent to Auschwitz-Birkenau, or marched to the nearby Plaszow labor camp, led by Amon Goeth, a man whose reputation boasts of cruelty and sadism. Little hope can remain for their fate. In other news . . ."

I jumped up and ran from the bunker, almost blinded by tears and anger. It was the "in other news" that sent my temper over the edge. How could they move on to *other news* as if the fate of those ten thousand Jews was only one piece of a nightly broadcast? As if they hadn't just announced something that sent my world flying apart?

Yitzchak must have followed me. He put his hand on my shoulder, and I turned around and folded myself into his arms, sobbing. I knew I was the older sister and that I should be comforting him, but tonight, it was the other way around. What did it matter if I'd known this was coming? Nothing could prepare me for actually having to deal with such awful news. Hundreds of people still lived because of my work. Why couldn't I have saved my own parents?

"If they were taken to the labor camp, they might still . . ."

That was all he said. That was all either of us said.

Yitzchak held me until no tears were left, the last time I would cry for our parents. Nor would I hold on to any anger toward them, not for refusing to believe me when they could have, or for staying when they should have left. Instead, I would remember the best of who they were: my father, strong and kind and ever loyal to my mother. And my mother: tender and loving and always ready with a word of advice when we needed it.

I was proud to be their daughter, and before this war was over, I would make them proud of me as well.

When I'd collected myself, we returned to the bunker to find Tamir and Rachel in close conversation with Esther. She looked over at me with tremendous sadness in her eyes and shook her head. I knew what that meant.

"No!" I shouted, indifferent to whether the entire ghetto heard, much less the people in this bunker. "No, you will not do this!"

Yitzchak grabbed my arm, holding me back. "I was

here when her father posted those lists. You have to understand—"

"That is not her fault!" I was still shouting. "If we accept that all Germans are not Nazis, and all Poles are not against us, then can't we accept that Esther is not her father? He did what he did, and those were his choices and no one else's. If Esther wants to stay, then she must stay."

"We have a place she can go," Rachel said. "Maybe it's better—"

Ignoring her, I turned to Esther. "What do you want?"

Her answer came immediately. "I am supposed to be here in the ghetto, and I want to stay here." Then she spoke more loudly, to the whole group. "And if you allow me to stay, I promise to prove that I am as much a part of this resistance as any of you. I will fight!"

I looked them over, my expression as serious as ever before. "And if you make her go, then I promise that I will not fight. I will leave with her and you will have two fewer members for the coming battle."

"Three." Yitzchak stood at my side with his arm around me. And suddenly, I loved my dear brother more than ever. I loved Esther too, truly loved her, as if she were my own sister.

Tamir and Rachel exchanged glances. Then in a softer tone, Rachel said, "You may stay if you wish, Esther, but you will have to prove yourself to the others. I cannot do that for you, nor can your friends."

"I will."

When we were alone again, I pulled her into a hug and she thanked me, though I'd certainly done her no favors.

She whispered, "Does this mean you forgive me, for Lodz? Do you trust me again?"

I wished I could give her the easy answer. I'd forgiven her a long time ago, but trusting her was very different. I held her hand and said, "Tell me the truth about the package you were supposed to deliver. It's okay to admit there never was a package."

"There is, Chaya, I promise."

"What is it? At least tell me that."

"I can't, I've promised not to say anything until the right time." She lowered her eyes. "I'll deliver it when it's needed most."

"And that's not yet?"

"No, not yet."

She still wouldn't look at me. What package could she possibly have that was such a secret?

Over the next several days, I became aware of a strange incongruence within the ghetto. People here seemed happy, wearing easy smiles and waving with friendly hellos, as they would have done before the war.

They were, in fact, entirely out of step with anyone I'd met in Poland since the war began, and particularly in the ghettos.

We were hungry, of course. We had no idea how long our meager food supplies would last, and so rations were imposed that were nearly as strict as what they were under control of the Judenrat.

We were exhausted. If I wasn't digging a bunker somewhere, then I was stocking it with supplies gathered from elsewhere in the ghetto. Not only food, water, and weapons, but blankets, clothes, and books for those who would be confined here while the fighting took place on the streets.

And if I wasn't working on a bunker, then I was building handmade weapons. We made Molotov cocktails, filling glass jars and even light bulbs with sulfuric acid, bleach, or whatever else we could find that would either burn or explode. We sharpened the edges of sticks or flattened them into handles, which our welders fashioned into knives.

Every item we found in our exploration of the apartments was considered for its possibilities as a weapon. A broom handle, a rolling pin, or a pair of scissors. Knitting needles, wiring from the walls, and certainly every tool from the workshops.

I thought Esther could sense people knew about her father. Few people talked to her, and those who did were soon pulled aside by others for a hushed conversation, and then Esther was left alone again. Each day, her shoulders slumped further, and her eyes remained longer on the ground.

She was, in fact, the only person I saw who looked the

way I expected everyone here to look. Even I found myself smiling more than usual, sometimes laughing as I worked among other resistance members.

And eventually, I understood why.

It was because the ending of our story was already written. We knew what was coming, and that it would happen soon, and that even at our best, most of us would never walk away from this ghetto, if any did.

In the knowing, there was peace.

And with our action came joy. Finally, after years of endurance and suffering, and the pain of having our lives stripped away from us one piece at a time, at last we had something that restored our dignity and pride and our common feeling that this was the moment when we would make a stand.

That time was coming, probably sooner than any of us knew.

Until then, I had work to do.

THIRTY-SIX

April 18, 1943
Warsaw Ghetto

Another month passed with the same routine. The snow had melted away and warmer days brought hope for a better future—a cruel tease, considering our circumstances. I'd never experienced a springtime such as this one. It had been three months since the Germans last attempted to enter this ghetto, and almost two months since we'd arrived.

In all that time, we'd discussed theories, debated options, and considered opinions from everyone who claimed to understand what the Germans were thinking. But no one really knew.

And for three months, the only thing that truly mattered was that every day they waited, we improved another bunker, created more weapons, and solicited help from the outside world. Every day gave us another few hours to live, to tell ourselves that anywhere the Germans didn't dare to go, there we were free.

ZOB leadership divided the ghetto into three separate zones, each led by a different commander. Other resistance groups were here too, some divided by political beliefs, others by location, but all of us united with one purpose: to make a final stand with honor and dignity. We were joined by several people emerging from the wild with offers to fight on their own, wherever they could, however they could. It was nearly impossible to travel from one zone to another because they were separated by German patrolled areas. After the fighting began, we would have little idea in one zone what was happening in the other two.

In that time, we'd dug or built over six hundred bunkers. Their locations were disguised so that only a person who knew of the entrance would be able to find it. Some were larger than others, but we'd scavenged from abandoned apartments to try to make each one as comfortable as possible, since they were to hold civilians who might be in there for weeks or even months. Most bunkers locked from the inside, so in the end, the Germans would have to either break in or lure us out. Many had fresh water supplies, electricity, and air vents, allowing those who were not fighting to stay in hiding for as long as a year, if they were careful. Every bakery within the ghetto had been operating nearly nonstop to create rusk bread, which, although dry and crusty, lasted far longer than regular bread.

We'd acquired pistols, rifles, and at least one machine gun, with ammunition for all calibers. We had grenades, both military and homemade devices, and hundreds of other containers that would explode when we lit them. We had several hundred pieces of armor stolen from the Germans, including steel helmets and bullet-resistant tunics. We spent a great deal of money on the black market to acquire these items, thanks to the Judenrat treasuries, which the resistance was happy to take for itself.

But as I looked over what we did have, I couldn't help but think this wasn't nearly enough. I remembered Cyganeria, how quickly we went through our supplies, how much it took for what little we accomplished.

We also didn't have support from the outside world, not like we needed. How many times had our leaders begged the Polish Underground Army to join us? With their help, we'd have a chance to bring a fight to the Nazis that could make a difference, maybe even turn the tide within Warsaw. They gave us a few weapons and a symbolic pat on the back for good luck, but that too was inadequate.

Then one evening, after three months of preparation, three months of wondering and planning and hoping for even one day more, a man I knew only as Chaim burst into our bunker in the Central Zone, his eyes wide with fear and only two words on his lips: "They're here."

The Germans had come.

Just like that, the last of the sand ran through the hourglass.

Chaim and the other lookouts on the rooftops reported

that thousands of soldiers were gathering in Warsaw, setting up camp like we were the new front line of the war, and maybe we were. It suddenly made sense why the Germans waited this long—it took time to organize an army of this size, extensive planning to prepare a ghetto of seventy thousand people for total liquidation. No doubt those were their orders.

By six o'clock, they had the ghetto surrounded.

Our day had been spent hastily moving the last of our supplies into the bunkers and helping people get to their assigned places.

I crowded into a bunker with Yitzchak, Esther, and Tamir, and at least a dozen other fighters. We were all tense—wanting to move, to race, to test our strength and courage against the invaders. I'd already faced them dozens of times when entering the ghettos. Very soon, I would face them again, but in an entirely different way.

It was the evening before Passover, and the tension was so thick throughout the ghetto, every move I made seemed to require me to push myself through solid air. As important as it was every year to observe Passover, I couldn't think of any other night of my life when we needed God to save us more. Our bunker would hold the Seder. Every bunker would hold it.

Someone had located a white tablecloth for ours, and we gathered around it. The same women who had worked tirelessly making food for the bunkers pushed themselves yet again to bake matzos and hard-boil the eggs, and some of the men provided wine. It wasn't a complete meal, but what we had was kosher and it reminded me of the sacred nature of that last supper with Akiva. How long ago that seemed now.

This was my second last supper. I didn't expect to ever celebrate a third.

An elderly man behind me whispered, almost under his breath, *"Oyf lebm un toyt."* Yiddish for "On our lives, on our deaths." Those who heard him quietly repeated the words as a vow, another pledge of honor. I said it too and felt my courage rise.

Tamir read from the Haggadah. As I sipped from my wineglass, listening to the recitation of God's deliverance of the Israelites from bondage in Egypt, I couldn't help but wonder if He would deliver us now.

Tamir answered my unspoken question, perhaps the question no one dared to ask. "Didn't Moses once say to our people, 'Be strong and courageous! God is the one Who goes with you.' My friends, if we do not see the end of tomorrow, then know that we have fought for the deliverance of others. If our deaths give the chance of life to others, we have done well."

The rest of the group moved on with the Seder, but my thoughts remained there. Tamir sat nearly across from me, giving praise and honor to a God who might not save him from his fate. But he did so, confident that this coming fight was worthy of God's blessings.

My mind returned to that small apartment in Lodz where Avraham and Henryk and Sara believed that their deaths were to honor God. I understood that now. The resistance was not about who lived and who died. It was about the way we lived, and the way we would die when our time came.

Which might be sooner than any of us wanted. Near the close of the meal, someone behind me mumbled, "Tonight will not be a good night."

If other words were spoken afterward, I didn't hear them. We huddled in close together, all of us pretending to sleep and no one doing a particularly good job of it. Time crawled forward without mercy, each minute an hour, each hour a lifetime. And yet, it felt as if I'd only blinked once when the boom of a tank's gun echoed above us, so forcefully that bits of dirt crumbled beneath the cracks of the bunker ceiling.

It was very early in the morning. Someone called out the time: 2 a.m.

Those without weapons had been told to remain in the bunkers until an opportunity came to escape into the forests. I didn't know when, or how such a thing was to be accomplished, but they couldn't remain in here forever.

To the rest of us, Tamir issued the call that was no doubt being given in every ghetto bunker. "All armed Jews, the time has come to fight."

I looked over at Esther, then at my brother, and found joy in their fixed expressions of determination. We shared a grim smile, grabbed every weapon that had been assigned to us, and followed the others up our narrow ladder.

It was exactly ten months since I had officially joined the resistance. Since the day I had promised Gusta Draenger to fight against the Nazi occupation in any way I was needed. Every experience of my life since then had prepared me for what was about to come.

And I was ready to be tested.

The Warsaw Ghetto Uprising was about to begin.

April 19, 1943
Warsaw Ghetto

Esther positioned herself near me on the third floor of a former soup kitchen building overlooking Nalewki Street. Yitzchak had been assigned elsewhere, which felt like losing him all over again, but this was only the beginning. We were bound to be separated eventually.

Below us, a single-file line of SS troops entered the ghetto, their precise march making it difficult to know how many soldiers were here. Maybe fifty or five hundred or five thousand—anything was possible. When the full moon finally emerged from thick clouds, I caught a look at the uniforms, but at this distance, I couldn't read their markings, although they definitely didn't look German. Tamir passed by to say they were mostly troops from Lithuania and the Ukraine. There was a third group too, the Jewish police.

Beneath my breath, I cursed, but it was loud enough for Esther to hear.

"Chaya, don't speak like that!" she scolded.

Inwardly, I smiled. It was fine that I was waiting to kill as many soldiers as possible, but she would not tolerate my cursing.

Tamir heard me as well. "The OD had no choice. Those who refused to participate were already shot near the Gestapo building."

"And what do these men think will happen to them after this is over?" I countered.

Other than the lengthening column of soldiers, the streets below were deserted. They marched past numerous banners and posters. Some called for Poles outside the ghetto to join us in the fighting. Others for courage until the end. But my favorite was a poster of two hands shaking each other through a break in the ghetto wall with text reading all people are equal brothers: brown, white, black, and yellow.

Perhaps one day.

Perhaps.

While the column advanced, we waited. Patiently. Silently. My finger on the trigger, my muscles ready with anticipation. Between Esther and me sat a dozen grenades, a matchbook, and three homemade explosives. I also had a few extra rounds of ammunition for my gun.

But we did nothing to this initial column of soldiers. These men were only pawns. We awaited the true enemy.

At the first hint of dawn, the Germans entered, perhaps

after assuring themselves that since nothing had happened so far, they should be fine too. How wrong they were.

I didn't know who was the first to fire on them, nor who gave the order, but once I saw the action start, I was ready. I started with one of the explosives, lighting the fuse inside a bottle filled with petrol, then dropped it from the window on an entire detachment of soldiers. It exploded, bodies fell, and the troops who survived it scattered.

Next, members of my team reached for our grenades. For many of them, this was the first live grenade they'd ever thrown, much as it had been for me at the Cyganeria Café.

Esther turned to them now. "Count after you throw, not before." The reminder probably wasn't necessary, but better safe than sorry, I supposed.

Esther and I pulled our pins. Her sights were on a group that had already scattered to the far end of the street, and I found a group of soldiers who were aiming their rifles upward, toward another building. Both grenades exploded, sending debris high into the air. When it settled, I counted five Germans down, either injured or dead.

This was a good start, but it wasn't enough. This was not enough. Never enough. The words rang through my head.

Orders were shouted below for the Germans to retreat, and from nearby, Tamir ordered us to stand down as well. We needed to save our strength for Germans who were advancing, not retreating.

Esther and I rolled back against the wall, away from the windows, and my pulse was still racing when Tamir ordered us to gather up our weapons. "They'll target these windows when they return," he said. "Let's move below."

He ordered some of my team into the buildings at street level, but Esther and I were sent down into one of the many tunnels constructed beneath the streets. From here, we could secretly access small holes that allowed us to shoot from almost ground level, or to roll grenades under the feet of the marching soldiers. They wouldn't even know where the bullet that caught them came from.

We were barely in place when the soldiers returned again. This time, they weren't in formation, and Tamir was right, they shot wildly at the windows, taking aim anywhere they thought we still were. In return, I fired at targets ahead of me, while Esther rolled at least three more grenades at passing troops.

We were close enough to the Germans to hear their confused shouts. They didn't know where to aim, or where we aimed from, resulting in orders to advance shouted out at the same time as orders to retreat or to take cover. The soldiers' reactions were equally confused, panicked men running or diving to the ground, or standing frozen, unsure of which order was meant for them. They hadn't been trained for this.

Which made me smile. They'd faced down whole armies, conquered countries with Blitzkriegs on land, sea, and air. They boasted of their superiority in technology, manpower, in their very race. Yet for all of that, the Germans were not prepared for *us*.

Within a half hour, the Germans retreated a second time, and shouts passed through the streets that they had left the ghetto entirely. Tamir dashed through the tunnels, asking for reports on how many of us were injured or wounded. With each response, a swell of pride rose within me.

"We're fine," I called out, as all the others had.

"Not one," Tamir said, hope thick in his voice. "Not one of us is injured yet."

Yet.

That single word remained locked in my mind. But for now, the victory was ours.

"They'll be back," Esther whispered. "Twice as strong as before."

No, not twice as strong. The Germans would return with ten times the strength. Or more.

Tamir and a few other senior leaders crept out onto the street. After they determined it was safe, they called for the rest of us to come out. I was nervous, remembering what had happened to those in Akiva who were out in the open when the Germans responded to the Cyganeria attack, including my friend Jakub. I was still alive because I knew how to blend into the background and when to hide. But I did want to see the effects of what we had done, knowing that I might never have another chance for it.

The narrow street was covered with broken glass and plaster, and the shrapnel left behind from our explosives. Fallen German soldiers littered the streets. Some were dead, some wounded, uttering pleas for help from the very people they were intent on slaughtering.

I stared at one soldier's face, his eyes closed in death. He couldn't have been much older than me, little more than a boy. Who was he before the war? Had he sat at Hitler's feet, absorbing the doctrines of anti-Semitism? Had he volunteered to be here, hoping to rid the earth of everyone who looked different from him, who believed differently? Or had he been torn from a loving mother's side, forced into this ugly war against his will, against his beliefs?

Whoever he had been, he was no longer my enemy.

Most of the other fighters who emerged wrapped arms around each other with cries of *"Mazel tov."* Even if this was only our first scrape, it went far better than any of us could have expected.

Then we were hushed and immediately fell silent. From outside the ghetto walls, we heard orders shouted for soldiers to come in and retrieve their injured.

We waited, listened, and nothing happened.

Nothing happened.

How could that be? Those were direct orders. Where were the soldiers who'd been ordered in?

Still there was nothing, and no one.

Esther leaned over to me. "They're scared. They won't come in, because they're afraid they won't come back out."

They were right to be afraid, while we were full of confidence and pride, and feeling for the first time in years that we were no longer victims, but that we controlled our own future. I would remember this moment always, the morning I stood with my fellow resistance fighters to claim our own destiny again. Even if it wasn't the future we wanted, this was the day I stood on my feet, faced my enemies with my own name—Chaya Lindner—and took my life back.

Someone farther down the street called out, "Let's get to work with the fallen soldiers. Everything that can be scavenged from their bodies must be taken."

Esther took a few steps back, shaking her head. "I can't do this, Chaya. Please, let's find another way to help."

I agreed. I knew that salvaging everything from them was a necessary disrespect for the dead. But Esther and I could be of value elsewhere in the ghetto.

We headed toward Mila Street, where ZOB had its headquarters. This was where Yitzchak had been assigned, and I hoped we could join him there. I had one round of ammunition left in my gun, two Molotov cocktails, and three grenades. Despite the continuing cheers and self-congratulations behind me, I knew we'd need much more than this.

More than we had.

More than we could possibly get in time.

THIRTY-EIGHT

April 19, 1943
Warsaw Ghetto

Esther and I found Yitzchak in a building overlooking Mila Street, inside what must have been very nice apartments at one time, and there we joined one of four groups that had been ordered to hide. They hadn't seen much fighting yet, but I described to them our success and warned of the consequences of humiliating the Germans the way we had.

Yitzchak was too excited about their plan to have properly heard me. With a smile of naïve enthusiasm, he said, "We've seen them lining up outside the gate. This is the most likely road for them to come down. When they do, our orders are to wait."

"Wait?" Esther asked. "No, if we allow them to get deeper into the ghetto, that's where the civilians are. We have to keep them—"

"Our orders are to wait." Yitzchak put his head down as if to end the conversation, and I followed his gesture. There were many times over the past few years when it had been my job to think on my feet, to make my own decisions. This was not one of those times.

It wasn't long before another column of soldiers appeared, hundreds of them, mostly Ukrainian SS men and Jewish police officers, similar to what had happened early that morning. My gun was trained on the SS officers. It infuriated me to see the OD march with the enemy, traitors to our people, traitors to their own beliefs. But I couldn't fire on them.

"Did your father send in the OD?" a man hissed over to Esther. She shrunk behind me, and I glared at the man until he looked away.

"He's afraid," I whispered to Esther. "He's afraid and angry and he doesn't know what to do with all that emotion. What he said wasn't about you."

"It was," she replied. "I loved my father, Chaya. I still do. But being in the Judenrat was an impossible situation. I remember at the beginning, he thought he could help the people here, and he did a lot of good. But very soon, the choices weren't between good and bad, they were between bad and awful."

"A choiceless choice," I mumbled. "There is no winning, only a decision as to how we will lose." How many times had I faced that very problem myself?

Esther nodded. "Exactly. Either my father cooperated with the Nazis or they'd punish his family."

"So he sent you away."

Her voice cracked. "I asked to go. I had to go. Of course I'd rather have stayed with my family, but not if I was a tool used against my people."

I put an arm around her, drawing her in close. "Your own choiceless choice." And just like that, I wasn't angry with her anymore, for lying about her past, or about Lodz, or for any of the mistakes she'd made. I'd made many more mistakes myself and not had to pay half the price for it that she had.

Orders were shouted to the soldiers on the street, reminding me of the need for silence and to pay attention. I looked outside again, waiting until the lines passed. But my mind became a constant zigzag between three thoughts. The first was for Yitzchak and Esther. How much I loved them. How much I wanted to protect them. I would give my life for either of them if necessary. If it would matter in the end.

Then I thought of Akiva. Our leaders, the Draengers, could have left Poland before the war took effect, but they came back to fight for us, just as I'd come here. I missed my friends in Akiva too, Rubin, and any others who continued to fight from the forests. Those who were gone. Without their training, their example, I would not be here today. And even if I had the choice not to be here, but living in freedom a thousand kilometers from here, I'd choose to stay and fight. This was where I belonged.

Which pulled my mind back to the present. To the rows of Jewish fighters on either side of me, each of us waiting.

Each of us hoping our contribution to the fight made a difference.

The column of soldiers passed us by entirely. Their eyes were focused directly ahead, as they'd been trained to do, but that was a mistake. We were to the side of them, and above them, and below. Nothing was ahead but a dead end.

Literally.

Because once they were ahead of us, with a shouted order in Yiddish, the fight began. It was mostly gunfire and a few grenades, but it took surprisingly little to scatter their lines and force a retreat.

"That was easy," Yitzchak said.

Too easy. They'd be back.

And they were, only fifteen minutes later. But this time, the advancing army was accompanied by three tanks. Again, we were ready.

"Let's stop them," I whispered, holding my hand out to Esther.

But she only grinned over at me. "This one's mine." She pulled a match from our matchbook, lit the rag on the outside of a fuel-filled wine bottle, and threw it into the street, smashing the bottle directly on the nearest tank. The spilled liquid immediately ignited and would have done little good, except others had the same idea. Something must have leaked inside the tank because suddenly the top hatch burst open like a popped cork. Flames shot from within the tank. The entire thing was on fire.

"Evacuate!" someone shouted from within our bunker. "That thing's gonna explode!"

Esther, Yitzchak, and I grabbed what remained of our weapons and scurried to a lower floor, but we were still only halfway down the stairs when the explosion shook the walls and chunks of ceiling fell around us.

"Now there are two tanks," Esther said, nimbly dodging another piece of falling plaster as we ran. We followed the rest of our group into a neighboring building and were told to find new positions. Esther and I ran up to the third floor, where I hoped to see another round of explosions, but by the time we found a window, the remaining two tanks were retreating. An entire column of German soldiers had been hiding behind the tanks, but our grenades and gunfire took care of them.

A woman at the far end of the room from me sat back against the wall, nodding as if an enormous weight had been lifted from her shoulders. "German blood. At long last, the blood spilled in the ghettos is not from the Jews."

She was right, but I couldn't cheer for that either. I wanted a world in which *no* blood must be spilled. A world free of hatred that made a fight such as this necessary.

The walls rattled sharply, ending the celebration around me. We rushed to the windows, but wherever that explosion came from, it was at least a few blocks away, a reminder that success on one corner did not guarantee success elsewhere.

"They're in retreat!" a man shouted up from the floor below. "Wait where you are until we get further orders."

The same woman who spoke earlier passed around some rusk bread and we shared drinks from a few bottles of water. It was rust-colored, which couldn't possibly be healthy, but then, I was hiding in a war zone surrounded by impassable walls and German soldiers. Dirty water was the least of my concerns.

After an hour, Tamir came with a radio and a report from elsewhere in the ghetto.

"The Germans have left . . . for now," he said. "One of our fighters is dead, only one, which is a miracle, but still one dead."

I almost couldn't believe my ears. Only one dead, when so many Germans had fallen?

Don't feel hope, I reminded myself. Don't let yourself believe that this is over.

But I did hope, and I did wonder if maybe we had a chance. I knew it was foolish, even dangerous, to dwell on what I knew to be impossible, but I couldn't help it. What if we did make a difference here?

The radio was switched on and tuned to the German broadcast; everyone who was not assigned to keep watch elsewhere huddled around it to listen. For those who didn't speak German, Tamir gave the translation.

At first he smiled. "They call us bandits. Perhaps we are."

I smiled too. I considered that a compliment.

Then his face darkened. "The commander of this first wave is being replaced. That means they will return with a new strategy, and an officer determined to prove himself to his superiors."

Another smile now. "The new commander has rejected a call for aircraft bombers. He says it's not necessary against vermin such as us."

This was good news. It meant the Germans were underestimating us, just as we underestimated them early in the war. They believed we were incapable of sustaining an attack fierce enough to require a bomber. They'd think differently before this day was over.

Which left a pit in my stomach. Before this day was over, they would have changed their minds. They would send in a plane to bomb us, sooner or later.

Despite what the radio said, I was sure it'd be sooner.

THIRTY-NINE

April 19, 1943
Warsaw Ghetto

By noon, the strategy of the Germans' new commander became clear: mass force. Our radio alerted us to his call for more troops and vehicles.

Good. If they were here, they could not be on the front lines or tormenting innocent people in the death camps. I *wanted* them here.

Esther took the news better than I expected, but I leaned over to her. "That package you were supposed to deliver. Could we use it now?"

"No," she said. "Not yet."

Yitzchak leaned over to me with a wry smile. "There's no package, you know."

Perhaps not, but even if there was, it was probably already too late. Esther could not have brought along anything that could save us now.

The Germans entered the ghetto once again through the

north gate, but this time, rather than marching in organized columns that were easy for us to pick apart, they came in fast, shooting, then diving for cover, then shooting and moving again. We fired back, of course, but by the time we found one man, he'd already moved on to a different place. Some of us were good shots, but many of the fighters had never held a gun before today.

Tamir shouted for us to move to the rooftops and attics. There, we hoped to be out of reach of the German bullets, but plenty able to drop explosives on them.

I set my gun into the makeshift holster at my side. Then Esther and I followed our group up the stairs. Once we emerged onto the rooftop, four stories high, I drew in a sharp breath. I'd never been up here before. In fact, I'd never been this high up in my entire life.

From here, I saw much of Warsaw, and the view unnerved me. In the distance, the Polish and German neighborhoods were full of spring blossoms and children playing in a park, while mothers cradled their infants and gossiped with one another about the struggles of feeding a family with far more rations than my people were ever allowed.

More important, I saw the gathering of German troops and tanks outside the ghetto walls: ten times the number of soldiers who had been ordered in here so far. Some were spreading out across the city to quell any further uprisings before they started.

"They must be afraid of the violence spreading," Esther whispered.

"Why?" I asked. "Do they really think those people would skip their midday tea to help save lives?"

"I need more ammunition," a man nearby called out. "Who has extra?"

No one responded. No one had extra. I had only three or four shots left in my gun and had to conserve them for now. Between Esther, Yitzchak, and me, we had just five grenades left. More supplies remained in our bunker, but we'd have to break through a hundred or more enemy soldiers to get there.

By four o'clock in the afternoon, another mass of troops began to roll in, far greater than anything we'd seen yet. From our count on the rooftops, there were several more tanks and armored cars, our estimation of two thousand SS men, two battalions of German police, as many as four hundred Polish police, and perhaps other forces as well. We'd also begun to see some signs of fighting outside the ghetto, individual Poles who were finally taking their own opportunity to fight.

But as always, it wasn't enough. It would never be enough.

We dropped grenades, Molotov cocktails, and for that matter, anything we could find that might create trouble for the Germans below. The bulk of the fighting moved north of us, where another ZOB cell was firing at the Germans with a machine gun they'd acquired. It represented the fourth battle of the day in our area alone. I wished I knew what was happening elsewhere in the ghetto.

"Leave the rooftop!" Tamir called to our group, his tone taking on a sudden urgency. "We've got to move deeper into the ghetto. Now!"

"Why?"

Even before the question left my mouth, I got my answer. From our vantage point, a single airplane crossed the horizon. A bomber.

They had called in a bomber.

I knew they would, but I didn't expect it today. The order would have come from the same commander who only this morning dismissed our threat as a mild skirmish. Now he'd seen what we could do.

I should've been terrified at the sight of the bomber, its sights already fixed on us, perhaps on the very building on which I stood. But I felt no fear. If we required such a response from the Germans, then this in itself was a victory. Perhaps on our own, the resistance fighters of the Warsaw Ghetto could not get the attention of the world. But we'd certainly demanded the attention of the Nazis, and their response surely would be noticed by the Allies.

Not in time to save us, of course. But maybe we'd prove to the world that the Germans *could* be defeated, that this war could be won.

Yitzchak bundled up our few remaining weapons while I took Esther's hand to ensure we stayed together along the way. We hurried down the stairs, now on a race against a weapon that could flatten every building on this street.

It was obvious where the bomber would drop its load. We only had to look for where they were clearing the ghetto of Germans. Tamir directed us to find shelter in the bunkers as far from the north gate as possible.

But before we could join the others, Tamir grabbed Esther's arm, nodding at the matchbook she was carrying. "I need that."

"The matches?"

He cocked his head toward a warehouse behind us. "Nothing gets left behind for them to scavenge."

Esther handed him the matches and then he ordered us to leave while he ran back into the fighting. We darted into the street, jumping over fallen bodies and debris, but I kept looking back until I saw a plume of black smoke rising where the warehouse had been. Judging by how fast the smoke was spreading, whatever was in that warehouse would be a total loss, a major blow to German supplies.

The Allies had done nothing for us, but Tamir had just done them a great service.

By then, the bomber had arrived over the ghetto. It was painted camouflage green with Nazi symbols on both wings, and trailed a thin line of smoke. I hoped we'd guessed correctly about where it would drop its bomb.

Two doors swung open from beneath the aircraft and three or four objects dropped, not three blocks from us. From here, they looked like oversized animal droppings, but when they landed, the ground beneath us shook twice. The first time from the explosion, and then again from the weight of buildings around the drop site collapsing.

Yitzchak took Esther's arm to steady her, but I fell to my knees and immediately looked back for Tamir.

He still hadn't rejoined us. I didn't know if he was alive or if he'd been caught in that explosion. I didn't know if all our people escaped the area, or if any of them were now trapped between the Germans and the downed building. There was so much I didn't know.

Meanwhile, Esther pointed out an entrance into another bunker, one we had helped to build. It was behind a false brick wall in a former apartment but was accessed through an air vent. She crawled through first, then I followed, and Yitzchak went last. Esther shouted out our names in Yiddish to warn the occupants we were coming and not to attack.

When I emerged into the bunker, I stood against the back wall beside Esther, neither of us saying a word. Yitzchak started to speak when he came through but quickly fell silent. Both fighters and civilians huddled together inside, holding each other in obvious grief and utter despair. But it wasn't about the bomber. Something else was wrong.

"What's happened?" Esther asked.

"They found the hospital," a man said, not even looking

up at us. "They killed everyone inside. Revenge for our fighting."

"They were all going to die anyway," someone behind me said. "We knew that from the beginning."

"It wasn't that they killed the people there," a woman added. "It's *how* they did it. Pure evil, nothing less."

I didn't ask. I didn't want to know, or think about it. I took Esther's hand again and whispered that the victims were at peace now.

But the mood in the bunker grew heavier with each passing minute. No one talked, no one looked at anyone else. We sat in silence to wait until we received orders otherwise. After an unbearable half hour, Yitzchak began singing. Softly, respectfully, in honor of our dead.

My brother's song made me sad, but I also felt it healing me. As he sang, I took his arm and leaned against his shoulder, reminding myself to keep breathing. For now, that was all I could ask from my body—I was exhausted both physically and emotionally. Tomorrow would come far too soon, and when it did, I'd still have two good legs, a fresh supply of weapons, and an increased certainty that I was right to have come here.

When Yitzchak finished, we sang another song together, and then another. And when we became silent again, I felt a little better.

By eight o'clock that night, a note was dropped into the bunker inviting anyone outside who'd like to come. The

Germans had left our part of the ghetto for the night and there was something out there that the ghetto commanders thought we'd want to see.

Yitzchak and I were among the first to leave, but once we got down to the street, many other people were already there. I followed their line of sight to the top of a building in Muranowski Square. Someone had placed two flags on the roof, large enough and high enough that they should be visible from most places in Warsaw. One was the red-and-white Polish flag. The other was the blue-and-white Jewish flag.

It was supremely defiant, and I couldn't help but smile. No doubt it would add fuel to the Germans' anger, and spirit to the hearts of Polish citizens. It simply made me proud.

Together, we gathered to say a quick prayer for the dead before returning to our bunkers, waiting on the streets to give time for the civilians to go in first. As they did, Esther turned to me and said, "I'd forgotten."

"Forgotten what?"

She shrugged. "What it feels like to be free."

Yitzchak chuckled. "We're hardly free, Esther."

"We've never been more free. Don't you see? They don't control us anymore. Since we already know how this will end, they can't even use the fear of death against us. There is nothing more they can take from us, but today, we have taken their superiority, and their belief in our submissiveness. No matter how this ends, history will recognize today for its greatness."

Yitzchak smiled beside her. "You're right. Perhaps we have already won."

I took both their hands, drawing us into a circle. "Tomorrow will bring a new day of freedom, then. Whatever else it brings, we will never live in a finer time."

FORTY

April 20, 1943
Warsaw Ghetto

The second day of fighting was also the fifty-fourth birthday of the Führer, Adolf Hitler. For his birthday, he would likely have sausage and potatoes and a hearty slice of birthday cake to go with a glass of wine. He would dine seated on a padded chair with his closest friends and dogs nearby, and be surrounded by high-ranking Nazis who would assure him that the genocide of the Jewish people would be complete any day now. And they would toast to that.

I woke up determined to disappoint him. So when we heard a vehicle driving through the ghetto streets, I reached for my gun. But Yitzchak's quick peek from our bunker informed us that this was not a soldier, only a man in a black coat with a loudspeaker. His car stopped thirty meters from our bunker, making it easy to hear his introduction of himself as a member of the former Judenrat. Or, rather, making it impossible for us *not* to hear him.

I scowled and checked the ammunition I'd loaded into the gun last night.

"My fellow Jews of the Warsaw Ghetto, listen to me."

I snorted with disgust at the mention of *his* fellow Jews. We were nothing of the sort. "Is it your father?" a man near us asked Esther.

Others within our bunker must have been wondering the same thing. Or, at least, they leaned forward to hear her answer, failing to notice how her back stiffened and fists clenched. As far as we knew, Esther's father was dead. That man couldn't have known how unkind his question was.

After a few shallow breaths, Esther shook her head. "But I know his voice. I know him. They must be forcing him to do this."

The Judenrat official continued, "Lay down your arms and surrender. If you refuse, the ghetto will be razed to the ground. My friends, I beg you to surrender or everyone here will die."

Everyone here will die? Yes, perhaps we would, but what did he think the consequences would be if we surrendered? We would not give up so easily.

I looked around at the others within this bunker, most people leaning against the walls, grim-faced and with heads hanging low.

"Well?" I asked. "If you want to leave, now is your chance. Although you must know where you will go from here."

They all knew. No one moved.

I creaked open the door of our bunker to get a sense of what was happening in other areas of the ghetto. The streets remained silent, except for the lone car escorting the Judenrat man.

Then a single shot was fired from a building overhead. It hit the car, which might not have been the intended target. But it was a decisive answer. Our official refusal of his generous offer to go to the death camps today. But thank you for asking.

Within an hour of his hasty departure, the Germans returned. This time we met them at Muranowski Square with fresh Molotov cocktails and a renewed determination to make yesterday's fighting seem like a warm-up.

We also had two stolen machine guns, each one capable of firing six hundred rounds of bullets per minute. These guns could chew up concrete streets faster than the Germans could escape on them, emptying our ammunition so fast it would sound like pulling a zipper.

Esther and I watched it unfold from a building overlooking the square. When we could help contain the retreating soldiers, we did. She filled each bottle with flammable liquid, lit it, then immediately passed it to me for throwing. My arm should've been getting tired, but if anything, each throw felt stronger than the one before. Our side was taking casualties today, but so was theirs. After an initial skirmish, they backed off to regroup. It wouldn't last long, but it did give us time to collect our wounded.

Which was the beginning of one of the first truly awful choices we had to make. We were ordered onto the street, now strewn with far too many of our own, either dead or wounded. I didn't know where to begin.

Because who should we help? Our medical supplies were limited. We had only a few civilians in this part of the ghetto with any significant medical training.

"Not everyone can be saved," Esther whispered.

She was right. Some of our fighters had wounds too serious for us to treat. Maybe we could make them comfortable, but nothing more. When the Germans returned, the dead would have to be left behind, unburied, unceremoniously abandoned. But who of the living could we save?

I hated this.

Reluctantly, we entered the streets, each breath drawing in the chemical residue of the explosions, the odor of sweat and fear, the smell of blood. From my position, I saw at least twenty fallen Jews. Half were already dead, or so near to it that I already knew they were beyond help. But close by was a woman with a gash on her arm, the same one who yesterday morning had celebrated the German blood in the streets. It was easy to send her back into the bunker. From there, the decisions became harder.

I knew very little about medical care, and apparently no one else had any better understanding of what we should do. How should we choose? Would we save one life at the expense of another?

To my right, a man was lying on the ground with some sort of head wound. If it was wrapped, could we stop the bleeding, or did the damage run too deep for the few bandages we had? To my left, a boy near my own age seemed to have a broken leg. It wasn't life-threatening, but we had no way to set the bone. When it came time to evacuate the bunkers, would he be left behind anyway? Or would we have to risk two other lives to carry him out?

I didn't know. How was I supposed to know?

I was a courier. I was the person who figured out ways for people to live. Not the person who decided which people must be left to die.

Esther walked toward the man with the head wound, the most serious of the injuries around us. "I'll stay with him as long as I can, or until it's no longer necessary." She sat beside him, putting his head on her lap and talking to him. Whatever she was saying, the tension seemed to leave his body.

I helped carry the boy with the broken leg back to the bunker, but by the time we emerged, the sound of vehicles rumbled into the ghetto. They were back.

Yitzchak handed me my knapsack, filled with what remained of my allotment of weapons for the day. There were fewer than yesterday, which meant I had to be smarter, bolder.

Bold enough to attack the armored vehicle lumbering down this street, looking like a cross between a tank and a Maybach car. The gunner sat up higher than the driver, with a long-barrel machine gun capable of shooting through an entire floor of an apartment building in only seconds.

It could kill hundreds of us, even thousands, before the end of the day.

We had to stop it.

Just after it passed me, a sniper from somewhere above found the gunner, who keeled over his gun, dead. The vehicle stopped as its driver realized they had been targeted, making it easier for me to dart out from the alley where I'd been hiding. I already had a grenade in hand, pulled the pin, then tossed it into the gunner's open hatch. I began counting: 3 . . . 2 . . . 1.

Although I was running away, the explosion knocked me off my feet. My ears rang with a high-pitched squeal, but I knew enough to get up and run. I was barely up again before another armored car arrived, larger than the one I'd just attacked. It rolled almost directly ahead of me on the street, seemingly unaware that I was there, and immediately began pummeling the apartment buildings surrounding us. I fell to the ground, almost exactly where I'd helped the boy with the broken leg, covering my head with my arms, screaming against the deafening noise of shattering glass and wood. Brick shrapnel flew around me like thrown confetti, some of it landing on top of my legs and back. I didn't know how many of our resistance members were already stationed inside the buildings, or how safe it would be for them to escape. These buildings were already dilapidated.

Bullets would bite through them as though the walls were made of paper.

When the gunner paused to get into a new position, I ran farther from the vehicle, my ears still ringing violently from the blasts. I stayed low as I headed toward the nearest building, hoping I hadn't been spotted. Hoping even more that Esther and Yitzchak were blocks from here by now.

Down a narrow alley between buildings, I found a trash bin made of thick metal. Maybe it wouldn't be thick enough, but it was the best of my options. I dove in, covering myself with the garbage and pushing it all in front of me as if that might make any difference. I gagged from the putrid odor but forgot it entirely only seconds later when the machine gun began firing again, somewhere near me. Near enough that I was sure the gunner had spotted me, but wasn't sure exactly where I'd gone.

It's impossible to know how long it went, maybe fifteen minutes. Maybe half a lifetime. Even fifteen minutes with a gun like that, and he probably turned the buildings into Swiss cheese. They just might collapse on their own.

What if Esther and Yitzchak were in one of them? What if they were trapped or injured or out there searching for me? I had to know.

It terrified me to come out, but I had to know.

Cautiously, I emerged from the trash bin. Smoke lingered in the air and the street echoed with collapsing pieces of the targeted buildings. The one behind me was full of holes, but

I darted inside anyway. It seemed to be empty, but I knew people had hidden in here earlier today. Where was everyone?

The fighting had stopped on the streets, and when I peered through a hole, I understood why. German soldiers had arrived, hundreds of them. They were sweeping through the buildings and dragging our fighters out with them, forcing them onto their knees in long rows on the streets.

I counted the number of captured men and women. Ten, then twenty. Forty and growing. I didn't see Esther or Yitzchak. But they were still bringing people out.

Worse, another squadron of Germans came from deeper in the ghetto, escorting with them long lines of civilians. I didn't know if they'd figured out how to breach our bunkers, or if these were Jews from the wild territories. It didn't matter. They kept coming, endless lines of my people, hands on their heads, marching to their last moments of what little freedom we'd had these past few months. Each was placed on their knees, row by row by row.

Then the corner of my eye caught a bit of movement. A fighter rose from her knees with a gun she must have been hiding before. She took aim at one of the commanding officers and fired, hitting him squarely in the chest.

Immediately, another officer gave the order to shoot, and every Jew on the street was killed.

Every. Single. One.

I crouched low, closing my eyes tight and covering my ears with my hands. But no matter how hard I pressed them in, trying to block out the brave final words of *Shema Yisrael*, it wasn't enough.

Just as our manpower was not enough. Our weapons were not enough. Our help from the outside was not enough.

And death. How could the Nazis *still* have not had enough of death?

FORTY-ONE

April 20, 1943
Warsaw Ghetto

By midafternoon, I began to see the first major flaw in our plan. We'd expected hand-to-hand combat with the Germans. Expected them to separate as they searched the apartment buildings, one room at a time. In that way, we would divide and conquer. Hence, the knives and sharpened sticks and wires.

But with one armored car, they'd made an entire street corner uninhabitable and instantly killed several hundred of our people. People who never had the chance to fight close up.

People who never had a chance to defend themselves. We knew this was how it would end, didn't we?

I knew it, and I didn't. I had never expected the scent of death to be so raw, the very air around us as brittle as ice. I never expected to be one of the fighters still on my feet when so many others, far more experienced than I, had fallen.

For now, the fiercest fighting had moved into the Brushmakers District, away from my area, which allowed me time to find Esther and Yitzchak. I hoped that wherever they'd gone, they were together, helping each other. Keeping each other alive.

I began searching bunkers, apartments, anywhere a person might hide, but it was no use. No one had seen them, and when Esther's name was mentioned, I got the response that maybe she'd joined the Nazis, like her father had.

"Since the day I met her, Esther has been fighting to save Jewish lives," I argued. "She could have hidden, could have surrendered, or she could be sitting here in a bunker like all of you. You owe her more respect than this."

That humbled them. It certainly humbled me. Esther had never been my burden for this mission. Not when I'd learned so much from her.

By four in the afternoon, I'd made my way to Lezsno Street in time to see an advancing tank accompanied by an entire German column. I knew we buried a land mine just ahead, so I wouldn't waste my weapons here. Instead, I ducked into a nearby building that at one time had been a furniture store, where women in high heels might've stood for hours debating which cabinet best displayed their china. Now I waited beneath a hole where a window had once been, crouching on top of shards of shattered glass and empty bullet casings.

"Chaya!" someone whispered.

I turned to see Yitzchak headed toward me. Just Yitzchak.

"Where's Esther?"

He shrugged. "I haven't seen her since this morning. But I was sent here." He lifted himself enough to look through the hole above us. When he lowered himself again, his face had darkened. "It isn't going well. We can't hold out for much longer."

The tank had passed us and was nearly to Smocza Street, where we'd planted the land mine. It was one of our key plans, to lure the largest groups of soldiers here.

I put a hand on Yitzchak's arm and we peeked out the hole again. "Then let's make each moment count. Now, watch!" The explosion would be massive.

But it crossed the street and nothing happened. Nothing. Not a puff of smoke or a bump in the road or any sign of trouble. A sinking feeling filled the room around me. The land mine had failed. This was a heavy disappointment.

Until someone inside the building said, "All right, then, let's take it down ourselves. Go!"

Nodding at each other, Yitzchak and I ran back onto the street. I had a gun in one hand and a Molotov cocktail in the other, waiting to be lit. I intended to use both.

From one of the buildings above us, fighters were already dropping lit cocktails onto the tank, just as we had done the day before. The first five or six merely rolled off, but then one fell directly inside a partially opened hatch, and after a contained explosion, smoke began rising. One soldier crawled out, badly burned. The rest didn't.

The German soldiers on the street responded, firing weapons into every window of the tall buildings around them. The sound of shattering glass came at us in a terrifying pitch, and when larger pieces began falling near us, we ran. I heard an order given in German to shoot any captured Jew on the spot. As if that weren't already their plan.

Gunfire echoed from every direction. Behind us. Toward us. From above and below. Some must be ours. Most of it would be theirs. A bullet whisked over my shoulder. Too close. A hair's difference in aim and I'd be dead.

In response, we dropped lit Molotov cocktails as we ran. They'd create smoke to mask our escape, and hopefully enough heat to discourage the soldiers from pushing through the smoke to chase us. I knew why we had to throw them, but hated the waste of what few supplies we had left.

So if I was going to throw mine, I wanted to make it count. I stopped, turning just long enough to light my cocktail, and took aim at an advancing German. He dodged the worst of it, but before I turned back, an explosion lit into my leg, knocking me flat onto the ground. I leaned up and saw blood spurting from my thigh, almost like everything was happening in sudden slow motion. I'd been shot.

I'd been shot, which came with an indescribable pain. But far worse was my anger that I'd let it happen to me. It wasn't supposed to be like this. If I died in this battle . . .

when I died, I needed to make my final moments count for something. Not this.

I wrapped my hand around the wound and felt Yitzchak's hands beneath my arms, dragging me away. "It's okay," I muttered, gritting my teeth against the fire in my leg. "It's okay."

"It's not."

He dragged me inside a building, out of immediate sight of the advancing Germans, but that left a trail of blood behind, a road map to find us. Once we were inside, he tried to lift me, but it was a clumsy attempt that left me gasping and begging him to stop.

I tried to be firm, the bossy older sister he used to know. "Leave me here, Yitz. They can't help me in the bunkers."

"You don't know that."

"I do! If I saw someone with this injury on the streets, I'd have to leave them, and you have to leave me."

"Stop that! We just need—"

"Chaya?" Esther ducked her head into the building. "They told me you were in here. They told me—" She stopped when she saw my leg. "Oh no." Without a second's pause, she knelt beside me and removed her shoulder bag, then used a knife to cut the handle off. "Yitzchak, I need your water."

He had a half-full bottle with him, but immediately passed it to Esther. She poured it over the wound, then pressed on my thigh, apologizing the entire time if it hurt. I choked back the scream inside me, gritting my teeth while she tied the shoulder bag's handle over the wound, getting Yitzchak's help with the knot.

She leaned closer and whispered, "I can see where the bullet entered and then exited. We've got to stop the bleeding, but any of the women in the bunkers with a good sewing kit can take care of that. Let's go."

A sewing kit. They'd stitch me up like a wool skirt. I was already feeling nauseous at the thought of it. Then I remembered what the Germans did to Esther's hand, how much more that must have hurt, and I vowed not to complain anymore about my injury, at least, not aloud.

Once the column of Germans passed, Yitzchak carried me out a back entrance of the building and down into a nearby bunker. By the time they lowered me onto a bed, my stomach was in knots. Yitzchak held my hand while Esther explained what needed to be done. That wasn't necessary. An older woman with a kind face and a nearly threadbare head scarf was already pulling out a needle and thread.

"My name is Rosa Kats," she said. "I can help you, but you must be a very different kind of brave down here."

Rosa Kats. Why did that name sound familiar?

The question soon escaped my thoughts, especially when alcohol was dumped over the wound and I wanted to leap from my skin. I was determined not to yell or cry out, but when she stuck the needle in, it hurt almost more than being shot. Esther had my hands and Yitzchak held my leg down, but that was to keep me still, not to comfort me.

I felt each stitch, and stars swam in my vision, but Rosa continued to work, mumbling phrases the entire time about how I needed to be strong. Minutes later, the thread that was meant for darning socks and patching holes in pants closed a gash in my flesh. She wrapped the leg with one of the bandages I'd brought in here when we first came and offered me an aspirin. I wanted as many as was safe to take, but these too were rationed. I got one, only one. It would barely touch the pain I felt, but I swallowed it anyway.

"You've got to stay in the bunkers now," Yitzchak said. "And we're needed out there."

"I can help." I wasn't sure how, but I was useless in here.

Esther smiled. "Remember the advice you gave me once? Sometimes the best help you can give is to stay out of the way."

She was right, and besides, I couldn't stand on my leg right now, much less fight on it. Ripples of pain ran in currents throughout my whole body and I was having trouble keeping my eyes open.

Outside on the streets, the fighting continued amid shouts and screams, explosions, and the sound of vehicles that seemed to roll almost on top of our underground bunker, crowded entirely with women and a few children. Together we prayed, held one another close, and talked in soft voices about what would happen when we were discovered.

When, not *if*.

A pretty young mother leaned in to me and whispered,

"Those who are captured up there, are they being arrested, or is it . . . worse?"

For the first time since I joined the resistance, I lied to my own people. "They've been arrested, nothing more. For now, they're fine."

Everyone who heard me breathed an audible sigh of relief and the tension in the bunker calmed. I shouldn't have lied; these people deserved to know the truth. But the truth would do them more harm than good. And as they settled in for the night, so did I.

The sound of gunfire and explosions above me became nothing more than a backdrop for my dreams.

CHAPTER
FORTY-TWO

April 21, 1943
Warsaw Ghetto

I slept all night and for most of the next day. At some point during that time, I got up long enough to try balancing on my injured leg, but it collapsed. When I tried again that afternoon, I could stand and even hobble about with a little help, which was good enough for me. I asked for my knapsack.

"You're not going back out there," the older woman who stitched me up said. What was her name again? Rosa Kats?

I remembered! With a smile, I touched her arm. "I met your son, in Lodz."

A spark appeared in her eyes. "My son? He's still alive?"

"He wants you to know that he loves you, and that you were right."

It was all I had to say. She nodded. "Mothers always are." She put her hand over mine as it rested on her arm. "Our children never know how much we love them."

I thought again of my parents. Did they know that I loved them? Did they think of me in their last moments? I wished they could have known Yitzchak was still alive. It would have given my mother so much peace.

"Now you must get back in bed." Mrs. Kats was already leading me there. I started to protest, but she added, "You'll only get in the way out there. Back in bed."

Thirty people were crowded into this bunker with only one bed available. Whoever was supposed to have their turn in it right now, I doubted they wanted me still using it. At the same time, it felt good to have a mother again, even for one more night. And her advice must have been wise. Within minutes, I was asleep again.

I awoke later that same evening to the sound of static filling the air. The women in here had my radio and were trying to find a signal to connect them to the outside world. Finally, they caught a broadcast in English from the BBC in London, and the young mother began translating for the rest of us. The reporter was describing some sort of conference with several European and American leaders. They were discussing what should be done for the Jews still trapped in Nazi-occupied Europe. The Allies had almost completely ignored us thus far. It was astonishing that they even bothered to meet on our behalf.

For two minutes, the reporter blathered on about the complex issues surrounding our situation, and about Allied priorities and disagreements. But he said nothing about solutions, about the death camps, or even about basic compassion.

I scowled. "It sounds like the only thing these leaders agree on is that there *are* Jews in Europe."

"And that's probably all they will agree on," another woman added. "What more must happen for them to help us?"

They wouldn't help. Not when the American president spoke of "spreading the Jews thin" and dismissed the atrocities against us as "sob stuff." When Canada responded to the question of how many Jewish refugees they would accept with "none is too many." At least the British government seemed more sympathetic.

I sat up, again reaching for my knapsack, but the older woman pushed me down. "It's gone quiet for now. There's no one out there for you to fight."

"I'm feeling better—"

A woman waved at us to be silent, then turned the radio a little louder. This time it cut to a different message. I heard only the end of it in English, but the announcer repeated it in Polish. Then before anyone could translate, he spoke in Yiddish. "This message is from the Allied armies to our Jewish friends in the Warsaw Ghetto in Poland."

"Our *friends*?" a woman began. "A minute ago they couldn't even agree we need help and now we're friends?"

She was quickly hushed in time for the announcer to continue, "We know what is happening there, but we also know you are dying as heroes. For every one of you who falls, we will take revenge."

He quickly moved on to another story, but here in the bunker, each of us was still pondering every word in our heads. It was the first time I'd heard any of the Allies acknowledge our situation, and certainly the first time they'd called us heroes.

If only that were true. The fight here had nothing to do with heroism. It was about taking a final stand, defending our dignity and honor, and drawing the world's attention to us, even if only for a brief moment. Nothing about that was heroic, but still, I liked hearing the word.

The old woman offered me a bowl of cold soup and caught the lingering smile on my face. "You want to be a hero, child, then eat with us now, and take one more night to rest. I'm sure plenty of trouble awaits us tomorrow."

I listened for any sounds of gunfire or tanks, or shouts of orders. Hearing nothing, I was satisfied. One more night.

FORTY-THREE

April 22, 1943
Warsaw Ghetto

As it turned out, I didn't have the entire night. Rounds of gunfire erupted early in the morning, echoing throughout the ghetto. Even with my injured leg, I knew I had to be out there.

I clumsily rolled my pants leg down over the bandage, avoiding the looks from the other women, everything from disapproval to respect and appreciation, none of which made it any easier to leave. It hurt terribly to walk on my leg, but I could walk on it. Running was another matter.

I left the bunker and heard them immediately seal it again from inside. That was good. Those women had probably saved my life. I wanted them to remain safe too.

I hobbled toward Muranowski Square, ignoring the protest in my leg and walking much slower than I wished I could have done. Hopefully, the fighting would still be there when I arrived.

It was, and that was awful news. The exchange of gun-fire in the square was worse than my darkest imaginings. Bullets flew from every direction, explosions burst without warning, and no one seemed to be in command of either side.

A square-faced SS officer suddenly turned and our eyes locked. His hand unfolded, revealing a grenade. From his widening smile, I knew I was his intended target. I started to run, knowing full well I wouldn't get far enough away. He pulled the pin and raised his arm to throw it.

Then a bullet whizzed past my ear, hitting the grenade itself, which exploded in his hand. I didn't know whose gun had just saved my life, but I owed them something better than running away from the fight.

Because of my injury, I would have no chance in any hand-to-hand combat. But I dug into my knapsack for a Molotov cocktail, lit it, and threw it at a soldier who held a machine gun aimed upward at the nearest building. When he fell, I saw some of our own fighters moving in to get the gun. A double victory.

But it was one of the last victories I'd see that day. More soldiers continued arriving, dozens of them replacing every single man we'd brought down. For every bullet of ours, they had unlimited rounds for machine guns. For every small explosion we could create from old light bulbs and petrol, they had tanks with firepower to cut through build-ings and bombers that could level them.

Yet we fought.

I pushed through pain and exhaustion and a mounting death toll that surrounded me on every street, down every alley. Throughout the day, I caught occasional glimpses of Yitzchak, who had joined up with a group of other teen boys to fight. But I never did see Esther, and that bothered me more and more with each passing hour.

By afternoon, I'd emptied my supply of grenades and then did as much damage as I could with my gun. As evening approached, I still had half of my rounds left when a new sound entered the ghetto, somewhere behind me. It turned my stomach and made me retch.

Only one thing could create a sound like that. My worst fears were confirmed when I saw enormous flames shoot into the sky, accompanied by smoke as black as midnight.

Flamethrowers.

The Germans brought in flamethrowers. The ghetto was about to burn.

Orders were shouted for any fighters to move deeper within the ghetto, anywhere to escape the buildings, already glowing with fire.

I found a temporary shelter in a bunker built on a building's rooftop, which was filled with other fighters whose faces probably mirrored my own, where dirt had become encrusted to the brow from sweat, with lips dry from heat and worry, and eyes that had finally accepted what the mind did long ago: It was no longer about *knowing* how the battle would end. We *felt* down to our bones how near the end was.

Still, I nearly cried out with joy and relief when a coded knock came to the bunker door and both Yitzchak and Esther were admitted inside. Yitzchak had blood on his shirt, although I didn't think it was his, and Esther had lost a shoe, but they were both on their feet and I couldn't pull them into a hug fast enough.

When we separated, Yitzchak simply said, "We heard you were here." On any other occasion, they would check on my leg and I would ask about their adventures while I was recovering.

Not tonight.

Now we only looked at one another, empty of any further conversation. Drained of hope. The flamethrowers had gone quiet for now, but their earlier targets inside this ghetto were still burning, and they'd return tomorrow.

The pungent odor of fire filled the air, burning our nostrils and making our eyes water. We headed outside to where we might have a chance for some air, when, above the gunshots and crackling of fire, the strangest noise caught my attention.

Music.

Not hymns of Shabbat, or even songs of comfort or hope.

No, it was a simple tune for children, like what would come from a barrel organ at a carnival. How was that possible?

I limped to the ledge of the building, ignoring Yitzchak's warnings that I'd be seen if I went too close. From here, just past the ghetto walls, a merry-go-round had been set up for Polish children. I couldn't see much through the smoke and haze, only the occasional reflection from the mirrors or a flash of a young girl's pretty skirt. That hadn't been there a few days ago, I was sure of it. The ride would have been hastily set up by the Germans, perhaps to mock us or to pacify the people from joining our revolt.

My fists clenched at the sight of it.

Even if the Germans provided such a sick carnival, no one had to come! No one had to bring their children next to our wall, where they could surely smell the gunpowder and the acrid stench of fire. No one was forced to sit their child on a carousel where they could hear the cries of other children in here, begging to be rescued from their doom.

I clutched my stomach, utterly disgusted, until Yitzchak put an arm around my shoulder.

"Not everyone on the outside is like that," he whispered, pointing to a nearby hillside. "Look."

I followed his gaze to a gathering of Poles in their wagons and on horses. Many of the women and even men looking toward the ghetto walls appeared to be shaking their heads in despair. I was reminded of the hundreds of people who had provided help to us, all at risk to their own lives.

But as I limped back into the bunker, I felt the noose tightening yet again. Surely everyone else in this ghetto felt it as well. But none of us talked about it. None of us talked at all.

It was also true that we had lost much of the joy we felt only a few days ago in anticipation of this battle. Perhaps because the plans we had made with hopefulness were now collapsing beneath the reality of what it was to face an enemy a thousand times stronger than ourselves.

Yet when we settled in for the night, Esther whispered, "Do you regret coming here? We could have stayed in Krakow or even left the country."

My answer was simple: "No regrets." And I meant it.

FORTY-FOUR

April 23, 1943
Warsaw Ghetto

didn't sleep well that night. No one in the bunker did. Who could sleep when we were packed in so tight that only the most seriously injured could lie down? When unidentifiable noises clattered and knocked and banged near the bunker's walls? When every thought was a question of what another day of fighting might bring? Before I was ready for an answer to that question, gunfire erupted below us. Night was over.

"The fires must be spreading," someone observed.

That was obvious. Smoke had wafted into the bunker overnight, stinging my throat until I finally allowed myself a small sip of water from our dwindling supplies. It did nothing for my hoarseness or dryness.

Nothing for my hope.

We prepared for another day against the Germans, more exhausted than when we'd fallen asleep, and nibbled on some rusk bread, which was probably all we'd get today. No one looked directly at anyone else. Few words were spoken.

Until Esther pulled a belt buckle from her shoulder bag and held it out. "When we were gathering weapons from the wounded Germans, I took this. What do these words mean?"

It was a gold buckle with an eagle standing on top of the Nazi swastika. Arched over the image were the words *Gott Mit Uns.*

I closed my eyes and drew in a deep breath, almost unable to answer. "It means 'God With Us.'"

For her to bring that up, today of all days, was stunning. As we celebrated Passover this week, the Christians were preparing for Easter. As part of that, today was their Good Friday, a day that was supposed to be dedicated to seeking forgiveness from God.

How could these soldiers commit such atrocities on this day, all while wearing an emblem that suggested God supported their actions?

This morning, our radio was tuned to a feed that connected us with the Polish Underground. The latest news was announced by the Polish woman in Warsaw whose voice we'd often heard before. Whoever she was, she'd become a vital bridge between resistance groups, broadcasting information from one group to another. I imagined how eagerly the Germans were searching for her. Information was power, and she'd become a source for both.

She said, "Members of the Polish Underground, citizens

of Warsaw and surrounding areas, all those who yearn to be free. Surely you have noticed the Jewish Quarter here is under attack by the invaders. Their resistance leaders have issued a plea for help. They need weapons and ammunition. They need people who will fight, both from inside and outside the walls. They need your help, not for their own sake, but for the freedom of Warsaw, the freedom of Poland. Please help."

Yitzchak snorted. "What help? Many of the weapons we bought from the underground are defective. They jam, or worse, they backfire. They took our money and gave us weapons they can't use anyway."

I cursed again and didn't care if Esther heard it. Maybe the underground didn't know. Maybe their own weapons were just as bad.

But maybe they knew exactly what they were selling. They wanted our money and cared nothing for our lives.

"We can't expect help from outside the ghetto," Yitzchak said. "And if we do get any, it will be too little, too late."

I agreed. Though by the time we returned to the street, my mind snapped to another day's fighting, already under way. The pink-colored clouds suggested that anywhere else in Warsaw, a beautiful spring morning was rising, the hazy sunrise fueled by the fires still burning within these walls. And here, among ashes and debris and the growing scars of our battles, we saw far too many fallen resistance fighters, a few of them people I considered friends, people I'd laughed with only a few days ago as we pledged our lives and our honor to one another. They held to their pledge, and probably very soon I would have to do the same. It had been a terrible night for the ghetto. And today promised to be worse.

Without the advantage of nearby buildings in which to hide, we were forced to attack from half-exposed positions behind still-burning walls, in open ditches, and always at greater distances than we wanted.

"We're stationed too far away to be effective," Yitzchak said. "But if we get closer, we'll be shot." He thought about that a moment. "I'm going in closer."

"Don't go!" I wanted to make Yitzchak obey me, just as I used to make him do chores or clean up his messes. But I saw the determination in his eye, the desire to stand tall, the same glimmer of strength I used to see in my father's eyes. Perhaps Yitzchak was meant to finish the fight my father never started, to honor our parents and all they had taught us in our early years, long before they knew where fate would lead us. As hard as it was to say "Be safe," I did, and then turned my attention back to the battle, whispering under my breath, "Find me again soon."

While he ran one way, Esther helped me limp down the street until we found a half-standing building with a hole torn through the wall. It would've taken something more than a machine gun to blast through these thick layers of brick, wood, and plaster, something monstrous. Maybe it accounted for the explosions I heard yesterday.

A small group of Germans ran down the street, unaware of our presence. I injured one with my gun, less than I'd wanted for the sacrifice of a bullet. Esther and I ducked low while several rounds were returned in our direction, but most of the Germans only scurried away.

Once they'd gone, another small group of fighters passed through the room where we were hiding. "Did you hear?" a woman asked. "Fighting has begun from outside the ghetto! It's happening!"

A new surge of hope swelled within me. Could the people of Warsaw truly be responding to that plea for help that we heard on the radio? This was what we'd wanted all along, to spark a movement beyond these walls.

"There aren't many," one man said. "But if it's even one or two, it's a start."

A woman dressed in German armor ducked her head into our room. My first instinct to aim at her was calmed as soon as I recognized her as Tamir's friend Rachel, whom I hadn't seen since the fighting began. As angry as I had been with her for trying to send Esther away, I was glad to see her now. I admired her expression of focus and determination, and tried to mirror it when she looked at me.

She said, "We need your help, down in the tunnels. A fresh supply of weapons has come in from the Polish Underground."

Esther and I followed her out, though I wasn't expecting to see much. Were they the same high-quality toys we'd already paid such dear money for? Weapons that jammed and misfired?

"If they delivered the weapons, they should have stayed here with us to use them," I said.

She smiled back at me. "The delivery came through the Catholic convent near the ghetto. The church allowed us to dig a tunnel into their catacombs, which we've used to evacuate many of our children already. The nuns delivered these weapons, though I daresay we won't ask them to stay and fight."

Despite our grim situation, I found myself smiling too, reminded that there were good and bad people everywhere. The more I embraced those who were good, the more I hoped to dispel the evil from my life.

Whenever possible, Rachel avoided the streets, leading us through buildings when possible, and through back alleys when necessary. About halfway there, we stepped into an alley, and a German shouted at us and fired a shot. It grazed my shoulder but I returned fire until he fell. Seconds later, Rachel had collected his gun and packs of ammunition. Since my gun had just been emptied, Rachel gave me everything she'd found.

We reached the tunnel beneath the square, and indeed, a small pile of weapons and ammunition awaited us, as well as some fresh bottles of water and a little dried meat.

"We've got to take all of it out in one load," Rachel instructed. "We can't risk another trip back here."

"There's too much," I said. "Even if we divide the load into thirds, we can't carry our share."

But Esther stepped forward with a white tablecloth that must have decorated someone's Passover table a few days ago. "Today is the Sabbath. Would it be wrong to use this?"

"I'm sure it is," I said, then reached for the tablecloth. "But it is a good solution."

We laid out the cloth and piled everything on top of it. Then Rachel took two corners, and Esther and I each took one, to lift the weapons. It was still heavy, but together, we were managing.

The problem was the thickening air around us.

Smoke.

"The flamethrowers," I said. "The building above us is on fire!" Which meant there would be Germans at the exits to shoot us as we left.

If we left. I was already coughing from the smoke, and my eyes were stinging like needles had been poked into them.

"We can load these weapons," Esther said. "Shoot them before they get us."

Rachel shook her head. "There will be more of them than us. And if we die here, then we lose this entire cache. Listen carefully: Go back to the tunnels, and stay there until it's safe to come out. You must get these weapons into the hands of our fighters!"

"What about you?" I asked.

"We've stashed other supplies on the upper floors. I'll collect what I can."

"No." I didn't want her to go. "The fire—"

"Is burning fast. I can't waste time here. Obey your orders."

She waved us away, back into the tunnels. I hoisted my half of the tablecloth higher over my shoulder, determined to bear more of the weight than Esther. When I turned around again to look for Rachel, she'd already disappeared in the smoke.

It would be the last time I saw her alive.

FORTY-FIVE

April 24, 1943
Warsaw Ghetto

Night had given us little sleep and no rest. Exhaustion was wearing on my concentration, my ability to respond to our widening losses. Beyond that, my leg ached fiercely, whether I put pressure on it or not, and I'd lost track of what day it was. It didn't matter.

When I mentioned that aloud, Esther reminded me. "We missed Shabbat last night. I don't suppose we'll be honoring it today either."

I didn't have the energy to shrug that off. "Perhaps not. But we will honor our people today as best we can."

It wouldn't be much of an honor. Estimates of our dead now numbered into the hundreds, far more than the number of Germans we'd killed. And their plan to burn the buildings was working better than they could have imagined. By the end of the day, there would be more fires and more deaths.

It had taken Esther and me most of the night to drag the

heavy cache of weapons out of the tunnels, ready to hand them over to friends and fighters who no longer existed. Once we emerged, I wished we had never come out.

Building by building, the soldiers were shooting flames into every floor, turning the air around us into a furnace. With fewer places to retreat, our people were being discovered in greater numbers. Some threw out mattresses and jumped from upper-story windows, only to be shot upon landing. Others remained where they were, their final *Shema Yisrael* swallowed up in the smoke. Some were finally forced to surrender, offering up any weapons they had. They were arrested and put onto the waiting trains. I didn't want that fate, but if it came, I would find a way to continue fighting from within the extermination camps. I would always find a way.

I'd lost track of where Yitzchak might be, but after Esther and I delivered the weapons to a supply bunker, we moved deeper into the ghetto. By then, my goals had changed. At my core, I was a courier first. It was my job to get into the impossible places so that others could escape them. When I shared my plan with Esther, she readily agreed.

We had to move ahead of the fires and warn everyone still in bunkers to leave the buildings. We didn't have much time.

We had no time at all, and far too much ground to cover.

It was slow work. I still couldn't run, and the smoke had tarnished my throat to the point that my yells carried on the wind like whispers. I banged my gun on anything metal, hoping that at least it would be heard by those in hiding. I dragged myself up each flight of stairs, yelling, "Get out, get out!" and did the same on my way down. I accepted every offer from others to help, but begged them to move ahead of me and clear the buildings.

By the time I was on the street leaving my second building, Esther was at least a block ahead of me, trailing civilians behind her as they moved to safer quarters. I was angry with myself for having been shot, for having been slowed down by one careless moment. I had to go faster.

But as I headed toward the third building, I heard the buzz of another airplane overhead. My knotted stomach twisted tighter. Another bomber had come.

It turned at the last moment and dropped its load several blocks ahead of us, leveling a building we had yet to enter. Explosions rattled the ground beneath me, and a massive cloud of dust and debris rose into the air, enough to flatten that quadrant of the ghetto. Most of those who had emptied out of the bunkers ran down side streets, hoping to find new bunkers that might escape the soldiers' attention. But Esther and I only hurried forward, hoping to get more people out before the bombers returned. Or before the fires caught up with us.

Behind us, four Nazis were headed this way. Two held flamethrowers and the other two were watching for snipers. Flames spurted both right and left, creating so much light in front of them that they hadn't seen me yet.

I turned and ran, hoping to get into hiding before they

noticed me. My leg screamed with pain, as if the fire from those Nazis was already inside my flesh. Somewhere back here was a bunker, partially hidden between these buildings, but when I found it, the door was open and the space had been abandoned. Smoke poured from vents that were supposed to have supplied fresh air to the bunkers, not choked them out. This would be the fate of every other bunker eventually.

I couldn't see Esther anymore, but still I ran, heat licking at my back and spurring me on even faster. The flamethrowers swept in fiery lines across the building I'd just been in.

"A Jew girl!" one of the Nazis called. They'd seen me.

Shots were fired, but I'd already fallen flat on the ground, the bunker door almost within my reach. If they saw me fall, I hoped they'd think I was hit. Or better still, I hoped that through the thick smoke, they could no longer see me at all.

They moved on to the next building without checking for me, which wasn't a surprise. They understood as well as I did that I was trapped. The tall ghetto wall was behind the bunker, but I could never scale it with my injured leg. From here, I couldn't see any gaps beneath the walls, nor could I dig one out with my bare hands. Not in time.

The only way out of the fire was through the fire.

I drew in a breath of thick air and darted into the bunker. If I was correct, a tunnel passed beneath this one, extending back toward Mila Street. I desperately hoped I was correct.

Smoke had completely filled the upper half of the

bunker, but I bent over and began feeling my way around. I didn't know the layout of this room, and even if I did, items from the people who had stayed here were scattered randomly about, as if they'd left in a hurry. I tripped over a small ladies' bag and fell face-first onto the dirt ground, scraping my hands in the fall. My leg lit with pain, but at least this low the smoke was thinner. I dug into the bag and found a head scarf, which I wrapped around my nose and mouth. Then I crawled, dragging my injured leg behind me, until I found the tunnel entrance at the back of the bunker. I rolled into it and, belowground, took my first breath of clean air. Or slightly cleaner air. There was still smoke down here.

From there, I limped away from the soldiers with the flamethrowers, but I didn't get far before panic rose in me again. Footsteps were coming my way and I'd already caught a glimpse of the person farthest ahead.

German uniforms. The Germans were in the tunnels.

Now I really was trapped.

I backed against the wall and pulled out my gun. I'd lost track of how many bullets remained, but I'd empty what I could on the squadron ahead.

"Don't shoot, don't shoot!" The words were spoken in Yiddish and the accent matched. I didn't fire, but I didn't remove my finger from the trigger either. Not yet.

"You're Chaya Lindner," one man said. I only knew his last name, Pilzer. Or something like that.

I lowered my gun. "What are you all doing?"

Mr. Pilzer gestured to his group. "We're going back up to the streets, to try to stop the flamethrowers. If we're spotted, hopefully the uniforms will fool the Germans, or confuse them long enough to let us get close. Are you all right?"

"I'm fine." It was such a relief to be surrounded by friendly faces, regardless of how they were dressed, that I forgot the pain in my leg.

"I thought you might be OD or Judenrat," I said "They're helping the Nazis now."

He frowned. "The Nazis must have decided they no longer need them. All of the remaining Judenrat and OD were shot earlier today outside Gestapo headquarters."

"Oh." That was all I could spare for them. I knew I should feel something more for those men, but I didn't. They had bargained with a wolf, thinking that could save them. But in the end, the wolf always bites.

"You need to get out of this tunnel," Pilzer continued. "The Germans know about it. That's how we got these uniforms, but more will come through here."

"Where can I go?" I asked. "Where is the fighting?"

"Go wherever there are no soldiers, and do what you can for as long as you can. We are losing the fight. Every minute that passes, more of us fall."

We wished each other good luck before leaving. We said it. But none of us believed in luck anymore.

FORTY-SIX

April 24, 1943
Warsaw Ghetto

Evening slowly approached, following a horrible, endless day passed in a literal haze due to the thick smoke around us, an unyielding, suffocating blanket. Fire roared from nearly every building within my sight, some with flames consuming whole floors at once, and some buildings where the flames had already hollowed out everything but the brick walls, leaving them as empty shells. I stared at the one where I'd hidden after leaving the tunnel, where I might still have been if Pilzer hadn't warned me to leave.

I was in another building now, one of the few in this area not already on fire. I knew that was a risk, that it was surely one of the next targets for their flamethrowers, but it had offered me the best angle to continue to attack soldiers on the street.

So from a broken second-story window, I'd fired the last of my ammunition, and now I was waiting for an opportunity to escape and join the others . . . if there were any others. An hour passed, and then another, but whenever I looked out, SS soldiers seemed to be everywhere. I had to wait and hope this building would stand for as long as I was in it.

The SS was using the street in front of me as a collection point for captured Jews, both unarmed civilians and resistance fighters. The people were separated into two groups. Most of the civilians would live another day on their journey toward the death camps. The other half, mostly the fighters, would die here. At this point, I didn't suppose it mattered which group they were in, not really.

And if I didn't get out of here, they'd find me too. I crept to the main floor of the building, preparing to leave through a hole in the side of the building. A ten-meter gap separated me from the next place where I might hide. I waited for a distraction, taking advantage of the horrible moment that I knew was coming for those on the street. When the soldiers lined up with rifles aimed at the resistance fighters, I ran, faster than I thought possible, considering my injury.

But still not fast enough.

"You, girl!" I didn't turn around, but I knew the soldier was shouting at me. I'd been spotted.

Shots fired in my direction but they hit the building, somewhere over my head. I turned around only long enough to see a handful of civilian Jews back on their feet, fighting with the Nazis. They attacked them for me, as a distraction, giving me a chance to live. Knowing what they'd done would cost them their lives.

The piercing shots of gunfire were the last sounds I heard before darting into the next available building, parts of which were still on fire. I hurried through it, choking on the smoke and dodging falling planks of wood, until I found an entrance to another tunnel. I hoped the Nazis hadn't compromised this one too.

I climbed down inside, closing the latch overhead before too much smoke filled this small space. Then I curled into a ball, wrapping my arms around my legs and trying to keep my thoughts together. What now? Should I go left or right or back to the surface?

In the end, I didn't go anywhere, because I didn't know where to go. I had no more ammunition, no food or water. I didn't know where Yitzchak was, or Esther, or any of the leaders who might yet have another strategy.

Except there were no other strategies, and maybe no more leaders. It felt like the Cyganeria attack all over again. When I was left alone with no idea of what to do next. Only this was far worse.

I closed my eyes to consider my options. There were no more options. Nothing I could do to help save the Jewish people. Or to save myself. Hardly a comforting final thought before I fell asleep.

FORTY-SEVEN

April 25, 1943
Warsaw Ghetto

Chaya!"

I bolted upright, instinctively ready to take a swing at whoever was shaking my shoulder.

Esther was crouched in front of me with Yitzchak beside her. Both had smoke-blackened faces, but they were smiling to see me still alive. It was nothing compared to how I felt seeing them.

"You're both safe?" I asked.

"Safe?" Yitzchak tilted his head. "You can't be serious with that question."

"The fires?"

They exchanged a glance, then looked back at me. "Everything is burning," Yitzchak said. "Now they're flushing out the bunkers by dropping poison gas grenades into the cracks."

I leaned back against the tunnel wall and closed my eyes. "It's over, then?"

"No, the fighting continues," Esther said. "But we have our next set of orders, directly from the top. We're going back to the beginning."

That got my attention. "What beginning?"

"We're couriers," Esther said. "We've done all we can inside this ghetto. Now it's time to get out, and to take as many people with us as possible."

I shook my head. "It's different this time. The ghetto is surrounded. It'd be a miracle for any of us to find a way out."

She took my hand and lifted me to my feet. "Come on, Chaya. I'll show you! It's time."

My eyes narrowed until I finally understood. "Every day for a month I've asked if you delivered that package and you've said—"

"I've said no." Esther smiled. "Until now."

"Because *you* are the package to be delivered." I stepped closer to her. "Or more accurately, you are the package that will deliver us from this ghetto."

She nodded and looked over at me as we walked. "We're leaving through the sewer lines. They're a maze, and some lines have to be avoided because they carry too much water. But this is how I escaped the ghetto before. I know the way out."

For the first time in days, hope seeped into me. "Then let's go."

Yitzchak climbed up to the street first, to make sure everything was clear, then helped Esther up, and they both helped me. My leg was stiff and sore, but the injury was healing. It hurt to walk, but I was steadier on my feet than before. I could manage the sewers. I was determined to.

However, once I was on the street, I forgot my leg entirely. The air was thick with black smoke, creating a morning like midnight. If we were careful, we could use the smoke to get from one place to another without being seen, or burned. The roar of the flames was as loud as a train and the heat was nearly unbearable. Gunfire could still be heard in echoes around the ghetto, so I knew some fighting continued, but most of the resistance seemed to have already collapsed.

SS officers dotted the streets, staring up at the buildings, which were slowly crumbling to ash. I hoped no one had taken shelter in them, believing they'd be safe. Believing they'd survive right up until the moment fire shot through their windows.

I wondered how many fighters and civilians had been killed on the streets. How many survivors had yet to be flushed out from their bunkers? Those who already had been captured were here too, being divided just as I'd seen them last night.

Some groups were lined up against a wall, hands visible, heads down. Others were made to kneel on the stone street. Someone there spotted us, then quickly turned away, unwilling to give us up. I was sure they hoped we had one last grenade or round of weapons to frighten the soldiers away and give these people a chance to escape, but none of us did. Esther only led us out of their sight.

Between the buildings, where the smoke gathered thickest, I choked, my head already swimming from lack of oxygen. The scarf I'd used before had disappeared somewhere, but Yitzchak pulled some empty glass bottles from a bag he carried and pushed one against his face. "It's not a lot of air," he said through his jar, "but it will help."

It did help, a little. At least I wasn't directly inhaling smoke and ash, and death. It helped enough to get us to a sewer entrance on an abandoned street.

The entrance was missing its manhole cover. One side or the other had probably used it during what appeared to have been intense fighting here. I hoped our side had used the heavy metal cover, and in the best possible way. Yitzchak offered to go down last and when he did, I noticed he'd dragged a fallen tree branch over the open hole. It wasn't a perfect disguise for our escape, but it was better than nothing.

Accessing the sewer line required a twelve-meter descent down a rusted ladder, every step darker than the one above it. The metal was cold and slimy, an immediate contrast to the suffocating fires above us, but it was no easier to breathe. The smell was worse than simple sewage. It was rot and decay and fetid air that felt like acid to my lungs. My leg protested the steady climb down, but I refused to fall or even to let it buckle. Each bend caused it to scream with pain, though, and I hoped it would carry me through the darkness below.

Twenty Jews were already waiting in the sewers when we arrived. Four men, seven women, and nine children. The only one I knew by name was Mr. Pilzer, the man who had worn the German uniform before.

"Only twenty," I mumbled.

"Twenty," Yitzchak said. "But we are not the only group. There are others. These are ours to save."

Esther stepped in front of us. "Everyone listen carefully. The Nazis know about this route, so we must not do anything to alert them. No one talks or splashes or switches on any kind of light, not even for a blink. We'll travel in a single-file line. Put one hand on the shoulder of the person ahead of you and keep your other hand on the sewer wall for balance. Beneath your feet it will be rounded and slippery. Choose your steps carefully. This walk will take hours. If you cannot do this, then do not endanger the rest of us. Does anyone need to leave?"

I'd never heard Esther speak like this. Yes, I'd seen glimpses of this person over the past few months, but she was in charge now, and she knew it. This Esther was going to lead us to freedom. I knew she would. The rest of the group seemed to trust her too, despite some of them no doubt having gossiped about her father before now.

No one left. No one said a word.

"Then let's go," she said firmly.

Esther took the lead and asked me to follow directly behind her. I knew it was because of my injured leg. She was worried that I might not make it. Frankly, so was I. It was already straining on the rounded paving stones. Yitzchak would be near the last of our group, and I didn't like that at all.

When everyone was lined up together, we began to walk. Occasional bits of light filtered in through other manholes, but they were few and far between, and here, still inside the ghetto boundaries, any light was darkened by the smoke aboveground. Before we crossed beneath each manhole, Esther stopped us and looked up.

Without her explanation, I understood. We didn't want to trek a group of twenty-three people beneath a squadron of soldiers. One of them was sure to notice the movement, or hear the soft splash of water. It was the sole reason that I was glad for the fires. They were loud enough to give us better cover than we otherwise might have had.

It wasn't long before I lost track entirely of how far we'd gone and where we might be in relation to the ghetto. We must still be inside, simply based on the smoke that continued to trickle in, but whether we'd gone a half kilometer or three times that, I didn't know. At least everything was going smoothly.

That is, until a cover opened behind us. A German-speaking soldier was midway through a casual explanation of what he was doing. ". . . occasionally throw in a little poison gas, in case there are any Jews."

And a grenade dropped, trailing tendrils of poisoned white smoke.

FORTY-EIGHT

April 25, 1943
Warsaw Ghetto

A child coughed near the back of the line as her nostrils picked up the first waft of poison. As innocent as it was, even that simple cough threatened us all. If Esther hurried us forward, the soldiers directly above us would hear our splashing. If we moved as slowly as we had before, the gas would claim every one of us.

I felt a break in our chain somewhere behind me. Esther turned and waved an arm, hoping to silently calm everyone, but no one was paying any attention, if they could even see her.

Then I heard a splash, and in the light beneath the manhole, I saw Mr. Pilzer's body go down. He didn't fall like a dead body would. Instead, he used himself as a shield from the gas, deliberately spreading out his clothes to contain as much of the smoke as possible.

It was one of the most heroic things I'd ever seen, and this after living a month in an entire ghetto full of heroes.

"Go," I hissed at Esther.

We returned to our single-file line, hurrying onward. Steadily moving forward, trying not to think about Mr. Pilzer, or, rather, thinking so intently of him that we seemed to form a silent pact that his death would not be in vain. We would escape the ghetto, and once on the Polish side, we would find a safe place for everyone. I knew how to find safe houses. I'd done it before, I could do it again, for all of these people. And in honor of the man we left behind.

Gradually, the smoky manhole covers offered us tiny glimpses of sky and fresh air. I wasn't sure how long we'd been walking, two or three hours at least, but every part of me was soaked through, my injured leg throbbed, my muscles were sore, and I was chilled to my core. A small price to earn our lives back.

When I couldn't contain myself any longer, I whispered in Esther's ear, "How much farther?"

"We take the next left turn, then walk straight for about an hour until the line hits a dead end."

I smiled. "Dead end? Did you really just say that?"

"Shh." She stopped walking and our line came to a halt. None of us were moving. The water should be still too, but it wasn't. Something splashed behind us.

We weren't alone.

Occasionally, a low-ranking Nazi was sent into the sewers to ensure nobody was using them for escape.

We weren't alone, and we all knew that was why.

Although the sounds behind us were still far away, they seemed to be coming closer.

Esther drew in a slow breath. Resolute, as if she'd already decided what must be done.

No.

No.

"Do you remember my directions?" she whispered.

"Don't ask me that, Esther. You must lead us out of here." The tears filling my eyes stung them, worsening the pain inside me.

"This was always my mission. I always knew if it came to this moment, what I'd have to do."

How could she sound calm, even as the reality of our situation was crushing my heart? I gripped her shoulder, needing her to feel my desperation. "I'll go. Not you."

I'd meant what I said and even turned to go, but she grabbed my arm. "Last time I was here, it cost people their lives. Now I'm here to save lives."

"No, you can't—"

"They knew my father, so I can talk to them better than anyone." She pushed a small folded paper into my hands. "That must be read on every underground radio station you can find. Promise me, Chaya."

I shook my head, feeling desperate. Feeling more helpless than I ever had before. "Please don't go."

"One more thing. A truck will be waiting at the exit in a

little over an hour, arranged by the Polish Underground. But they'll only wait fifteen minutes. You must hurry."

The splash of footsteps was coming closer. She squeezed my hand and gave me a quick kiss on the cheek. "We are couriers, my sweetest friend. Didn't we always know the risks? Go now. We can still save these people."

She pushed past me and disappeared into the darkness. I gritted my teeth for the courage to take my first step forward. But it didn't come. I couldn't leave her, not after all we had gone through to get this far. Not after I had learned to love Esther like a dearest sister, like a most trusted friend.

I was the one who was supposed to save her.

But she was saving me instead.

We waited there in absolute silence. Thick tears rolled down my cheeks, blinding me inside a black tunnel where I was nearly blind anyway. I heard only the splash of her footsteps away from us, and the heavier footsteps of the soldier who had followed us.

Then the splashes stopped. They had come face-to-face.

"My name is Esther Karolinski," she said. "My father was a member of the Judenrat and he served you well. I'm afraid I've become lost in these sewers. If you will take me back to the surface, I will gladly surrender. There are rats down here and dead bodies filled with disease."

At best, that was a half-truth, but she was hoping to spook the soldier who found her. They hated the sewer lines, knowing they were used by underground fighters who waited for an ambush opportunity.

The soldier aimed a flashlight down the pipes toward us, but we were already around the corner, none of us daring to breathe, except Esther. She had dared more than any of us. "Are you alone?" he asked in Polish.

"I traveled with a man who was my guide, but he succumbed to a poison gas grenade a few kilometers back. Please, sir, I surrender."

"Let's go, then."

And she was led away. Her footsteps, then his, louder splashes growing fainter as we waited until it was safe to move again. A few minutes later, the silent darkness was broken by a single shot fired inside the sewer line. I jumped and covered my mouth with my hands so that I wouldn't scream.

I wanted to scream, and felt it exploding inside me. I wanted to find that soldier and make him pay. But mostly I wanted to collapse right where I stood. How much easier that would be. The final splash where Esther fell was so . . . final.

Time stopped while its echo reverberated in my heart, creating a wound that would never fully heal. I gasped with pain, but choked back any further tears. Much as I wanted to stop here, I had to keep going. Because Esther was right that we were couriers, and this was what we did. She was right that we always knew the risks. And that if these people were not saved, then her sacrifice was in vain.

A hand went to my shoulder, a girl a few years younger than me, who nudged me forward, and somehow, I lifted a leg and began to walk.

Every step I took after that felt heavier than the one before it, but I forced myself to keep moving until we found the exit. Yitzchak and an older man climbed the ladder together so that one could pry it open while the other peeked out. As soon as the manhole cover opened, bright spring-time sunlight poured in, hurting our eyes. Then I caught the sound of a running engine motor humming down at us. Yitzchak climbed out first to verify the truck driver was our contact, then hissed that it was safe to send the others up.

The children went first. If their mothers were not here to help, then I boosted them onto the ladder and pushed them as high as I could until Yitzchak took their hands and helped them to the surface. One by one, they disappeared from the sewer. The women went up next. I was included with this group, although I feared that with my injured leg and bro-ken heart, my climb was too slow. When Yitzchak grabbed my hand, he gave it an extra squeeze and whispered, "If only our parents could see us now."

If only.

I reached the surface and pulled in a deep breath of fresh air while peering back toward the ghetto. It was easy to spot from the fires and thick plumes of smoke rising in the sky. I wished Esther were here with me, but I was glad she wasn't back there.

Mostly, I just missed Esther. Nothing would ever feel right again without her.

"I knew you'd make it out," a familiar voice said. I turned to see Rubin hurrying from the passenger side of the truck.

My eyes widened in disbelief. "Rubin? How did you know?"

"We've been monitoring coded radio transmissions from your leaders. One indicated that they needed a truck to meet a courier. I knew in my gut that it'd be you. I had to come." By then, we'd reached the back of the truck. He gave me a quick kiss on one cheek, then said, "We need to hurry."

There were no homes at this far end of the street, but that didn't mean curious eyes were far away. To look at any of us, it'd be obvious where we'd just come from. I climbed into a truck marked for dairy deliveries. For everyone to fit, we had to stand and squeeze together, but no one complained.

I was soaking wet, and somehow still filthy from black smoke, blood, and sewage, and a thick bandage was tied around my thigh. I had a homemade holster at my side with a German-made gun in it, and a German knapsack that was completely empty except for my false identification papers and a kitchen knife I once bought to free Esther . . . who in the end freed us. And I was standing proudly among twenty other people who had fought for their survival. By getting this far, they had won that battle.

As soon as the last of us was in the truck, Rubin shut the doors behind us, and we drove away.

A beam of sunlight streamed in between the doors, and I remembered the note that Esther had placed in my hand.

It was signed by Mordecai Anielewicz. He wanted this to be broadcast over the radio to everyone who would hear it. I read aloud, " 'Sensing the end, we demand this from you: Remember how we were betrayed. There will come a time of reckoning for our spilled, innocent blood. Send help to those who, in the last hour, may elude the enemy—in order that the fight may continue.' "

I looked around the group. "That is our message to the world, my friends. Our fight must continue."

I would find a way to honor Mordecai's final wish. I would carry on the fight.

FORTY-NINE

April 25, 1943
Warsaw

The truck drove us fifteen minutes from where we had escaped the sewers to a farmhouse on a quiet hill where we were quickly ushered into an attic room. There were no windows up here, but even then, the farmer, a shy-eyed man who couldn't have been any older than Dolek would have been, lit only a few candles and asked us to keep our voices low, a warning that was hardly necessary. Soon after, a Catholic priest and a pretty girl I assumed was the farmer's wife entered with trays of hot stew and fresh bread and real milk. The aroma of the food nearly overwhelmed me as I realized for the first time how little I'd eaten all week, surviving on crusts of rusk bread, a bowl of cold soup, and more raw nerve than I thought I had. It wasn't just me. Most of us accepted the bread and milk, but looked at the stew as if it was too much to manage all at once. I noticed the children broke their slice of bread in half, stuffing the rest inside their coats. One day they would remember again what it is to have enough food. But that would take time.

We were also provided with new clothes. Polish-looking clothes, though I couldn't imagine where they'd come from. I was more than happy to get rid of the ones I'd worn for far too many days, stained by sweat and blood, torn and smelling of gunpowder, sewage, and death.

"We have a few blank identification papers," the farmer said. "And we'll find safe houses for all of you until this terrible war comes to an end. There are many of us in Warsaw who want to help."

If he'd already arranged for safe houses, then he'd done my job. Which meant it was time to move on. When I walked past the priest, he noticed my necklace with the Catholic crucifix.

"Ah," he said. "You are a—"

"I'm a courier," I said, proud of the title. Proud of who I was.

He nodded respectfully. "Then you have seen too much of this war."

"I have seen too much of a war that reveals people for who they truly are."

"Indeed it has." He stared at me, the corners of his eyes glistening in the candlelight. "Some are revealed as cowards, others as villains or thieves." Now the corner of his mouth tilted up, very slightly. "But I hope you have also seen those with uncommon courage, those who will look evil in the face and say, 'This is where it ends.'"

In my mind, I saw Esther again. "I knew such a girl," I mumbled.

He reached out to pat me on the shoulder. "I believe I am also looking at such a girl now. History will count you as a hero."

I stepped back, unwilling to accept the title. "No, sir, I'm not." Not when compared with those who made sacrifices far greater than mine. Not when I was far too aware of my flaws, my mistakes. My failures.

"The world will take notice of what is happening in the ghetto," he said. "Mark my words, it will be a turning point in this war."

Maybe, but I couldn't think of anything that big. I hoped he was right.

When the priest clasped his hands in front of him, I happened to notice something curious on his forearm. I gestured at it, so he rolled up the sleeve of his robe enough to show me the prisoner number tattooed there. "Auschwitz. Hitler wants no Gods other than himself."

It was a reminder that hatred runs deeper and wider than a single race or nationality, and if love was not stronger, hatred would run through the generations. I intended to be stronger.

The priest offered me a nod of respect; then I returned

the gesture as he turned to help the others. It felt good to use proper manners again, like a civilized person.

The farmer's wife pulled me aside and tended to my leg wound properly. Infection had begun to set in, and the sewer waters had only made it worse, but she treated the injury with a generous dose of alcohol and then wrapped a new bandage beneath my pants leg. These were new pants. Designed for a boy, perhaps, but the fit would work after I cinched the waist with a belt.

"If you are leaving us, then a dress will blend in better around Warsaw," she said, showing slight disapproval for my choice.

"I'll keep the pants," I said. "I won't be in Warsaw for long."

"Where are you going?"

Yitzchak looked at me for our answer. Behind him, I saw Rubin sitting with a few of the children, helping to clean their faces with a small towel and bowl of water. He must have felt my eyes on him because he smiled over at me.

"We'll join the partisans," I told her, and beside me, Yitzchak nodded in agreement. The war wasn't over, and the fight inside me was as strong as ever.

At sunset that evening, Rubin, Yitzchak, and I returned to the truck, along with a few other refugees who had also chosen to come with us to the forest.

Before climbing in, Yitzchak and I lingered behind

an evergreen tree near the farmer's home. Farther down the street, a church was just releasing its parishioners from Easter services, a worship to mark their deliverance from death. How pretty the women's dresses were, how fine the men's suits. Their children had clean faces and full stomachs and probably hadn't spared a thought this week for the lives that were still being lost within sight of this church. Their lives looked . . . normal. I didn't even know what the word meant anymore.

But at the end of the exiting group, one couple paused to look in the direction of the ghetto. The air was clear here, but it was impossible to avoid seeing the fires and hearing the occasional round of a machine gun. The wife wiped tears from her eyes and her husband shook his head and held her close.

"What now?" she asked her husband.

I was asking myself the same question. Tomorrow we would mark the end of Passover. As Yitzchak and I were saved from the ghetto, we would find a way to save those who could still be saved.

Rubin crept up behind us, whispering in my ear that it was time to go. He added, "There's a large group of partisan fighters in the woods outside Warsaw. It's not only Jews, but anyone who is determined to play a role in ending this war."

"We'll keep fighting," Yitzchak said.

We would fight there for the Draengers, and Dolek, and for all of Akiva. We would fight for the mother on the train, and Wit, that kind man in the woods who sheltered Jews on his farm, and for Avraham, Sara, and Henryk, and all who died in the Aktion in Lodz. We would fight for Mordecai Anielewicz and for ZOB and for all those who rose up in the Warsaw Ghetto to defy an entire army of evil.

We would fight for my mother, who could no longer fight for herself, and for my father, who gave his last breath in devotion to my mother, and for my sister, who was taken too young, too innocent.

And we would fight to honor Esther's life. Esther's courage. I may never again meet anyone as strong as she was.

Historians might say that the Jews lost every uprising we attempted in this war, that every resistance movement failed.

I disagree.

We proved that there was value in faith. There was value in loyalty. And that a righteous resistance was victory in itself, no matter the outcome.

We got our three lines of history.

RESISTANCE

AFTERWORD

The Cyganeria Café attack on the night of December 22, 1942, was one of the first open acts of armed resistance by the Jewish people in occupied Europe. Although comparatively small in scale, and despite the German response, which eventually destroyed Akiva's organization in Krakow, it proved to other Jewish groups that resistance was possible.

As noted in the story, the Warsaw Ghetto Uprising was never going to result in victory over the German forces. But the effects of what the Jewish people accomplished there, in managing to stave off the Nazis for nearly a month, reverberated through Poland and all of occupied Europe.

Ultimately, the Warsaw Ghetto fighters held out longer than the entire country of Poland did against the initial German invasion. It inspired other uprisings in ghettos such as those in Rodzih and Bialystok, and in the extermination camps of Treblinka, Sobibor, and Auschwitz. It also was a foreshadowing and model for the Warsaw Uprising, launched by the Polish Underground army on August 1, 1944. Within the world of my imagination, I picture that Chaya was there for this fight too.

However, because this is a work of fiction, it's important to separate my characters from the actual people who chose heroism, courage, and honor in the face of certain defeat.

Chaya and Esther, their families, and many of the people they meet along the way are fictional characters so as not to intrude upon the personalities or actions of actual people involved. However, many details from their experiences are pulled from true stories.

In this book, most of those referenced in leadership positions within the resistance movement actually existed, and where it was possible to quote them exactly, this has been done. Where it was not possible, I attempted to preserve the spirit of their message.

The following are some of the many heroic individuals involved in the Jewish resistance.

AKIVA

Aharon "Dolek" Liebeskind would have been twenty-seven at the outbreak of World War II. He was described as charismatic and loyal. He was key in organizing the couriers and forming connections with other resistance groups. His motto was to "fight for three lines in history," even when the outcome was already known. He died in a shootout at the Akiva bunker on December 24, 1942.

Abraham "Laban" Leibovich is not mentioned in this book but was heavily involved with the Akiva raids in the fall of 1942. He died during an attempted prison escape on April 29, 1943.

Hillel "Antek" Wodzislawski stepped into the leadership of Akiva after the organization's collapse following the Cyganeria attack. He died in October 1943 during a retaliation strike for the murder of a Jewish child in hiding.

Justyna "Gusta" Draenger was the young wife of Shimshon Draenger and it is thanks to her that we know as much of Akiva's story as we do. After her arrest, she dictated the story of the resistance to the other women in her prison cell. Five copies each were made on pieces of toilet paper, which were then smuggled out of Montelupich Prison. Most of the narrative survives and was compiled into a book titled *Justyna's Story*. She was killed in November 1943 after fulfilling an agreement with her husband that if either was ever captured by the Nazis, the other would surrender too.

Maniek Eisenstein was the youngest Akiva leader and hid in the Tarnow Ghetto after the Cyganeria attack. He was killed on March 20, 1943.

Shimshon Draenger was twenty-two when the war began, and caught the attention of the Germans early on because of an anti-Nazi newspaper he published. He was the head of the Kopaliny Farm and had a talent for forgery. He was the husband of Gusta Draenger and had an intense focus on the cause of the resistance. He was killed in November 1943 after fighting with the partisans in the forests of Poland.

ZOB

Mordecai Anielewicz was twenty years old at the beginning of World War II but quickly began to understand the threat of the Nazi plan to exterminate the Jewish people. It took time to persuade the various resistance groups within the Warsaw Ghetto to unite, but once he did, and became their captain, he fulfilled the dream of many resistance fighters to prove that "not all sheep go like lambs to the slaughter." He died on May 8, 1943, in the ZOB bunker at 18 Mila Street in Warsaw.

Mira Fuchrer was nineteen at the outset of the war and eventually became a courier through the Warsaw Ghetto. She was the girlfriend of Mordecai Anielewicz and fought in the Warsaw Ghetto Uprising until her death on May 8, 1943, in the ZOB bunker.

Zivia Lubetkin was a leader during the Warsaw Ghetto Uprising and acted as a liaison between bunkers. When it became clear that the resistance headquarters was about to be raided, Zivia was sent through the sewers to find a connection on the Aryan side. She escaped but continued to run resistance operations from outside the ghetto. She died in Israel in 1976.

COURIERS

After the war, many of the young people who had been involved in courier work spoke little of their accomplishments, preferring to let those who died in their efforts be named as the true heroes. Thus, there is no complete list. However, I wish to mention a few couriers whose work saved countless numbers of lives and gave hope to a people in an otherwise sealed-off world.

Anka Fisher was a courier in attendance at Akiva's "Last Supper" meal. She had recently been released from prison following a brutal questioning and torture but never surrendered any information, remaining true to her oath of silence. Her fate is unknown.

Chajka Grosman was nineteen when the war began and almost immediately was asked to take a leadership position within her resistance group. Much of her courier work involved warning the residents of Warsaw about extermination plans for the Jews. She was actively involved in the uprising at the Bialystok Ghetto in August 1943, survived the war, and died in Israel in 1996.

Chavka Folman Raban was fifteen at the outset of the

war. She became well trained in the use of weapons, helped smuggle many Jews out of the ghettos, and was directly involved in the Cyganeria Café attack with Akiva. She was eventually arrested and sent to Auschwitz but survived. She died in 2014.

Frumke Plotnicka was the first courier in Warsaw to smuggle weapons into the ghettos inside a bag of potatoes. She joined the Bedzin Ghetto Uprising and was killed on August 3, 1943, in a basement with a rifle clutched in her hands.

Hela Schüpper worked as a courier between Warsaw and Krakow. She was once arrested while carrying forged identification but begged to use the bathroom before leaving with the soldiers. There, she flushed all the evidence so they were eventually forced to release her. Hela was later involved in and survived the Warsaw Ghetto Uprising by escaping through the sewers. She died in 2007.

Mire Gola was a courier throughout Poland and a key player in encouraging Akiva to begin fighting back after the ghetto Aktions in Krakow. She was shot to death while trying to escape from Montelupich Prison on April 19, 1943, the same day the Warsaw Ghetto Uprising began.

Rivka Liebeskind was Dolek Liebeskind's wife. Her courier work focused on finding safe houses and distributing false identification papers. When other Akiva leaders were arrested or absent, she played a key role in keeping the resistance moving forward. She survived the war, and died in 2007.

Vladka Meed was a Warsaw courier and expert smuggler, who brought dynamite, gasoline, and pistols into the Warsaw Ghetto and helped many children to escape. She survived the war and died at age ninety.

When thrust into a situation as intense and traumatic as war, and facing possible extermination, no two people will respond in the same way. Some will collapse, others will betray, and others will try to ignore the calamity. But in those same circumstances, some will emerge with honor and rise as heroes. However, it is important to note that because of the horrifying and extraordinary nature of the Holocaust, any attempt to judge the actions of anyone through a "normal" lens will likely reflect a poor understanding of just how difficult the circumstances were.

May we never forget. May we live with honor at all times, regardless of our circumstances. And may we choose love, a weapon that will defeat hate every single time.

Love is the resistance.

Jennifer A. Nielsen
2018

After words™

JENNIFER A. NIELSEN'S

Resistance

CONTENTS

About the Author

Jennifer was born and raised in Northern Utah to parents who couldn't possibly know what they were getting into. She rode bicycles no-handed, climbed trees with power lines running through them, played the outfield on her three-person baseball team, and found many other activities that shall remain unnamed (i.e., stuff her mom still doesn't know about, and she's not about to find out here).

She also grew up with a love for books and an imagination that often interested her far more than the real world. Stories and characters and fictional worlds were constantly in her head.

However, it never occurred to Jennifer that becoming an author was a real career option. That changed in sixth grade when she discovered that S. E. Hinton, the author of her then-favorite book, *The Outsiders*, had written that story while she was a teenager. Inspired to try writing her own book, Jennifer began a story about a girl with a wild imagination (sound familiar?) whose daydreams come alive one day and get her into heaps of trouble. The writing was going fine until this girl became locked in a closet and needed to pick the lock. Jennifer had no idea how to pick the lock, but now that she was a serious author like S. E. Hinton, it was no problem to call a locksmith and ask.

The locksmith disagreed. Believing that Jennifer was misbehaving, he yelled at her on the phone. She hung up and found a place to hide. Eventually, she left the hiding place, but her character never did. Jennifer never wrote another word of the story.

In fact, Jennifer didn't begin seriously writing again until she was an adult. Her first few manuscripts were catastrophic attempts at storytelling that are now mandated in her will as items that must be buried with her one day. Seriously.

After much failure—followed by the requisite consumption of ice cream—her tenacity and study of writing began to pay off. In 2012, Jennifer released *The False Prince* with Scholastic. Since then, she has published thirteen novels—and counting.

Jennifer is married to an awesome guy whom she met in her senior year of high school when they played husband and wife on stage (stage kiss!). She has three children and a dog that won't play fetch, and has recently acquired a cat that hallucinates. She lives in the mountains of Northern Utah and there enjoys spending time with her family, watching movies, and writing snarky biographies of her life.

Q&A with Jennifer A. Nielsen

Q: *What was your inspiration for writing this story?*
A: It was never in my mind to write a story like this one, but once the idea grabbed me, it refused to let go.

Resistance began on a trip I took to Poland. As part of that trip, we visited a Jewish cemetery in Krakow, which was a humbling and profound experience in itself. However, I happened upon one particular grave marker that caught my attention. The marker was for an entire family, all with the same date of death—April 1, 1943. All of the family, that is, except for the oldest son, who died in 1986. And I asked myself, why him? Why had he been the only one of his family to survive the Nazi horrors? The longer I stared at the grave marker, the more I noticed something on the marker was not right. Below this son's name was a second name, and it wasn't Jewish. I wondered what a Polish Christian name was doing on this family's plaque, and it bothered me enough that I could not let the question go until I had found the answer. It took some digging, but eventually I did.

It turns out that when the Nazis invaded Krakow, this boy managed to obtain false papers for himself, assuming the Polish Christian name now on his grave marker. His looks were Aryan enough that he was able to pass himself off as someone he was not, but that, and his false papers, kept him alive.

He wasn't the only one. I discovered other young Jewish people in Krakow who had used false papers and their abilities to pass themselves off as Christians to resist the Nazi occupation. This was the Akiva resistance movement, a group that history had largely forgotten, much as it had forgotten that young man on a grave marker in an overcrowded Jewish cemetery. I became determined to give these young resistance fighters a small amount of the recognition they had earned with their courage, their honor, and their lives.

Q: *What resources did you use in your research, or, what did your research process look like?*
A: Early in the research process, I began to understand the need for accuracy in every word I wrote. If I misrepresented a part of this history, it would allow someone who denies the reality of the Holocaust to say that if one fact was false, maybe other facts are false as well.

So I dug into deeper research than I had ever done in my life, in books and original resources from Holocaust Museums and foundations. I watched the testimonies of Jewish resistance fighters from the Nuremberg trials, and video and audio interviews of Polish survivors and fighters, particularly those from Krakow or who had been in the Warsaw Ghetto. I downloaded the Nazi aerial maps of the Warsaw Ghetto, then translated their codes from German to determine what every building was. I found maps of the Ghetto sewer lines from the wartime era, including manhole entrances and exits. I scanned pictures for every possible detail, and through all of it, took detailed notes, learning far more than I knew I would ever need.

I also learned the importance of verifying information by getting more than one source. This is particularly important because the Holocaust and the war in general were traumatic events for those who were part of it, and sometimes the names, dates, or places would vary.

Above all, I learned that the words I wrote only scratched the surface of the story that was there. Every single resistance fighter had their own dreams and hopes and fears. They all found courage in their own ways, and contributed to the resistance movement as only they could. Every one of them deserves to have their stories told.

My gratitude to those archivists, researchers, and documentarists who continue to work on gathering their stories and preserving this much needed history.

To those with any family or local history from World War II, please do your own research to recover or preserve their histories.

Q: *What was the most inspiring or your favorite piece of information that you learned during your research and writing?*
A: When Akiva was formed, the leaders knew they had no chance of winning against the entire Nazi army, and little chance of surviving. But they did fight for a reason. They called it their "three lines of history." Three lines in a history book to remember who they were—regular, ordinary people. Most of them were in their early twenties or teenagers. None of them had military training, or the resources to stand against an entrenched occupation. And their three lines of history was to remember what they fought for: freedom, the right to live, and the right to be recognized as a person, the same as any other.

But aside from a few mentions on websites or out-of-print books, I realized they never got the one thing they wanted—their three lines of history. That's why I had to write *Resistance*, to give them at least that, if I could.

Most profound to me was the realization that we each have the opportunity in this life to earn our own three lines of history. If they could stand for what they believed, against such odds as they faced, why can't any of us? There is so much need in every country, in our communities, or in our homes. Imagine what a world this would be, if we each simply worked to earn our own three lines of history.

No matter how small we feel.

No matter the odds against us.

Every one of us can make a difference for good.

A destitute youth in the Warsaw Ghetto.

Portrait of a woman wearing a striped blouse and an armband in the Warsaw Ghetto.

Young boys caught smuggling by a German soldier in the Warsaw Ghetto.

The ruins of an apartment building destroyed by the SS during the suppression of the Warsaw Ghetto uprising.

SS troops walk past a block of burning housing during the suppression of the Warsaw Ghetto uprising. The original German caption reads: "An assault squad."

Jews captured by the SS during the Warsaw Ghetto uprising are interrogated beside the ghetto wall before being sent to the *Umschlagplatz*. The original German caption reads: "Search and Interrogation."

An SS Lieutenant (*Untersturmfuehrer*) interrogates a Jewish resistance fighter captured on the twenty-first day of the suppression of the Warsaw Ghetto uprising.

Jews captured by the SS during the suppression of the Warsaw Ghetto uprising board a truck.

Jews captured by SS and SD troops during the suppression of the Warsaw Ghetto uprising are forced to leave their shelters and are marched to the Umschlagplatz for deportation.

Survivors of the Jewish underground pose atop the ruins of the Mila 18 bunker in the former ghetto.

Turn the page for a sneak peek at another thrilling World War II story from Jennifer A. Nielsen: *Rescue*

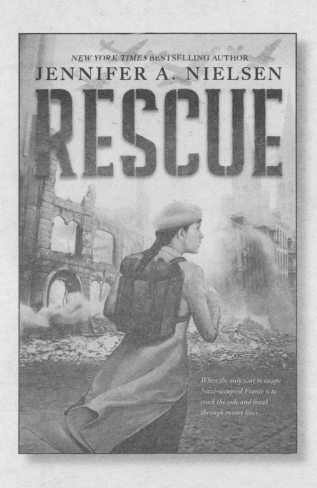

PROLOGUE

May 11, 1940

Papa stood at the gate by the road and waved goodbye.

He wanted me to wave back at him, but I didn't. I couldn't. Even if I tried, I couldn't make myself smile and send him off as if he were only going for a simple walk.

Not going to war.

Maman stood beside me, her arm tight around my shoulder. "One day you will understand this, Meggie. France needs him now."

No, *we* needed him! What if the war came deeper into France—what if it came to this same gate—and he wasn't here to protect us?

He wouldn't be here. I did understand that. If the Nazis came, we would have to defend ourselves.

All this had happened so fast. Four days ago, as German troops began lining our border, Papa received a telegram from London, one that had kept him and Maman awake all night in a whispered conversation I wasn't supposed to hear. I did catch a few words: resistance . . . sacrifice . . . secret.

Two days later, on the eve of the invasion, we abandoned our home near the German border and fled to an area known as the Perche to stay with Grandmère on her farm. She lived much farther from the border, and we hoped that would be safer.

I doubted anywhere was safe. Because only one day after the Germans stormed through our border, Papa was leaving us.

And no, I could not understand that. So I didn't wave.

It was something I would regret every single day that followed.

Read these thrilling stories
from *New York Times* bestselling author
JENNIFER A. NIELSEN

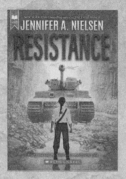

When the Berlin Wall divides her family, Gerta finds herself in a race against time to escape to the West.

When the Nazis occupy Poland, Jewish teenager Chaya decides to fight back…to resist.

When the Russian Cossack soldiers occupying Lithuania arrest Audra's parents, she becomes caught up in the deadly struggle to save her nation.

When one girl fights to save her father from the Nazis, she works with the French resistance and finds herself racing against the clock to crack a crucial code.

When World War I stretches its cruel fingers across Europe, five young people hold the key to one another's futures.

Dive into the fantasy worlds of *New York Times* bestselling author

JENNIFER A. NIELSEN

THE ASCENDANCE SERIES

MARK OF THE THIEF TRILOGY

THE TRAITOR'S GAME SERIES

 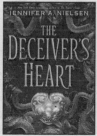 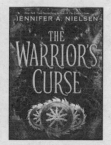